Bumshoes and Chromeboys

Walt Crocker

Bumshoes and Chromeboys

By Walt Crocker

Copyright 2007

Online editions may be available for this title. For more information Please visit LuLu.com.

ISBN: 978-0-6151-5087-1

Introduction

This book is a sporadic labor of love and hate that has been almost four
years in the making. My first book, "Out To Lunch," on the other hand, took
about four months to write. Out To lunch is a book about working in the
restaurant industry for some twenty-five years, and all the crazy and
impossible things that can happen and all of the crazy and impossible
people that you meet. The whole boo was already in my head, all I had to do
was stumble home from working a fifteen hour shift, exhausted, and write it
all down. There were many nights that I fell asleep, face down on the
typewriter.

A couple of years later, I wrote Beam Me Up Scottie with Patrick Pippen.
Patrick is the nephew of basketball legend Scottie. We became friends while
working in a restaurant together and decided to tell his life's story, (or at
least what has happened so far in his short life). Gathering the material was
a lot of fun. We met once a week at a favorite local coffee shop for a period
of about two years. I brought a tape recorder and we just talked, at random,
in no particular order. Then I would go home and put it all down on paper.

So, I enjoyed doing both of my previous books. But, over the past fifteen
years or so I've also had an interest in metaphysics and spirituality. I was a
member of a traditional Japanese Incense School for a couple of years,
studied Tarot, Celtic Mythology, and Lucid Dreaming. I became a Druid, a
Pagan, and a Buddhist. Now my belief system has become a personal one.
I've sort of picked up different elements as I went along.

After the first two books came out, a lot of my friends and acquaintances
asked me when I was going to write a book of a "more esoteric and
spiritual" nature. The thought lingered in the back of my mind for some
time, but quite honestly, I wasn't sure if I could pull it off. I still don't know

if I have. The writing that was always easiest for me came from my experiences, both in the crazy restaurant business and growing up as a street thug on the streets of St. Louis. What I wrote about usually explored the darker side of things, so how was a person like me to write about the white light of lofty ideals and ethereal kindness?

Then I realized that most of the religions and belief systems that I had studied view the Otherworld as a place both light and dark. Both are needed there just like in the plane of existence that we physically occupy. Writing about someone like Cloud's past lives and current traumas was a perfect medium for both my writing style and what I was trying to accomplish. I could take him not only through several other worlds and planes of existence, but also explore my love of history and other cultures. So Cloud sort of became a yoyo being jerked up and down by the silver string. Connected to the universe in a powerful way, but not really understanding how it works. Maybe in the end, we all come through a little wiser, if not worse for wear and tear.

Walt Crocker 2006

Acknowledgements

I would like to thank Robert for his great friendship and spiritual support, Patrick, for being a kindred spirit and just hanging out from time to time, Kay, for always being there, Jim, for saving my butt more times than I care to admit, and Ellina, for being one of the most fun and talented people that I have ever met.

"Our chief want in life is somebody who shall make us do what we can."

Ralph Waldo Emerson

Chapter 1

He lies on the concrete slab like a miniature Mount Rushmore that has been toppled on its side. High forehead, strong Jaw, curved Patrician nose with a bump in the middle, patterned spider-like vein explosions. Crying cigar store Indian, wooden features framing thin lips that are screwed into a grimace. An Ace of spades sticks out of the chest pocket of his rumpled blue suit; dead man's hand partially covering the card. He had been a gambler in life, losing most of the time at cards and the roulette wheel, but winning the life gamble. Able to wake up most days and stand up, even though allot of the time he didn't know where he had been or even where he was. He was sixty-two when he died, the gamble finally failing to pay off one last time. Spend the last couple of years on skid row in Chicago, fighting for his space on the grate. Sometimes when .he rolled over in a drunken stupor the steam from the grate would boil his face like a par-boiled tomato and he would tell his panhandling clientele that he had just got back from the beach, lost his wallet and needed money to make a phone call. It rarely worked, but he enjoyed the acting part. The steam grate was warm and considered a reservation at the Hilton, but sometimes lesser accommodations were in order and he spent the night in a cardboard box or the bowels of an abandoned building.

"I smoke old stogies I have found, short, but not too big around. I'm a man of means by no means…." He hadn't traveled much last few years for health reasons. The nagging cough-rattle in his chest had gotten worse and his sole method of treatment was a stiff bottle of Mickey. He hated Chicago and fantasized about moving to warmer climes, move to the beach and wash his hair with herbs in the salty water and strike it rich selling his concoctions door-to-door like Paul Thomas. But gathering food had become the order of the day. The dumpster behind McDonalds had food that was pretty fresh, and sometimes when he felt like a Pizza, he would call Pizza Hut, give them a false name and address, not show up at the scheduled time and then retrieve the thing from the trash can when they finally gave up and threw it away. The advent of caller I.D. had changed all that though since it was obvious he was calling from a phone booth. Damned technology was like a vulture on a drunken bum's life. Sometimes a right wing born-again would show up with a ratty blanket and some cookies, but there was always a catch. He had to listen to some goddamn sermon about where you were going to end up in the afterlife. He didn't want to talk about hell and purgatory, he was living it day by day.

Let them spend a few days in the scum slum and they wouldn't think much about what was to come after either.

"It was a hot summer night and the breeze was burnin' there was fire spreadin' over the sand ….." He felt like he was looking at the world through a broken piece of green bottle glass, it's ragged edges cutting deep into his trembling hand. Primordial in it's outlook, grinding back to a more natural form. "Is there anybody in there?" Just nod if you can hear me.....is there anybody home?" Home alone...In your deserted warehouse loft, spare furnishings, and a broken bloodstained cardboard box. Red stained teeth without the luxury of dental floss, hungry Vampire who doesn't remember where he got his last fix.

Bad blood gave him a headache. Have to choose his victims a little more carefully in the future. He staggers over to the broken window, gazes out on the street traffic below, dirty thumbnail scraping off pieces of lead-encrusted paint on the windowsill.

He feels a little lightheaded and weak, but then these days this was pretty much the order of the day. A wave of nausea suddenly makes the little boat-brain almost capsize. He staggers back over to the cardboard bed and notices that there are little spots of blood soaked into the fibers. He hiccups, sending a stream of blood and spittle cascading down his chin. It tastes salty and metallic, like licking the fender of a rusty car. The sea his brain is~floating on gets a little more turbulent now and he slumps to his knees. No panic yet, this sort of thing has happened before. Nasty oozing scab on the lining of his stomach. Never had a chance to heal. Wiping alcohol continuously on an open wound. After a few hours it would go away like it always has, and he would be looking for a new pair of underwear, black tarry shit defiling the ones he was wearing. Underwear, socks and shoes, these were the important things. It was the only contact with the outside world. The shredded smelly suit only lends a slight air of formality to dealing with outsiders. But there was a catch this time, the wounded artery in his stomach refused to

spasm shut. Instead it lay there in the murky acid depths, jerking
and spurting like a tiny orgasm. It was the little death turning large.
He lay there for about an hour, heart pounding in a desperate adrenaline
attempt to keep 'his blood pressure from falling. The sun cast fleeting
shadows across the room and he imagined that there were other people
there. This was a good thing, no sense in dying alone.

The realization finally came over him that the time had maybe finally
Come. This event couldn't be soothed away by a bottle of cheap wine. He
felt oddly at peace, but where was the damn tunnel of light?

The shadowy figures in the room were dancing on the wall, hummed and
moaned, but didn't say anything. Where were the ancestral family members
waiting to greet him?

He feels very hungry. The wounded vessel that is his stomach contains only
his own blood and a small quantity of Campbel's Chicken Rice soup. A
rusty, leaky can of it being his last meal. They were miniature white
maggots collecting around the ulcer, animated, swimming around the hole,
waiting their turn to spill out into his abdomen. There is no pain. He feels
comfortably numb, but his thoughts race with amazing clarity. He smells
smoke. Wood smoke. He wonders whether the damned building is on fire or
maybe he's in hell already. The voice of Mahalia Jackson rises softly
through the ether. It's his mother's voice, lilting, and rising softly on the
smell of his favorite food; fry-bread cooked over an open fire.

She calls out his name: Robert Stevenson Skyfeather! How long it had been
since he had been called that. He was used to the nickname he had picked
up when he was a child, Cloud. He didn't remember how he had gotten the
name. Maybe because he was quiet as a child and people thought that his

head was always up there. He laughed, remembering an old joke about how Indian children got their names: the Chief to the   small boy explaining..."We name our sons and daughters after what the parents see as the child is being conceived.

For example, if a hawk flies overhead, the baby would be called flying hawk. Then the Chief turns solemnly to the child and says:

"Why do you ask, Two Dogs Fucking??" A car spits gravel as it takes off down the road, putting a ton of dust in the air. The white trailer with the rust-streaked roof sits quietly under a bright blue desert sky. A single tear wets the dust on his mother's face as his father leaves, he would never hear or see him again, until now. Now he decides to show up as a fleeting shadow...hovering over undigested mental fry bread.

He rides the tricycle around the dusty front yard in ever widening circles, his Grandfather trying to squirt him with a garden hose. Bam! It's a direct hit. The little boy gets off the bike and runs over, hugging the elder one. Familiar smell of old denim and leather mixed with tobacco. Indians and their tobacco; they rolled it, piped it, and threw it to their ceremonial gods. It was like sacrificing the lungs to the Deity of smoke and fire. Sometimes it was a blood sacrifice. The idea was to get to death before it got to your. Get familiar with it. Trek down the dreamscape and find the roadmap. Get over the hill and through the woods. There are guides and spirits all along the way. There were also monsters and tigers that will eat you if given the chance.

He had never been much on the old ways and now he regretted it. He wished he had taken Shaman 101.

Cloud sat off to the side, beyond the circle of Elders, hidden by shadow. A boY of thirteen, he was to be introduced to the old ways. The tribe still used chopping to circumcise 12-year-old boys.

The scar had yet to heal and he absentmindedly scratched at his private parts. Yanked from the security of his mother he was taken to the chopping block. After a brief ceremony, two small holes were made in his foreskin with a leather trowel, after which wooden hook-like devices were inserted in the holes and the excess skin. Was stretched cut over a wooden block. The boy was held in place and comforted with words spoken in an ancient dialect. Then, suddenly the small circle-knife was brought down forcefully, and with a single word it was naked penis time. Some herbs were applied to the wound to stop the bleeding and the foreskin was ceremoniously discarded of in the fire. Cloud was escorted back to the sweat lodge where he promptly passed out from the heat, smoke, and pain.

He awoke several minutes later in his mother's trailer and slept the better part of the day. The next day he was allowed to view, but   not participate in, one of the Shaman's rituals. Cloud looked around the circle...the chief sat in the East as the rising sun, wearing a full headdress of Golden Eagle feathers. To possess them now is a federal offense, but of course, these were old. It was rumored throughout the tribe that the old guy had needed just one more eagle-feather to complete the set, and as a young man had ventured to the top of the mountain, high up the clouds where the Eagles had their nest, and literally snatched the feather from the ass of a huge nesting bird. The pissed off Eagle came to the village, looking for the lost part of his bird-suit, and spotting the Chief walking along the road, tried to shit on him. This lasted about 2 days before the eagle finally gave up and had to fly off in search of food to feed his family.

The Shaman sat at the other end of the circle chewing on a raw piece of Buffalo meat. He would later kill the Buffalo, after all a considerable amount of meat had already been carved off the poor beast, and sleep in the bloody hide overnight to gain a vision and some insight as to what was going to happen to the tribe. Of Course the Peyote buttons he had swallowed earlier didn't hurt, He was rushed off to the hospital early the next morning complaining of stomach pains, no doubt it was from something he ate.

The Shaman looks wild-eyed and crazy, blood collecting in the bags at the bottom of his orbital sockets and spilling out into tears of red. He dances in a circle and waves his arms around frantically. The boy looks on in amazement, clutching his wounded genitals. As painful as his circumcision was, he's lucky the ritual had not taken place a thousand years ago. Back then the tribe would have constructed a beautiful mud and straw hut, decorated in the best baubles and beads. The boy and his female companion would have been dressed up in their finest regalia; he in his holy bloodstained animal skins and the pre-pubescent girl decked out and decorated at the first sign of her menses. He would wear a large sack over his newly cut manhood, into which would be placed a gourd filled, with magical herbs, all designed to exaggerate his newly-arrived at manly nature. She, on the other hand would be padded in all the right places. 'Looking for love in all the wrong places, looking for love in to many faces, watching their eyes .... "They would be led willingly towards the nuptial quarters.

This was after all a day of pride and accomplishment. Donated by nature, they had grown from children into the handsomest and most nubile couple in the village. There was much merriment and celebration the few days before the big event. Everyone was laughing and dancing, although the boy did detect a fleeting glint of sadness in his mother's eyes. Finally the time had come as they were led into the hut. There was a smoky fire lit in the center of the room and a bed of feathers, very soft, off to the side. The fire contained special mind-altering herbs that have since been long lost to civilization. The smoke made the couple a little dizzy, but with a very pleasant after-effect...they were becoming very sexually aroused. The elders removed their clothing and left the hut to prepare for what was to become next. They watched what was going on from behind small openings made in the straw, covered by God-Masks that were hinged and moved from one side to the other. The couple kissed and felt each other, and it wasn't very long before passion, aided by the drugs, took over. Meanwhile outside, all the adult males of the tribe were struggling with ropes, the ropes that held the rock. The large, flat stone, weighing several thousand pounds was suspended by the ropes and hovered precariously over the magic hut. The tribesmen struggled to keep the stone in place until exactly the right time. Veins popped out on their foreheads and the sweat poured from their bodies. Both of the youngsters inside the hut began to moan. The boy was thrusting harder, the girl bringing up her hips to meet him. Just as the climax for both of them occurred, one of the voyeur Shamans behind the Mask of God gave a pre-determined signal. The ropes holding the giant stone slipped through the hands of the tribesmen, burning their fingers. The boy's last powerful thrust to orgasm was aided by several thousand pounds of gravity. The male and female God-halves were reunited in one fell swoop as both the Children were crushed to death instantly. The tribe looked on in hushed silence as the workers tried to move away the stone with large poles. Finally they were able to move the stone to one side. The remains of the couple were pretty much unrecognizable. The boy's hand had been caressing the girl's face, and it had been pushed all the way to the back of her skull. The downward force had made both of the bodies look like a red-oozing plum that had been sat on by a very obese person. The Shaman walked over to the area that was the pubic region and scooped up what was believed to be bits of bone, blood and sexual fluid. This was to be used in later rituals. The rest of the mashed potato-cake couple was cooked and eaten by the tribe, each consuming their allotted lovin' spoonful. No representative fake wafers and wine, the blood and flesh were consumed for real here. The sacrifice was complete and the ceremonial stone was relegated back to its former position as a platform holding the throne of the ruler. God's appeased one more time, all was right with the world, the crops would grow strong and tall, and all the animals would willingly give up their flesh as homage to the ultimate example being set. The mothers of the children looked on as the fathers sat and chewed, wiping their faces and grinding the meal corn.

Cloud was somewhere up "there." Floating in a purple haze, tethered by the thin silver cord, bouncing around the stellar heavens like an over-inflated helium balloon. Looking down at the patchwork matrix containing his past, present, and maybe even future lives. There was something missing. In his present level of consciousness there was a dream-like state where everything had a fuzzy edge to it. He was too light and gravity no longer affected him. Lost on the interstellar highway without a roadmap. He wished he had paid more attention to the Elders and to his dreams. He was always told that the afterlife would look and feel like a very intense Lucid dream, and all the religion nonsense in the world was just practice for the reality to come. Every once in awhile there was a tremendous shift, sort of like being rocked by sea-swells of time. Right after this there was a northern light effect of color, and he felt in danger of losing what little stability he had left. Like he was going to go with the flow and dissipate into nothingness .... or "no thing" ness. The only thing that saved him was the Silver cord that came out of his navel, but it to was changing in color and intensity. He felt cold and alone locking down at his lives. Like watching a movie screen through a pair of binoculars. Everything was there at once like thumbnail pictures on a computer all melted together. The silver cord was his wired-in connection, but he was mouse less. He tried to focus what little will he had left through the dizzying ether. Suddenly, though the mist he noticed a small flickering light. Like a candle flame miles away in the deep, dark night. He tried to be still and focus on the light. It became a little easier the more he tried. Finally the sea of light parted a little, and he was drawn closer, almost against his will. He was clicking the mouse now, freeze-frame-by-freeze-frame getting closer, the satellite picture getting clearer. It was the village Shaman, looking up into the~ night sky with his arms wide-open, turquoise eye glowing in the firelight. He could see all the features of his face now and he had an intense, almost terrified look. Perhaps he had seen a ghost, and the ghost was Cloud.

The Shaman was still staring intently at the manifestation of Cloud. He held his rattle high up in the air, shook it fiercely, and made a magical sign. His turquoise eye seemed to give off a greenish glow as he shuffled his dusty feet, kicking up the well-trodden earth around the fire. Cloud was unimpressed...in his diaphanous state he felt invincible and he didn't appreciate the negative vibes that were rolling off the Shaman. He started zooming down towards the funny little man dressed in feathers and a grass skirt. Suddenly there was a voice in his right ear. It boomed, yet had a still, comforting quality about it. It seemed to rumble throughout his very being, speaking with authority. "Back off!" It told him. "You'll lose, he can destroy your soul" Cloud willed himself to stop advancing. He was amazed at how easy this was, and pretty soon the Shaman was out of sight. He wondered about the voice and tried to make contact with it, but it was no longer there. A broader picture was starting to take form. Looking down at the patchwork quilt that was his life, he realized that it was more like a web, connected with all the other lives and everything else. There were shapes of stars forming in the heavens around him. They were fuzzy and indistinct at first, but finally recognizable as points of light. Linear time no longer existed. He was beginning to feel the connection, the connection to the beginning of everything. This at first made him feel very small and insignificant, but then he was enthralled just to be a part of it all. Still there was no tunnel of light, no relatives, friends and loved ones there to greet him. He felt enormously alone, a tiny insect pinned under an errant pebble. He could but watch and wait. There was another sparkle of light on the quilted patchwork. He focused in on it. A picture slowly began to form. It was a lake, water of some sort.

No, it was actually the pond that he had gone fishing on as a young child, near the reservation. Droopy willows hung over it, heads bowed, their roots like heavily knuckled fingers clutching the mud. Young Cloud sat there on the bank, a broken piece of fiberglass glass fishing rod with a string tied to the end of it, stuck in the ground. Some kind of mist was floating around the scene, although there was no fog and the sun was shining brightly. He tried to get a look on the other side of   it, and a totally different scene came into view. Swirls of deep purple anger floated around it. Cloud was clutching the broken fishing rod and swinging it at another small child. It made a stinging whap as it struck the other child on his exposed leg. The scene was at a small way stop less than a mile from the broken trailer that Cloud and his family called home. A lone gasoline pump stood like an alien sentinel in front of the station. Scummy gasoline, stale and stagnant, filled the dirty glass head on top of it. There was a 25-cent Pepsi sign squeaking on a rusty sign pole as it swung in the breeze. John Paul Samson was enjoying a bottle of the drink inside the store, oblivious to the commotion that was going on outside. John Paul was one big Indian; over 6 feet tall and weighing about 350lbs. Most of his weight was in his upper body; his legs had been spared. Sort of a basketball perched atop of two toothpicks. He wore an old baseball cap and the remnants of a beard. Growing the beard was not an easy thing to do   for an Indian, and it sort of grew out in scattered tufts with large patches of brown skin in-between. His jeans were too small for his beer-induced belly and his ass was too skinny for his jeans. This made his midsection be in a constant state of flux, the crack of his ass, resplendent with dingle berries, was always threatening to spill out, like a smelly Maytag repairman on a hot afternoon. John Paul had finished his drink and his chat with the old lady that ran the station, and was walking outside to his old silver spray painted chopper that was parked outside. He glanced over and saw Cloud hitting the deaf and dumb boy with the remnants of the fiberglass-fishing pole. He walked over to see what was up. The deaf kid was taking a pretty good whipping, so John Paul grabbed Cloud by his sweaty T-Shirt and pulled him up to his feet. "Son, you ought not pick on someone who is much smaller than yourself."

John Paul said. Cloud yelled back at him that the little bastard had started it. Told him how he had been minding his own business at the fishing hole, when the deaf kid snuck up on him and hit him with the fishing pole. John Paul continued separating the two, when Cloud furious, turned on John Paul, who was at least 4 times bigger than he was. The boy, dusty and red-faced swung with all his might at John Paul's enormous stomach. John Paul just stood there, holding on to Cloud's shirt, laughing. The kid was wearing out and after a few minutes, slumped over to the ground; exhausted. John Paul walked back to the motorcycle his dusty split cowboy boots clunking on the ground. After numerous curses and failed attempts, he got the thing to start and sped off. The back wheel of the bike sent a dust devil of a cloud in Clouds direction. It clung to his sweaty skin and sent grit choking down his throat. He looked around, the deaf and dumb kid had long-since ran off. He sat there crying, hating the fat Indian. Someday. he would get even.

The Spirit-Cloud that was watching all this, suddenly felt the astral equivalence of vertigo. The whole universe was spinning around violently. He was in some kind of white room. There was a window along one wall, backlit by bright sunshine, but it seemed very far away. Red strings that resembled veins and arteries were all over the place, like being at a party with thousands of helium balloons floating near the ceiling with red ribbons hanging down from them. The room was spinning to the right and Cloud was getting caught up in the strings. They were sticking to him like some giant red spider-web. There was an odd looking tapestry hanging on one of the walls. It was a forest scene showing a wild boar being hunted by men on horseback. The boar's mouth was wide open, his teeth and tusks enveloped by foam-spittle. There was a bloody gash on the animal's back. It was obvious that he was wounded in the battle. The tapestry would at times glow and then darken to the point that it was almost unrecognizable. There was a book floating in the air in front of the wall hanging. The book would open and close as if driven by the same wind or whatever it was that was making the room spin. Sometimes Cloud could just about glimpse pieces of text inside the book, but the vortex of the room was Just to powerful to read any of it. The room was starting to slow down now; coming to a halt for a mere few seconds and then it started spinning in the opposite direction. It was like some crazy merry-go-round amusement park ride. If this was the Disney World of the other side, Cloud did not find it very amusing. He somehow knew that he had to move towards the window. When the spinning slowed, if he willed it just right, he could regain a little control. He started to calm down a little. The red vein strings were still attached to him however, and it was almost impossible to get free from them. Finally he decided to use the motion of the room to his advantage. He tried to spin his astral self in the same direction that the room was spinning. Finally he broke free and literally zoomed towards the window and the light. He lost it just as he entered the window and broke through. Everything was black and empty.

The great void, nothingness, what the Buddhists call no THINGNESS. Where you finally reach that point of enlightenment where all the illusions of the world and beyond the world are stripped away, and you realize that life is but a dream; a dream to some and a nightmare to others. What are you? I am awake. No mere dragging yourself back to the carnal quagmire to live through the pain and heartache of existence, sweet nothing, bliss of oblivion. Back to square one. Maybe that's what saves your mortal soul. It's the Alpha and Omega...the beginning and the end, where the end that cannot come fails to lead to the beginning anymore.

Cloud wasn't so lucky; he still probably had a few thousand re-incarnations to go through before it could all be over. The point was to learn something. But what was the lesson? In Nature you had to learn to survive. Propagate the species. Survival of the fittest, even if it took you millions of years to do it. A mouse twitching in the field, ripped to pieces by the red talons of a 200-mile an hour Falcon. "Fuck you!" Says the mouse as he is consumed. The last great act of defiance, middle finger thrust high in the air. We evolve and get better? Better than what? And what are we evolving into? There are always more questions than answers and who's in control anyway?

Cloud suddenly awoke from the darkness, a shame because he was kinda sorting to like not having anything to like or dislike for that matter. He felt the familiar pull on his bellybutton, the silver cord pulled tight to the point of breaking. It was like the mountain climber/window washer about to lose his safety rope. Hanging from the 20th floor with it wrapped around his neck. Shot by an automatic rifle on his way down. The press cries conspiracy. It was sort of like the Shamans out dancing under the sun in a field of yellow flowers, looking up at the sky, looking up at Cloud. The roadmap is open. Lay lines form endless cosmic roads and they all intersect. The cobweb shakes in the wind but remains unbroken. Cloud is older now and living in the city. When he was about eight years old, his mother moved there a few years after his father had deserted them. She got a job in a factory and struggled to support her family in a broken tenement flat deep in the city; almost downtown. She got up every morning and took the 6:00 a.m. bus uptown to the manufacturing district. Most of her co-workers were black and didn't take too kindly to an Indian from the Southwest infringing on their territory. She fought back, but without too much success, she was a minority within a minority. There was a lot of pushing and shoving and intimidation. They took her tools off of the grimy old workbench she sat at and broke into her locker at lunch and stole her cigarettes. But they were in no better boat, dealing with what was dished out on a day-to-day basis by all of the line bosses.

Cloud and his mom lived in a very old neighborhood, A couple of blocks of mostly Syrian and Lebanese immigrants that ran the local Mafioso for the Italians out of Chicago, surrounded by a ghetto comprised mostly of Blacks. The ghetto was anchored by recently built high-rise housing projects, the prison solution of the wayward fifties. Cold, buff brick imposing monuments to inequity, the Jects as they were called, took up about a six square block area. Surrounded by dirt-moats where the grass never grew, the buildings were linked by walkways enclosed in chain-link fencing. During the long hot summers when the air conditioning failed, families would sit in lawnchairs on the walkways to escape the brick oven heat emanating from the buildings. Sometimes the children would climb up the chain link fencing like they were trying to escape, not yet knowing that the only way out was to deal drugs or get an education, drugs being more lucrative, but the education safer. Climb up the fence almost to the razor wire; rattle your cage, no one else noticing except those already incarcerated.

Cloud was eight years old now with violent tendencies. He hung out in the basement and the attic of the old house depending on his mood. His first friend was Carl Jr. otherwise known, as Junior or J. Carl was a skinny poor white trash kid that was of a family from rural Arkansas. He was into weightlifting. Unable to afford actual weights, he filled bleach bottles up with sand and stuck an old broom handle in between the plastic handles. Carl was 14 and mainly hung around with a couple of older teenagers that had no Syrian family affiliations. Sometimes he would sneak a peek at them jacking off in the bathroom to a couple of Penthouse magazines they had stolen from the corner drugstore. He was rapidly learning the meaning of "pussy" and "hard on." He thought that making his muscles grow like those in his dad's old collection of Strength and Health Magazines would encourage other developing parts of his anatomy to do the same. He would lie in bed at night gently rubbing the tip of his penis until he fell asleep. One morning he received a wet sticky surprise all over his hand, and ran to tell the older boys that he now knew the meaning of "GUM." He had heard the street talk..."boy I'd like to give that chick some of my gum!" "Id have enough "GUM" for both of them" But he never really knew what they were talking about, thinking that they were referring to the chewing substance that came from trees. He couldn't figure out what was so great about chewing gum that would make all the girls go crazy and start taking off their clothes. They boys laughed when he said that and literally started rolling around on the ground. It's "COME" you stupid ass, they said walking away, leaving him even more confused than before.

Cloud spent many long hours on the back porch-reading comic books or throwing a rubber ball against the back brick wall, trying to hit a square "strike zone" that he had outlined in chalk. Carl Jr. lived in the run town tenement flat a couple of doors down. One day while Cloud was throwing the ball, Carl popped his head over the fence and asked Cloud if he would be interested in joining a club. "What club?" Cloud asked. Carl Jr. replied that it wasn't really any kind of club in particular, they could just secretly break into and commission one of the old deserted tar-paper covered sheds that lined the alleyways behind the houses, fix it up, collect weapons and "defend" it against all the other clubs in the neighborhood. He didn't know of any other clubs, but he was sure they were out there and would pose a threat sooner or later and it was better to be prepared. Cloud said that he would have to think about it, turned and ran back into the house, where he sat and worried about it for a few minutes, started playing with his deck of cards and fell asleep.

The next day Cloud was busy building his "city" in the dusty back yard. Actually it was more like an armed encampment than a city, holding his plastic soldiers and rubber cars. He was using a small camp shovel he had found to dig out the roadways in the powdery dirt. There was dust on his sweaty face and patches on his knees. Over and over again his mom had sewn the un-matching denim patches over his green pants where he had worn out the knees scurrying on his knees. He was ramming the Jeeps and tanks together and all the little toy soldiers were running for their lives. The final moment was at hand. Time to bring out the flamethrowers. He had stolen some Zippo lighter fluid and a can of his mother's hairspray. Holding a match right up in front of the toy tank, he aimed the can of hairspray in the right direction and let her rip. The alcohol in the spray caught fire and the resulting column of flame melted the plastic. It lay crumpled in a noxious, smelly heap, a wisp of acrid, very black smoke trickling skyward. Some of the smoke went up Cloud's nose and he coughed, and then spat on the ground.

He moved one of the toy soldiers like he was running from out of the tank's way, then doused him with the lighter fluid, lit a match and threw it at the fleeing, helpless toy soldier. The soldier rapidly melted into a pile of dusty goo.

He looked up and Carl Jr. was at his usual place on the other side of the fence; watching. "What do you want?" Cloud asked. "A club with you and me in lt." Carl replied. Cloud ran back into the gangway that separated the two houses. He was hiding, not really wanting any part of the "clubhouse" scene. "It'll be fun" a voice said next to him. Somehow Carl had gotten around to the front of the building and snuck in through the unlocked front gate. "Come here." he said. I want to show you something."

Carl led Cloud back through the gangway into the back Yard and over the saggy part of the wire fence. He then pointed to the sand-filled bleach bottle barbell set with the mop stick in-between, tied to the handles of the bottle with a couple of small rope pieces. "Think you can lift it?" Carl asked. Cloud was not one to step back from a challenge, no matter how much he disliked the person issuing it.

He bent over and grabbed what looked to be the handhold area of the mop stick. He tried to stand straight up and felt a sharp pain in his back. "Hey stop!" Carl yelled. "You'll hurt yourself doing it that way!" Carl went on to tell him how some bodybuilders preferred the wide stance as opposed to the narrow one, and that you always had to keep your back straight and lift with your legs. Cloud tried it again and got the bleach bottles a little bit further off the ground. "That's better." Carl said. "Wait here a minute." Carl ran into his house and at that point, Cloud thought about running back into the sanctuary of his own crib, but decided to rough it out and see what Carl had up his sleeve. Carl quickly returned with a handful of bodybuilding magazines. He told Cloud that if they both lifted weights everyday, that pretty soon they would look just like the musclemen posing in the mags. Then all the women would be crazy about them. "You DO like women, don't you?" Carl asked.

Cloud replied that he liked his Mom, sometimes, but all the girls that he had met were nasty, snotty little rags that scratched themselves in naughty places, told him he was cute, and tried to kiss him.

The wet slobbery stuff and Goo-Goo eyes were not to his liking. One time when Darla, a girl that lived about a block away, had tried to grab him, he picked up a two by four and hit her in the arm with it He got in trouble big time for that one as she had to wear a cast on her arm for six weeks, even though he claimed rightly so that it was in self-defense. Carl Jr. looked at him for a couple seconds, and then pulled a tattered picture out of his back pocket. It was a photograph from a sleazier rip off of Playboy Magazine. The kind that showed white trailer trash types fully stretched out and open like the gates of New York Harbor. Cloud stared at it intently, having never seen the likes of a full-blown naked bare lady before. Something about the configuration between her legs looked familiar though, the vagina reminded him of a keyhole. The kind of hourglass looking ones found in really old buildings like the one he lived in. The kind that accepted skeleton key the kind that he had peered through a couple of weeks ago as his mom was taking a bath. Looking at the picture oddly excited him, but he didn't know why. "Here, you can hang on to it for awhile." Carl said with a grin. Cloud was startled and a little nervous about this sudden intrusion into the adult world. He ran home and hid the picture behind a loose piece of stone that was chipped off the mantle of the fireplace in his bedroom. A couple of days later, he and Carl Jr. established a clubhouse, complete with a weapons locker. In it was an old pocketknife named Rusty that they found behind a trash dumpster and an old fishing harpoon, about 12 inches long stolen from Carl's Grandfather's tackle box. The old wooden tarpaper covered garage that they called home base sagged precariously to one side and probably should have been condemned. It was one of the few in the hundreds of years old neighborhood that had survived being burned down. It had a dirt floor and a wooden garage door in the back that was held together by rusty old iron springs that had long since ceased to function. The roof leaked really bad whenever it rained and Cloud and Carl searched the neighborhood looking for stray pieces of tarpaper that had fallen off of their buildings to repair the roof. Sometimes they would sneak atop old buildings and rip the shingles that were left and put them on the clubhouse. It was after all a matter of priorities. They then went about making a bathroom, a place to piss in, but not shit. It was as they called it, just a half-bath. Foraging through the alleys, they found a large piece of sewer pipe, the kind with a big flange at the top that narrowed down to a pipe at the bottom. They set about digging out a hole in one corner of the clubhouse, over in the corner by the defunct garage doer. They made it as deep as they could, given the hard, compacted dirt was not very easy to dig through.

They then jammed the sewer pipe down in the hole all the way up to the neck. It was Pretty stable, the idea that it would function like a cesspool, the noxious, stagnant urine eventually draining down into the Earth.

The next order of business was to cover over some of the dirt floor of the clubhouse with cement mix appropriated from Carl's father's tuck pointing business. Carl told Cloud that they must have some gravel to strengthen up the watery cement mix. They took brooms and started sweeping up broken rock about a block down the alleyway that ran behind the old shed. They mixed all this up in an old cardboard box until the powdery goo began to seep out of the sides. Using an old rusty trowel, again stolen from the tuck pointing father, they smoothed they gray mess out on the dirt floor. It got everywhere and took days to dry, but finally they had achieved a dirt-free portion of floor. Some days they just hung around the clubhouse, reading comic books and playing games. Other times when things got a little boring, they would climb up on the roof of the old garage and jump from building to building, finally climbing down after they had run out of roofs. They would then roam the alleys looking to kick the ass of rival gangs, but never found any. One day Carl had an idea: invade the basement of the old house and construct an gym to workout in. After all they had most of the equipment...several sets of bleach bottle barbells, some cast iron window weights taken from a condemned house where Cloud had almost fallen through the rotted floor, some chain, and an old set of springs from an abandoned mattress. They made their way down the dark basement steps after opening the slanted wooden hatch that covered the stairs. The skeleton key to the basement door was right where it was supposed to be, hidden by cobwebs on the ledge. They scampered around in the dark for a few minutes before finally finding the one naked light bulb hanging on a frayed piece of wire wrapped around one of the rafters. The basement was damp, cold, and musty smelling. Two very small windows with thick yellow-stained broken glass let in just a tiny fraction of light. In one corner at the front of the room was an old wooden sink that continually dripped water, even though it had been turned off. An ancient wringer washer stood hulking in the far corner towards the back. It had given up the ghost long ago, it's motor guts being ripped out to make a fan that cooled the house during the summer, air conditioning being totally out of the question. The floor/ceiling sagged at places, in eminent danger of collapse. It was hoisted up a little by floor jacks made of metal; the hundred-year-old wood fatally weakened by translucent termites. If you dare venture further back into the basement towards the front of the house, past the wooden wall that divided the place, you came to a hulking old coal furnace and the overwhelming smell of stagnant coal. It was still fun however to roll around in the stuff and put on your own personal blackface. There was a bucket of cinders that looked like it contained rocks from some distant volcanic planet. A gray striped engineer's cap hung on a rusty nail on the wall, personal property of the old black man that maintained the building. Sometimes the boys would find an almost consumed bottle of gin hiding up in the rafters. They would eerily consume the remaining inch of liquid and stagger around for a while, giggling, before falling asleep on an old mattress that they used as a workout mat. Carl shuffled Cloud over into the corner by the sink. "Does your mom have any rubbing alcohol? He asked. Cloud replied that he thought she kept a bottle in the bathroom right next to the Paragoric. He was sent to get the bottle and shortly returned with it tucked under his shirt. "We have to have an initiation. Carl said. "For both our Muscular Gym and the Clubhouse, after all we're in the same gang aren't we? Cloud nodded his head yes, but was wondering exactly what an "initiation" was. We have to become blood brothers, that way we can share secrets." Said Carl. He pulled Cloud over towards the sink. The idea of drawing and sharing blood did not really appeal to Cloud. "How can we do this?" Carl mused. Carl said that sometimes when he squeezed on of his zits, some blood would ooze out with the pus; he was after all 14 and prone to such maladies. He squirted some alcohol on his cheek and squeezed until there was an angry red splotch on his face. He turned to Cloud: hmmm, no zits. He felt in his pockets and produced a silver nail file. "This ought to do the trick." He said as he jabbed Cloud in the arm with it. "Ouch, you bastard!!!" Cloud screamed. There was a small dot of blood seeping out on Cloud's arm. Carl grabbed the arm and pressed it against his face. "Blood brothers for all eternity!" He yelled. Cloud looked at him with a puzzled look, and then walked over to the dripping faucet to wash the red and white bloody puddle off his arm.

The two gang members brought all their "muscular" gym equipment, bleach bottle barbells, ET All, down into the dingy basement and set up shop. They stripped off some old wood-grain contact paper that had been glued to the windows to better let in some sunlight. Before they could seriously begin pumping iron, there was but one thing left to do: BATTLE!

A game had been devised; one that took some preparation and the help of a couple of the Hadley boys that lived down the street. The Hadley's were mean, rotten and nasty, and there were a lot of them; four boys and three girls, all with blondish red hair, freckles, and an extra crease on their arms just below the elbow. It looked as though they could bend their arms in two places, but they couldn't, one of the local kids had tried, but just ended up breaking the arm. Retaliation was swift and painful. The father of the bunch was an alcoholic that occasionally would end up sleeping one off in one of the skid-row alleyways of the neighborhood, but mostly he would disappear for months at a time and never be heard from. The mother would dose herself up on whatever downer she could get her hands on, so the children had to pretty well fend for themselves. Cloud occasionally trailed into their house after the older kids, but didn't stay very long; the smell was pretty much overwhelming. Dirty dishes were stacked high in the sink and rotten and decaying food littered the kitchen table. Flies were everywhere, buss digesting the rotted food and eating the secretions off the eyes of sleeping children. Most of the family had red spots covering their bodies and blood oozing out of their gums. One of them was even called scab because he was continually picking at the crustiness and would occasionally shed his skin like a snake.

Now back to the battle, the balloon battle. This was the way that it worked. They would make a foray into Scab's kitchen wearing masks over their faces. They would collect things there. Bits of food, household chemicals that were smelly, like furniture polish, and other assorted nasty things. These were bottled up several days before the game, so they could get really smelly and stinky. They were then put into rubber balloons using a big turkey baster syringe type thing. The balloons were tied securely so they wouldn't leak. Trenches were laid inside of the covered basement steps and strategic spots were surveyed inside gangways running between the buildings. Then the war began, each side hurling the smelly balloons at the other. Biological paintball. A direct hit was worth 10 points and after a few, the victim was usually sent scurrying home to clean off the mess, except for Scab of course, he relished in it. That was why he was so valuable nothing seemed to faze him. After everyone ran out of balloons the game ended. Bits of broken rubber with unknown nastiness coming out of them hung off the doors and covered the walls of the buildings and the steps. Several days later they would sit around and point out how this balloon or that one had made an impact.

   Cloud and Carl were alone now, down in the gym, after things had settled down. Cloud remembered that at times Carl had an odd smell about him and it wasn't from the balloons. It was sort of a mixture of sweat, canned corn, and Comet cleanser. They were both relaxing after a muscle-burning workout with the bleach bottles. Cloud was lying down on the workout mat while Carl was next to him propped up on his elbows, looking at one of the nasty pictures he was so fond of carrying around in his pants pocket. "Will you look at that? He showed the picture to Cloud. Cloud wasn't really sure why Carl was so preoccupied with looking at nude women, but then he was only eight years old while Carl had Just turned fourteen. "You may not like these pictures now, but you will!" Carl boasted. Carl had his hands down in his pants, something he was often fond of doing. "Let's play a game." He told Cloud. He instructed Cloud to roll over on his stomach. "I'll be the man, you be the woman." Carl instructed him. Carl then proceeded to get on top of Cloud and put his arms around his waist. Cloud was unaware of what was going on, but he knew he didn't like it. Something just wasn't right about the whole situation. He tried to roll over and get away, but Carl had him firmly pinned. Carl moved around for a few minutes, squirming on top of Cloud. He moaned and rolled off of him, gasping for air. "Whew!" he said, as he grabbed his belt and moved it up and down. It was like something you would do after consuming a huge Thanksgiving dinner.

Cloud quickly got to his feet. Tears were stinging in his eyes. He looked at Carl. "My Mom told me about people like you! He said. "You must be a pervert." He was now breathing heavily. Carl looked at him sternly. "You're not going to tell her, are you?" He asked. Cloud slowly shook his head no. "Just don't let it happen again." He said. As Carl got up and started walking away, he turned to Cloud and said: "Remember the secret, we're blood brothers." He turned and walked out the door.

Chapter 2

The Cloud that was in the sky was bouncing around like a red rubber paddleball, and the staple in his bellybutton hurt. The light show continued and at times he thought he was being dipped into the fires of hell. Suddenly out of nowhere, a cool blue mist seemed to surround him. He felt singed, but hardened like a piece of clay pottery just removed from the kiln. "What doesn't kill you only makes you stronger." Sometimes however, you get so hardened that you begin to crack. The scene before him was something like a scrambled TV picture, but there were brief periods of clarity...he was being fine-tuned by some celestial technician. He watched as the picture formed and settled down a little. An occasional shock wave of violet electricity made his astral body twitch.

Cloud was thirteen now and staring at the cracked mirror in the bathroom of his mother's house. They had moved a couple of years ago, but just a few blocks away from the old neighborhood. Next-door and pretty much scattered throughout a few square block area, lived members of a Syrian family that had mafia connections. The elder of the family, the Godfather so to speak, had taken a liking to Cloud's mom, much to the disdain of his dyed, red-haired Arab wife. He would let her do the ironing for various male members of the family. The ironing always consisted of white cotton dress shirts. No pants or women's clothes. They had to be pressed and starched to perfection or she would probably have ended up tied to concrete at the bottom of the river. But mom did an excellent Job, making sure that no wrinkle was left unseated by the hot iron, and the extra money went a long way towards supplementing her factory job. The gangster house next door was well groomed and rather stately compared to the rest of the slum's houses surrounding it. A pack of wild German Shepard wolf dogs inhabited the back yard. The family was so good at killing things that no grass was able to grow in the yard, so eventually they covered it with concrete. Cloud was afraid of the dogs and his mother hated them. Cloud would run at top speed through the alley that separated the two houses and the dogs would run headlong into the wire fence, straining to get at him. The metal support poles were bent over in one area from the weight of the animals leaning against the fence. The dogs were deliberately made mean by adding liberal doses of red pepper to their diet. There was also an old lady in the neighborhood that would walk down the alley on her way to the store and throw a handful of the pepper at the dogs who were ~trying to get at her through the old wooden fence that bordered that side of the property. So the dogs were pretty fed up with the red pepper bit, eating away at their stomachs and continually irritating their eyes and noses. It made for a bunch of mean puppies. Cloud would summon up as much courage as he could possibly bear, then run at full breakneck speed through the gangway that separated the Tumis family from his own house. The pepper dogs would leap and strain at the old wire fence, bloody spittle dripping from their canines. Sometimes he could feel their hot breath panting on his neck they were so close. Other times a more stealthy approach was in order. When the dogs were sleeping or on the other side of the yard, he would sometimes try to sneak along the other side of the narrow passageway. Hugging close to the crumbling, musty smelling bricks, his breath coming in short spurts. Most of the time though, they were on to this trick, still being able to sniff him out through the effects of the red pepper. He could hear the familiar growl start, low and rumbling, then exploding into a ferocious howl. One time one of the dogs got out while Cloud was hanging around in the back yard. It knocked him over and was chewing on his jeans, ripping through to get at the flesh. His mom, hearing all the screams and racket, came flying out the backdoor with the first thing that she could grab, a pot of boiling potatoes. She threw it at the animal, trying desperately to avoid hitting Cloud. Some of the scorching liquid caught the dog on one of his bald mange spots that mapped out his scraggly back and this did the trick.

The dog went squealing back under the fence, tall tucked between his legs and hid in the woodshed for several hours.

Cloud hung around with a couple of the kids from the Thomis Family. They were mean and nasty, greasy and fat. Hair combed back in the fifties style, wearing Italian knit Ban Lon shirts and pointy Bannister shoes, patent leather all the rage at the time. The other kids on the block, not being quite so well endowed had to settle for white Levis, Boondocker boots, and tie-dye T-Shirts. The Thomis Family had truck hijacking as one of their business activities, so at times Cloud would help unload the stolen truck and receive a free pair of pants as a reward for his efforts. He also helped work the counter at the fake- front confectionary that the Thomis gang owned. A candy counter, some packs of cigarettes, and a few old cans of food were' all that littered the shelves, but you could get clothes, radios, and even TV sets for a bargain basement price if you were allowed downstairs. Message running was also another source of income if you were a young teenage kid like Cloud. On several occasions, he got to run back and forth between families delivering notes that contained explicit threats. "If you don't stop, you mother fucker, this is what's going to happen to your festered ass. Oh yeah, well after I rip out your fucking tongue and work your ass over with a blowtorch." That sort of thing. But it rarely escalated into any major conflicts, as the older members of the families would usually reign things in and keep the peace.

The Thomis family pretty much had the city under wraps. Their influence at one point went all the way up to the Mayor's office. The Syrians were really under the control of the Italian mob in Chicago, but it wasn't wise to talk about such things unless you were connected pretty high up in the family. There was one smaller rival family, but the elders of each one kept the peace. They were pretty much from opposite sides of the tracks so to speak, the Maliks controlled the more white-collar areas of the city, and while the Thomis family was more into petty theft, stealing trucks, controlling unions and engaging in some prostitution in the outlying areas. They were all involved in Democratic politics, extending all the way up to state senator. In addition to wearing the white shirts, smoking big cigars, and sporting gold teeth, they all rode around in black limos that were rented or in taxicabs. The likelihood of a bomb going off under those circumstances was a little less likely. You could never tell when the testosterone level would rise in one of the younger Clemenzas and the bombs and bullets would start flying. But the peace had been kept for some time now and they were almost respectable. They certainly were well respected in the neighborhood, as the poorer contingent would continually show up at Pappa Ray's bar asking for favors. The favors were on the menu and carried a price tag just like Baskin Robbins. Usually it was to speak politely to some judge to get a wayward son off the hook when he did something stupid like break into a factory to steal something.

Tiny Phillips was Just such a man, though no one was certain just whose son he was anyway. He was a member of a local motorcycle gang called the Saddle Tramps that became friends with Cloud's mother. The gang would sometimes park their hog Harleys outside of Cloud's house and sit on the steps; drinking the cheapest beer they could find usually something like Falstaff or Blatz and pop speeders. Eventually they would pass out, scraggly beards glazed over like jelly donuts, butt cracks halfway out of their smelly jeans. Cloud would occasionally fill up a plastic pitcher with ice cold water and trickle it down their cracks, in which case they would wake up with a startled scream choking, spitting and snarling, sometimes vomiting projectiles of bright red raw blood. Clouds mom would fix dinner for them, usually a pot of chili or stew, which they would ravenously swallow. The idea was to get one of the beans lodged in the ulcerous hole in their stomachs long enough to prevent them from bleeding to death.

Tiny was a large man, about 6'6", and 300 pounds. He was unemployed and when he wasn't drunk and crashing his motorcycle into parked cars, he busied himself climbing up on Churches ripping the copper ornamentation off of them and selling it at the scrap yard. He wore a pendant-shaped magnet around his neck to tell what was copper and what was useless base metal, one being magnetic and the other not.

Cloud and his Thomis Family friends liked to play games. There was a couple living a few blocks down the street from Cloud; Martin and Slyvia. Martin worked at the local garage and sniffed glue, paint, and gasoline, while Slyvla was fat, smelly, and mildly retarded. They were a perfect match for each other. Martin was in his forties, skinny, with freckles and reddish hair that was usually dirty and smelled of axle grease. It seemed that Slyvia never changed her dress, and probably not her underwear either. The boys were at that age where everything they talked about was disgusting and nasty, having just recently discovered an interest in the opposite sex. They would swagger down the street singing little ditties like...I was walking through the Jungle with my dick in my hand; I was the biggest motherfucker in the Congo Land. I looked up in a tree and guess what I saw, I saw a big motherfucker trying to piss on me...I picked up a rock and hit him in the cock, and that motherfucker flew a block" It really didn't matter that there probably weren't any rocks in the jungle anyway.

One day about three of them decided to pay a visit to Martin's back yard and see if he was staggering around, sniffing whatever chemical he could lay his hands on. They could then laugh, point and make fun. They looked through the basement window knowing that would probably be where he was...stoned and tinkering with some carburetor or something.

Instead, when they peered in through the dirty, broken glass, they saw the two of them, down and dirty on the basement floor, bare-assed and making out. Martin was on top, his red pimply ass thrusting deeply into the crack between Slyvia's legs. One of the kids remarked that the old broad must still have some pussy left on her anyway, while the Thomis boy standing next to him said that she really must be a dead fuck because she wasn't moving at all. They watched for a few minutes more and then left laughing, only later to discover that Slyvia actually was dead and had been so for some time. Martin the little glue-sniffing necrophiliac, would heat up her private parts with a blow torch until they were alive and moist and then have a go at her. This went on for a few weeks until she finally became too loose and squishy, not to mention smelly to get Martin off. He disposed of the body and was later arrested, but not before he was able to hump a few freshly mangled road kill.

Other days when the group was bored, they would hang around the old train tracks downtown, spraying the boxcars with graffiti or play project chicken. A large high-rise housing project was nearby and when the spirit of adventure overtook the gang, they would ride their bikes into the projects and then sit and wait until the word got out that there were bicycles to be had just for the taking. A vigilante group of natives armed with baseball bats and broomsticks would suddenly appear out of nowhere and try to knock the boys off their bikes.

The group, would then hop on the bikes and ride like hell to get out of. Dodge before they were seriously injured. They knew that if they could just make it a few blocks out of the projects, they would then be in their own territory and on safe ground. Most of the time they were successful at doing this and could then sit around and brag about how brave and bad they really were. One time however, Cloud's bike tire hit a bit of loose gravel and he fell. He regained his composure and his life just in the nick of time, escaping by a matter of inches. When the preceding sort of things got old, they would do things like going down on the local skid row and paying an old drunk named Red a quarter to swallow a lit cigarette. He would wheeze, cough and sputter for a 'few minutes after swallowing it, but down the hatch it went, a wispy curl of smoke coming out of his snot-infested nostrils. They thought that this exhibition was the neatest thing on Earth, but gave it up when Red was a little bit too intoxicated one time and booted up some of the most fowl and obnoxious vomit all over fat Johnny's shoes.

Chapter 3

The championship New York Jets football team, quarterbacked by
Joe Namath, who wore pantyhose but wasn't gay, were in town to play an
exhibition game with the hometown football team. This was under
sponsorship of the large brewery that pretty much ran things around town.
The Thomis family, being connected of course, was able to procure some
pretty nice tickets, and lots of them. Fat Johnny offered one to Cloud,
playfully suggesting that he would have to suck his dick to get one. Cloud
had never been to a professional football game before and decided to go and
not tell his mother, who might just object. She wasn't too happy with her
thirteen year old son hanging around with the sons and daughters of the
biggest crime family in town because there just might be a little bad
influence going on there, and him at such an impressionable age.

Cloud had already went cruising with a couple of the uncles down in~ the
red-light district on Washington Avenue. They would drive up in the
limousine and shout out "How much?" to the red hot pants clad in leather
hookers who would then reply back: "Ten and two plus the room baby!"
You have to remember that this was back in the sixties when you could buy
a new VW Beetle for about 1800 dollars and the price of a Filet steak dinner
at Best Steak House #2 was $1.69, and that included salad, potato, and lots
of butter-soaked garlic bread. Sometimes this is where the Thomis
hoodlums and Cloud and a couple of his friends that were related to the mob
would end up. After all, there's no better way to build up an appetite than
cruising for hookers on Washington Avenue. Sometimes they would get
together in the alley behind Cloud's house and play bottle caps. Bottle caps
was a game pretty unique to this part of town that was played with a stick,
broom, mop, or other type of stick, and a whole bunch of crown bottle caps

obtained from the corner tavern. This was never a problem because the family extorted money from them anyway. The game was pretty simple, but very difficult to win. One player would waft the bottle cap in the general direction of the batter and all he had to do was hit it. It was sort of like cork ball. One strike and you were out, and every hit was a homerun. One day the stick slipped out of one of the Family member's grasp and went flying through Cloud's window. No one dared to say anything of course. The Family member just reached into his pocket and pulled out a wad of twenties and started peeling a number of them off, asking Cloud's mom to tell him when to stop. She hurriedly told him to stop after the total reached about a hundred dollars, no need to push her luck.

Then of course, there was the curious case of Uncle Joe, as everyone in the neighborhood called him. Joe's source of supplemental income was to sell stolen weapons up North in the poor, black part of town. One day Cloud and a couple of his buddies were allowed to ride with Joe. Joe had the gun concealed, tucked into his trousers at the small of his back, it must have been uncomfortable sitting in the seat of the car with the cold steel of a snub-nosed 38 poking you in the small of your back. They drove about twenty minutes and Cloud watched as the sights became more and more grim. Men staggered out of corner liquor stores clutching brown paper bags close to their chests that held the cheap Night Train joy of life. Cloud thought back about the time that he and several friends had first tasted liquor; there was a sort of skid row in the neighborhood up by Leubon's Dry Goods Store. Right next door was Paramount Liquor and Cloud would watch, as the winos would stumble out of the door, draining the bottle as they went, too much in a hurry to feel the searing smoothness as the booze flowed down their throats to stop and socialize. They would stagger to the nearest doorway of the old abandoned dry goods building and usually collapse in a heap. One day the boys decided to play a game. They found an old empty bottle of Four Roses Whiskey, "the good stuff".

The bottle wasn't in too bad of a shape and it certainly was the right color, a rather dark shade of brown...dark enough to hide the contents of the bottle. Back in those days the only seal that whiskey bottles had was a stamp-looking piece of paper that was taped over the top and down both sides of the neck of the bottle. This was pretty easy to get off and then tape back on. The boys took turns peeing in the empty bottle until it was full. One of them then licked the liquor seal until it had regained some of it's stickiness. Then they waited. Waited for one of the drunks to come stumbling out of the store. After some pushing and shoving and getting up of nerve, they approached the bleary-eyed, stumbling man...hopefully he was already half blind and wouldn't notice what was going on. He clutched the fresh bottle of cheap wine close to his chest. "Hey mister!" one of the group shouted. "We found this full bottle of whiskey over in the alley, would you trade it for that bottle of grape juice?" A thought spread out like a slow moving amber current through the bloody-recesses of the old drunk's mind.... maybe a trade for a bottle of whiskey wasn't such a bad idea after all. The alcohol content certainly was higher and the stuff would last him a lot longer, maybe even for a couple of days, his damaged liver wasn't up to handling near as much these days as it used to be able to in it's heyday of week-long binges. He stumbled towards the boys warily, eyeing the bottle in their hands. He looked at it and reached out... the boys looked like they were ready to bolt at any time. They refused t to give up the bottle of piss-whiskey until he relinquished the wine. He grabbed for the whiskey as they grabbed for the wine...it was a face- off, each party successful in grabbing their own respective treasure.

The kids ran like hell down the street but just far enough to still see what was going on. The old drunk staggered back to his resting place, quickly screwed off the cap to the bottle of pseudo-whiskey, wrapped his parched lips around it, and eagerly took a huge swallow. His phlegm-encrusted eyes shot wide open at the salty taste of the fresh boy piss, and he spat, realizing what it was. "You little bastards!" he screamed, throwing the bottle in the general direction the boys had run. He sat down hard on the crumbled concrete of the sidewalk, tears streaming down his reddened cheeks. The boys were bent over to the ground in laughter, pointing at the sodden drunk. They ran a few blocks more, just in case the drunk would launch a feeble attempt to follow them. When they were pretty sure that he wouldn't, they cautiously screwed off the top of the Ripple and shared the sickly sweet contents therein. Pretty soon they were stumbling around, drunk and delirious. It was fun as the world began to spin. One of the group got sick and threw up on his shoes, but he didn't seem to mind it at all. Meanwhile, the drunk was crying himself to sleep and into troubled dreams. It was an experience that he hadn't had in quite awhile, the dreams that is, the alcohol usually knocked them out. After a few hours he awoke, but the nightmares didn't cease. They were playing out their sordid stage play right there in front of him. He held his shaking hands up to his face, occasionally trying to brush away the horrible imaginary insects that were crawling all over him. Cloud had drunkenly staggered away from his companions and snuck back to take a look. He felt sorry for the old man and what he had done to him. The drunk had finally passed out into some kind of fitful sleep, his body too exhausted with itself to put up any more of a shaky struggle. Cloud searched around in his pockets for some change and found about 50 cents, enough for the wino to get another bottle of wine when he woke up. He would do this every time he saw a fellow sufferer in the future, even when he was in the same situation. His first taste of darkness and he thought maybe the sun would never shine again, but it was just the booze talking.

"Hey!" "What're doin" back there?" "Beatin' your meat?" Cloud was shaken out of his revelry about the old Piss Drunk by Joe's gravely voice. They had arrived at their destination in the crumbling part of the North side of the city. The houses had at one point, about a hundred years ago, been as lavish and rich as the ones down in the currently more affluent South part, but had long ago been the seedy side of town. All this had taken place because of a lake. The lake ran along Peres Avenue and had dried up long ago, but not before it divided the city. Around the turn of the century, the lake had become stagnant. This was the days before there was much of a sewer system in the city and the lake was a convenient place to dispose of unwanted garbage. Eventually a foul stench began to waft off the body of water in the dog days of the good summertime and offended the rich folk living in the mansions on the north side. The urban exodus began en-mass to the suburbs with the introduction of the automobile. Some of the stately ornate houses were torn down to make way for the industrial factory boom. The others were converted into tenement houses for the workers from the factories. Eventually, the factories shuttered up and what Cloud saw before him at the current moment was the result.

Joe had stopped the car in front of an old redbrick building that had been whitewashed in a vain attempt to make it look stucco. He told the boss to wait in the car he would be right back. He slid the stolen gun down into the waist of his baggy pants and headed off. Joe didn't have the common courtesy of actually knocking on the door of the house he just barged right in. A few moments later, he emerged, dragging a nude black man behind him. The man had a huge erection and Cloud was staring at it, something like a veiny wooden cucumber sticking out from between his legs. "Look kids, that's all these motherfuckers do, sit around all day, get high, and fuckl" The black man was making sort of a fuss, being paraded around on his front porch in the nude in front of strange little white kids and the neighbors were somewhat embarrassed, but knowing that Joe would probably not sell him the gun, and most probably kill him, he decided to play along and maybe the ordeal would be over soon. Joe kept dragging him out towards the car, and at least his erection was fading, much to Clouds relief. The black man spoke to the kids in a deep southern accent. "Yeah, I was poking ma bitch." I'll tell ya somethin9 though, that bitch getting loose as a muthafucka, cracked my balls on that bitch twice, went in so deep, pretty soon gonna have ta' ties a board on ma ass." All this pretty much went past Cloud. Cracked his balls? They looked pretty intact to him. Pretty soon Joe tired of the exhibition, and let the black dude go back into his house to get the money for the pistol.

Part II

A Revelation of the Spirit

Starry, starry night, clouds of amber gray and the moon was shining bright. The ethereal Cloud looked down on this part of his life with what only could be described as sad amusement. If only there was some way to go about it all over again and correct his mistakes. But that was what this was all about wasn't it? Some kind of Karmic payback thing as he was well on his way to Nirvana or whatever any one man's particular religion called it. Walking on rings of Saturn on some kind of celestial merry-go-round. Still there was something about this that just wasn't right. Why, the idea that there was some kind of benevolent God meddling in people's day to day lives and taking sides in war-like or maybe Warlock combat just never made any sense to him at all. He was more inclined to take a more scientific, practical approach. If there was a God, then why did he let some people slide by with all kinds of atrocities and then turn around and punish the hell out of others. Or maybe it was punish the hell INTO others. His thoughts that you probably just became worm fodder clung to him despite all the wondrous things that he had seen recently. Or was it recently? How much time on Earth had really passed? He was certainly capable of looking into his own past, and other people's pasts for that matter, even entire races. When he was there, there was no concept of a past or future, no notion of anything passing, it all seemed right here in the present. Everything was laid out right in front of him in really no particular order.

He thought that maybe what the Indians had told him made more sense. That the afterlife was just like a never-ending dream of sorts. One that if you used the right techniques, you could actually access in your own lifetime before you shuffled off the mortal coil. If this was a dream, he certainly seemed to be increasing his ability to access more control. He felt weird, as though his thoughts were "things."

It was as if he had this antenna sticking out of his head like an insect and could "tune" into the wavelengths of things just by thinking about them. "I got you on my WAVELENGTH ......" He wondered if he could focus in on some people he hadn't liked back when he was alive and haunt their ass. He focused and tried to think of somebody's name. There were some scattered images of houses with some cars parked out in front of them, but the image was blurry and indiscrete. Maybe the particular person that you were trying to haunt had to also be thinking about you at the time or it wouldn't work. He tried to think of someone who may be thinking about him at the time, but no one came to mind. He thought maybe the liquor storeowner, since Cloud had missed his usual stumble-in afternoon alcohol score. An image of the Russian lady that worked at the store came into a fuzzy kind of view. But it was just a face. How could you haunt just a face? He concentrated and the face moved to the side, looking almost as if it was watching him, but still unaware. The store was old; it had a wooden floor with traces of sawdust. It had the warm comforting smell of stale tobacco juice and spilt beer. There was a creaky old elevator that once brought up barrels that were stored in the basement. It had long fallen into disuse. There were a couple of refrigerator cases with a flashing "cold beer" neon sign on top. He floated past the beer can collection and looked behind the counter. All his friends were gathered there. God bless their pointy little heads. They recognized him, their labels shouting, "Pick me!" Pick Me!" Jack was there and Jim, Lem Motlow and Johnny Walker Red, and Black and White. The little Scottish terrier was yapping at him happily. All the nationalities of the world had come to greet him. Jose, from Mexico was there, who was wearing his funny little red plastic hat and a shawl covering his dusty jeans. There was the wealthy class; the expensive French wines and Brandies, segregated from the poor side of town, where the entire crews of common bar whiskies like Kentucky Tavern and Four Roses lived. If one ventured too far into these bottles, they would kick your ass all over the place and make you throw up. At times, when he was lying in the gutter after a few day's binge, he felt seasick, like' a boat slave. Shackled to a type of backboard on the ship with your legs holding you in place because of the rusty iron shackles surrounding them. You were propped up on the outside of the ship, the board that you were tied to tilted up at an angle and a wooden trough below you. This was so the feces, urine and vomit could slide down the board into the trough where it was then hosed off down to the sea every couple of days. Condemned prisoner, to the life you had chosen. You always have a choice, choice being the most powerful word in the entire universe. Waking up and rubbing the Guillotine scar on your neck. The rumor was that if you survived the first fall of the blade, you wouldn't be executed. Receive your stay and live to be ninety in some rat-infested cell living on garbage until God's pestilence took it's toll. The alley was such a prison, only you could sometimes see a little more of the sky. You always worried about the axe however, even if It was in the form of a man carrying a Chromeboy, willing to sever your head from it's neck for the few cents that you had left in your pocket.

Cloud could once again see the lady's face behind the counter. She was smiling that smile. A smile of wisdom, souls winking at each other, a been there done that sort of thing. She had told him that before her husband had bought the liquor store and then promptly died, she also had struggled with the demon drink. Take a drink straight from the bottle then the bottle starts taking a drink from you, she liked to say. Well the bottle had been drinking from Cloud for quite some time now. He was about as dry as the Mojave Desert and that was the problem.

Which Devil do you dance with tonight? Jack, Jim, Johnny Walker, or just be content with Mickey, who smells and tastes so foul she makes you puke.

The bottles were Jumping, clinking, moving in unison. A mind- deafening cacophony of shattering glass ...... all the life blood slipping away ..... You're left with an old Vampire carcass withered by the sun, a stake protruding from your heart. There was a hot wind blowing as the scene of the liquor store faded from Cloud's sight. "Like the fires a burning from hell way down in the valley tonight....."

"Come on!" "Come on!" The beer can collection was shouting in unison. It's the holidays and we have to celebrate. They were smiling and jovial, not realizing that Jupiter was next in line from Saturn, the planet of war and death. He was in the German beer hall, Polka music in the background, yellow liquid turning into yellow urine, flowing in the trough. Clank down your tankard, pinch the golden-haired serving wench on the ass, slide down the bench and get a splinter in your own and a big red nose and beer belly to boot. It was still the holidays and tonight three spirits will visit you: wine, bourbon and scotch. The morning after party will be held in your shorts. The spirits have to go, leaving chunks of vomit and shit stains in your skivvies.

The Old Russian lady Cloud was trying to haunt was standing behind the counter. Once a source of comfort and solace, she was now holding a large plastic inflatable liquor bottle, shoving it in his face and laughing hysterically. She held it over her head like some over- exaggerated Zeppelin then shoved it between her legs like a giant phallus. He felt like magically turning it into real glass, after all he was a ghost, and then smashing it into her head. But instead he turned around and staggered out the door into the thin, cold December air. The neon signs in the window of the store hummed and sputtered. He looked across the street at the shuttered house with the red Christmas lights strung across the front. He stared intently at the lights, fixed in an almost epileptic state. A face formed in the contours of the bulb, fuzzy and indistinct. The mouth of the face was forming words, but no voice was heard. It was trying to speak to Cloud but somehow the message was not getting across. He felt cold, scared, alone and sick, about to lose grip on whatever reality he was in. He was tired and needed a place to lie down, but the lack of liquor drove him like an animal on the hunt. He had to consume or soon he would die. But wait. Wasn't he already dead? Was the afterlife as all consuming and unfulfilling as the other? More of the same seemed to be his reward. There was a shadowy figure standing a few feet from him. He had barely noticed. He caught a glimpse of brown paper. His salvation seemed to be within his grasp. He walked up behind the man and shoved as hard as he could.

Caught unawares, the man stumbled and fell hard to the frozen ground. The bottle bag was freed from his grasp, luckily it didn't break, or they would both be shit out of luck. Now only one of them had to suffer and it wouldn't be Cloud this time anyway. He kicked the fallen comrade in the throat. Phlegm filled sputtering sound resulted. Cloud reached over and picked up the bottle of cheap wine that lay on the sidewalk, alone and looking for a friend. He summoned all the strength that he had left and started running as fast as he could. A few blocks away he stopped, out of gas, face red, swollen and puffy from the effort. He shoved himself into a narrow space between two brick buildings. He tried to unscrew the cap off the bottle of wine, but found that his fingers were too cold, stiff and weak to even get the top of the damned thing off. He put the bottle top into his mouth and bit down hard, breaking a tooth in the process. It still wouldn't budge. Angry now, and getting more furious by the second, he stuck the bottle between two loose bricks and pushed down as hard as he could. The top of the bottle broke, lodging a jagged piece of glass into his finger in the process. He put the broken neck to his already bloody lips and took a large swallow. At this point he didn't care. The tart vinegar slid down his throat and gagged him.

The bastard was walking around with a fucking bottle of vinegar! The stuff was undrinkable even when mixed with 70% rubbing alcohol. He threw the bottle down the gangway and started sobbing, wiping red fingers across his face and finally realizing the metallic taste of his own blood.

Spectral Cloud was flying through the damn tunnel again; he was getting a little tired of being this damn haint on a mission. Peeling red rubber ball stapled to a wooden paddle. At the whim and call of some boy-God playing with himself and whatever other cosmic energies he could capture. He was on the outward fling, knowing that he would eventually be yanked back. Suddenly this very beautiful green-gold mist surrounded him. It was very soothing, like putting Aloe on a burn, ice cold water sliding very wet down your throat. There were stairs in front of him leading down into the abyss. For once, however, he was not afraid to float down the stairs. In front-of him there was a rather impressive looking door. It swung open very slowly as he watched. He went inside. It was a very large room, sparingly lit, that was divided into smaller rooms. Drifting through the corridors of your mind, which was now in the toilet. I have to unburden myself of a few things along the way. Karmic excrement shit down on top of the highest mountains. Slap some Laplander in the face with it. He shouldn't have chosen to become a Shaman if he wasn't prepared for this kind of thing. What part of the alley does your spiritual journey lead you to anyway? Smack dab perched atop the razor's edge, and I thought you were a fine English gentleman Mr. Maum. Cloud looked around the dimly lit room and started seeing things. Things that were objects from his life that now took on some kind of twisted meaning. Different parts of the room/rooms lit up as he floated through.

Where was the guide in this life mind museum that was in charge of turning things on as the tourists went on their merry way taking in the sights? Over in the corner lay a rag doll, one that he had when he was very small, about 3 years old. It had been sewn and re-sewn many times by an old lady on the reservation. It would be secretly taken from him by some horrible late night hag and thrown in the trash and the very next morning, knowing exactly where it was by some strange sixth sense, he would magically return it to it's rightful place. He now somehow had the knowledge that it was his first wife from some past life. She was white and the doll looked exactly like her, pale features, a white dress that was from the middle ages, and one of these pointy hats that angled straight back at an angle of about 45 degrees. He had a clear image of her now and recognized not only why he had so tenaciously clung to the doll as a small child, but also felt a tremendous pain in his chest, just about in the heart region. It was as if something was being violently ripped out and the hole was flooded with fresh blood. There was a dark man standing next to her in this particular image and Cloud's love had suddenly turned into hatred and contempt for this person. Cloud was looking now at another part of the room; a part that held a small metal box that he saw as an old tin that he had kept the few toys that he had as a child in. He slowly opened the box, but now instead of the old broken fire engine, it contained a shiny pistol with a carved wood handle. There was a flash from the box like the gun had gone off in a cascade of fireworks. Everything seemed to be exaggerated in this place. He stared at the canvas of his life and another image was forming. It was an image of a man. He was dressed in old clothing, Flemish or Dutch in the sixteenth century. Dark, striped silk suit and a fluffy collar that reminded Cloud of something he had seen on a clown at the circus. The man's head seemed to almost float above the collar like a fishing cork bobbing up and down on a turbulent lake. His face was thin and angular, thin lips and a long and pointed nose. Something about the nose struck Cloud as not being quite right, like it really didn't belong on the face, the tip didn't line up with the rest of it. It was the eyes however that was the most disturbing. Set close together, they stared out from the portrait with a burning intensity, filled with loathing, hatred, and anger. The lid of the metal box opened again and there was an even more bright flash of fireworks followed by a loud pop. The damn gun was definitely going off and had a will of it's own. In an instant Cloud knew that he had killed this man at some point in history and he was ethereally reliving that moment.

He also knew that it involved the woman. She was standing next to the man in the portrait now and was holding a child. Both man and woman stared straight out at Cloud, but the baby's attention was focused on the man. Looking up at him in an almost angelic manner. Looking up and to the right, eyes almost completely up in the forehead. Searching up in an undeveloped right brain for an image of the father that he could not see. With a last look of contempt, the father faded out from the portrait, leaving just the mother holding the child.

She was now looking at Cloud, staring at him with a feeling more of hurt than hatred. Her eyes were blank, but this feeling seemed to be expressing itself from somewhere right behind them. She too was fading from the portrait, taking the still searching baby along with her. Cloud began to cry, something that he had not done in a long time. Tears were soaking down his face and forming puddles in the folds of his neck. Some fell on the floor and burst into a cascade of color, like molten trailing from a roman candle. For a moment Cloud felt as if he was losing it, about to disintegrate like a cracked piece of glass shattered by the trembling of an emotional earthquake. He was going mad, mad to be loved, mad to talk to someone, mad to be saved by whose blood it didn't matter. He was a ghost that was being haunted by himself. He was the lesson master showing him how to do it. He realized why his own pathetic attempt to haunt the liquor store lady didn't work, there was no attachment to her, no bond forged in the smoldering ashes of time. The anvil had cracked and one more blow from the smith's hammer would end the entire weapon making. The museum was getting hot and stuffy.

Spirit sweat and ethereal ectoplasm juice, bodily fluids without the body, not worthy of glands. Blood, sweat and tears like manna from heaven watering a single weed that has no chance in hell of ever becoming a flower. Dried and withered Vampire too long exposed to the sun. Going through some kind of transformation process like a smashed grape, seeds exposed, insides all hanging out. There was a voice coming through the ether, haunting and melodic. He recognized it as the girl. His own personal Angel incarnate here on Earth.

Years ago he had stumbled upon her, going through an unlocked back door of the opera house. And he was stumbling, cold, hungry and particularly thirsty, hearing music and thinking that the heavy metal door would lead him to a tavern. He glimpsed her from behind the curtain, 16 years old, standing in the spotlight up on stage, every voice in the place quiet and every eye upon her, transfixed. She was the young virtuoso child prodigy that everyone in the arts district was talking about, singing classical music and still soiling her diapers at the same time. She seemed to glow in the shimmering light, and that voice, oh what a voice. The notes sprang forth effortlessly. Cloud noticed that it seemed to be coming from some place deep within her, yet from some power source that was somewhere else. Each time she would hit a high note, something overcame her, it was almost like she was possessed.

There was something transcendent about her, something that validated life and somehow proved the eternity of it all. He was in love not with her physical presence or even with her voice, but the ancient spirit that was within her. He knew that this was no sixteen-year-old singing since she was three, but rather a voice that came from inside all of us. Something that had been around forever, like the wind.

A hand grabbed him by his collar and yanked him out of his revelry. "WE don't need YOUR kind in here! He was told. The hand pulled him over towards the door that he had come in by and then pushed him so hard that he feel to his knees right outside in the alley. He stayed that way for a few moments, hands clasped together almost in prayer, feeling the blood soaking his pants from his scratched knees. Finally he rolled over on his side and was able to reach one of the trash cans that lined the alley for support. He walked around the corner and watched as people fanned out on the sidewalk in front of the theatre. He guessed that the concert was over. A black limousine lay in waiting less than a block from the entrance. He thought about waiting around to catch a glimpse of the young child star as she left, but then had second thoughts; he didn't need to be arrested and dry out tonight in some Jail cell. He started to realize how cold it was and knew he would have to find shelter for the night.

As he walked away, he heard the voice again. It swelled inside him, choking him a little. He remembered the face and realized who was looking out from behind her eyes, looking out at the audience, looking out at him. A hundred years ago and he still felt the applause.

Chapter 4

"As I look in the mirror this morning, on some dirty old restroom wall, it took awhile to realize it's really me there inside…" Cloud was very old but he, unlike most old people, hadn't remembered getting there. He looked at his reflection, a wispy lock of brittle gray hair hung out of place on his forehead. He felt very tired though it looked like he had just gotten out of bed. He shuffled his feet out along the bathroom floor to the kitchen. He had to think before making each step, the nerves in his legs long suffering from neuritis and the muscles mostly wasted away. There was an old metal pot on the stove, complete with rust spots, the kind you see hanging over a campfire. His face was lined and gray like weathered rock, deeply creased. A knarled cane stood propped up by the kitchen door. There was a fluffy little white dog asleep on the sofa in the living room. It was time to go for his morning walk down to the grocery store, but Cloud found it harder and harder to drag himself out of bed each morning and get through even the most mundane of tasks. He put on the old raincoat that he had worn for years, even though it was fairly warm outside. The plaid scarf that one of the grandkids had given him was firmly wrapped around his withered neck. He grabbed the cane and called for the dog that was jumping up and down and yapping hysterically at the prospect of getting outside and away from the stuffy apartment. The old man lived not too far from the sea and could hear the waves as he struggled down the stairs and out onto the sidewalk.

The dog tugged frantically at his leash, almost causing the old guy to topple over. He called to him and told him to please slow down.

The dog didn't seem to notice. Cloud zigzagged down the walk and past the shops, waving to passerby's and the people inside the stores. He walked past the shoe store where he had made shoes for many years and watched for a few minutes as the Korean guy that had bought it from him a few years ago struggled with one of the lasts.

He remembered the craftsmanship that had went into each pair of the shoes that he had made and was regretful that most of them were made by machines in factories now. He remembered telling his grandson to always put his hand in the shoes when he bought a new pair and make sure that someone hadn't left in a tack that could rip up your foot, but they no longer used tacks, everything was glued now. Weak glue that would dissolve in the rain. He went inside the corner market and chatted with the man that worked there for a few minutes. Bananas and kumquats in the brown paper bag, he headed back home.

There was a time when he would have played with the dog for a while down by the ocean, but today he was just too tired. He sat down at the kitchen table after struggling back up the stairs and then made himself a cup of tea. "Every dog has his day." He said to the little pooch that had been his companion for these last few years.

"Not feeling too well today." The old man muttered to himself as he finished his tea and shuffled off to his bedroom. Still in his overcoat, he stiffly lay down, his butt landing hard on the creaky old bedsprings. The dog jumped up beside him and snuggled up close, soon fast asleep in his doggie world of bone-dreams. There was something though that disturbed the dog, something deep down in that primordial dog brain that went back to the wolf's first association with humans, circling cautiously around the perimeter of the campfire begging for the marrow of half chewed human road kill. Something that made the dog uneasy, but also a little excited. The many years of domestication and his own pampered lifestyle, however, put a hazy patina around the feeling and he was soon fast asleep.

Ancient Cloud felt a little dizzy and a little sick to his stomach, but other that that he was ok, just a little tired and sleepy that's all. The little world that was his room slowly shrank around him. His vision grew dim and his eyes closed. He lay in a restful attitude of sleep, on his back with his hands folded over his stomach. He was having a swirling red dream, adrift in the sea. Everything in this dream was very vibrant and alive, but it contained no images, at least none of his normal everyday life. It was as if he was falling; ever deeper and deeper within himself. Inside his body there was a huge battle starting to rage. After eighty years of repairing itself everyday, the acid dwelling within it had finally outmatched the lining of his stomach. The caustic fluid had eaten through, heading for freedom in his lower gut. An artery had been in the way and was now leaking, squirting out blood inside his stomach like a rubber tipped medicine dropper being squeezed too hard. Cloud was slowly bleeding to death and he didn't even know it. The body has defenses against death, however, in a younger man the artery would have spasmed and narrowed, perhaps saving his life, but Cloud's had suffered from years of fatty abuse and were just too old to cope. His blood pressure was dropping from the blood loss and his body was sending out signals for his heart to pump faster to keep up with the demands of his brain, which was in his own right a greedy little bastard when it came to the blood supply. The old heart, however, scarred and clogged, refused to co-operate and couldn't have even if it wanted to. Finally it stopped and there was a deathly stillness within Cloud, one that hadn't been there since he emerged from the womb, actually since he was in the womb that he was now somehow returning to. His body temperature was beginning to fall after just a few minutes and soon the decay process would begin. At the moment of Cloud's death, the little dog awoke with a yelp and a howl of mourning, instantly aware of what was going on and not too happy about it. He tugged a little on the old man's coat, sniffed about and licked him on the face. Realizing that it was hopeless, he ran to the kitchen barking and howling furiously, trying to tell the pack that the lead alpha dog was gone and an election of butt humping and mock teeth gnashing needed to begin. But there was no returning call of brother and sister wolf, only the lapping sounds of the ocean banging on the beach. The little dog held vigil at the foot of the bed for several days, drinking out of the toilet bowl. He was getting very hungry and could see the box of dry dog food sitting up high on the kitchen shelf, but there was no way to reach it. The old man had made sure of that so there would be no late night puppy feasts and dancing in the moonlight. Cloud's body was rapidly decaying and the smell of it all was overpowering to the dog. The dog approached the bed cautiously, tail tucked between his legs, and thought about the unthinkable that he had thought about many times before as he lay and watched the man sleep. He jumped up on the bed and began licking Cloud's face, bit in and tasted human blood for the first time in his short life.

Chapter 5

Cloud was definitely repulsed at the thought of one of his re- incarnation's mortal remains ended up traveling through the alimentary canal of a cannibalistic canine. He was back up in the purple energy field, or whatever you called it, and something different was definitely going on. The broadcast was breaking up again. Fluttering flashes of the old warehouse where he had most recently passed on. He could smell the blood, piss, and vomit and even at times the wet cardboard he had been lying on. He found this last death to be the most unpleasant; probably because it was the most recent and still fresh in his astral memory. There emerged a black hole to the right of his perception that he hadn't noticed before, a hole that seemed to be sucking every- thing into it. It pulled him toward it, stretching the silver cord almost to the breaking point. How far could this thing stretch anyway? Finally he was trapped. He was falling faster and faster towards the hole and there was no way he could escape. Dizzy and full of vertigo, he was going through a black tunnel. Well on his way to oblivion. The darkness was heavy and almost peaceful and he contemplated spending the rest of eternity in it.

He awoke to the smell of wood smoke. A strange being was looking down at him, a robot of some sort. He wondered that maybe he had gone to some future place in time when suddenly the creature removed its face to reveal the countenance of a man underneath. The knight in the image was encased in armor that looked like it hadn't been polished in some time. There were red streaks of blood smeared at some of the openings, especially near the armpits and down between the legs. There was a large dent right across the backside of the knight that Cloud noticed when he turned to shout at someone in the background. The knight had incurred a huge-blow from the blunt side of a very heavy battleaxe that caused him to uncontrollably piss blood all through his suit; it found an escape hatch through the chain mail between his legs. Not exactly the fatal Dolores blow, but quite possibly fatal nonetheless. Cloud noticed the sounds of battle raging all around him. Grunts, shouts, cries and screams permeated the air. It wasn't at all like the movies, where you tasted popcorn instead of smelling sweat and tasting the metallic taste of blood. Cloud put his fingers up to his face and discovered a large gash running from right under his right eye down almost to his chin. In his most recent life, the scar would be replaced by a faint wrinkle that appeared right about the time he turned forty. As the blood flowed out, he felt pain flow in. He spat out blood and spittle along with one of his front teeth. The knight reached over to pick Cloud up off of the ground. He stood there quivering; feeling his body to make sure that everything was there. He noticed that he was not wearing a suit of armor; instead it was some kind of medieval shirt and pants trimmed in leather. "Squire!" The knight shouted. "We'll attend to your wound later, right now the others need help." Cloud reached down and picked up a rather heavy rock that was lying a few feet away, picked it up and heaved it in the direction of the retreating knight. It beamed him on the back of the head and knocked him unconscious. Cloud then turned and ran as fast as he could in the opposite direction away from the battle. He was a drunk, a gambler, a conman, and a sometimes lover, but this battle this just wasn't his cup of tea, or hog swill for that matter.

"He ran through the bushes and he ran through the brambles and he ran through the places where a rabbit wouldn't go ....." The song was playing in his head as he ran and stumbled his way through the woods. Suddenly he came upon a small path in the forest. There was a large rock at the entrance with strange rune-like inscriptions carved on it. He followed the path for a small ways through the woods and came upon a small cottage. "Oh come on!" He thought to himself. I'm in no mood for Hansel and Gretel at this point in my death. Whose directing this shit anyway? He crouched down and looked to see if there was anything or anyone moving near the cottage. The cottage was white in color with a green wooden door. He couldn't tell if it was painted that color, or if the wood was just extremely old and moldy. There was a thatched roof, made out of some kind of straw, and a smokestack that appeared to be made out of some kind of clay. Small wispy curls of smoke came out of the stack, like something that was wafting up from the dying embers of a fire. It didn't seem like there was anybody home, so Cloud decided to take a closer look. He approached the cottage cautiously, looking around in all directions. There was a flower box underneath one of the windows and next to it a very sturdy looking wooden door that had strange rune-like carvings on it. The door was open just a crack and Cloud opened it a little more and stared into the inside. The smoldering remnants of a fire glowed in the hearth. A swinging iron rod held ax~ an iron pot that contained a rather foul smelling herbal liquid. A primitive mechanical clock was perched on the mantle place

The curious thing though that really caught his attention was the table. When he looked at it he felt like he was starting to float up in the air a little. He tried to divert his attention away from it, focusing on the large bookcase that lined the wall on the other side of the room. The books were very old and tattered, appearing to be extensively used over their life of many years. There was a small bookstand in from of the shelves that contained an open book that appeared to be an illuminated manuscript. A white candle was on the stand. Just over the open book and all that remained of it, was a dripping stub. He tried to read some of the lettering on the books, but suddenly his head would turn back towards the table like he had a very large magnet implanted in his skull. The more he looked at the table, the more he felt himself floating up in the air, and the less he was able to ascertain the other details in the room.

He stared more intently at the table and realized that there was something rather large lying on top of it. Cloud was now floating about halfway up towards the ceiling, so he decided to direct himself over towards the table. As he got a little bit closer and the details became more explicit, he realized what was lying on the table. It was a body; a body that was covered by some kind of a shroud. The shroud was very old looking and appeared to be made out of some kind of off white linen. It was stained and parts of it had become threadbare. He noticed a faint sort of flowery odor emanating from it that wasn't at all unpleasant. He was now hovering almost directly over the corpse and seemed to have developed a strange attachment to it. He suddenly realized that he was being drawn towards the body by a very powerful force. Closer and closer he became. He felt anxious but strangely peaceful. All of a sudden, instead of looking down at the body he was in the same position as it was looking up at the ceiling. He could feel the faint heat from the fire and smell the flowers more intently. For what seemed like a few seconds, he was at one with the corpse and he felt a feeling of intense cold; intensely cold and alone. And his decent didn't stop there; he was still being drawn downwards. Down through the table, smelling the damp wood and even feeling the wood fibers and the rings in the tree that it had come from. Then he faced darkness, a huge gaping hole was beneath him and he started to fall more rapidly, almost like being thrown off a cliff. Pulled in the direction at first like the magnet, then pushed like a baseball bat swung at your back as you peered over the precipice. He was falling and falling fast, with no twigs to catch on to. He reached out in panic, arms flailing about in all directions. He cried out in a language that he didn't know. It sounded strangely and vaguely Latin. "Dominus Sanctorum... .....

It rolled off his tongue like a mouthful of slick spit, spilling out in the darkness around him. Then just as he felt he was losing it all and slipping away, he was snatched out of the dark belly of the whale and into the light of the room. There was a glimpse of a bearded man in a flowing white robe. The man had a smile on his face that almost denoted amusement. Cloud was back in his physical form again. He looked around the room, at the books, the fireplace, the tiny windows, then at the table. The body and the shroud were gone. All the colors were intensified, almost painful to look at. He caught a glimpse of something out of the corner of his eye. Something that was glinting and metallic, lying on the oaken table. He slowly walked across the room and picked it up. It lay there shimmering in his hand. He gazed at it intently for a moment and then clutched it to his chest. It was a small cross. He put the crucifix into the pocket of his worn faded trousers and walked outside.

Chapter 6

Cloud exited the cottage still wondering what had happened inside of it. Everything outside looked different now; the sky in particular had taken on a sort of golden color, almost orange. Rainbow-like streaks splashed across it, containing all the colors of a prism. Everything around him seemed to glow and seemed to be talking to him. Talking? Not really, more like some other type of communication that was hard to put your finger on. The were almost feeling him, his thoughts, feelings and emotions, and he was feeling theirs. One particular rock sitting in front of the house vibrated whenever he looked at it.

If some emotion welled up inside him, the color of the rock and the vibrations would increase. He was so well aware and in tune with every-thing around him that he felt he could stay here forever and just look and feel at things. He never knew before that things were really like this, or where they? Was this like some false revelation, long strange drug trip? Was he really just inside his own mind? Or was he dead or dreaming? He quickly dismissed the thought. All this was just too real to be some figment of his imagination, or the result of ingesting too many dregs at the bottom of a bottle of wine. The energy that was pulsating around him was now getting too intense, so he wandered around to the back of the cottage where things felt a little more settled. There was a path through the woods that came right up to the back of the place and he noticed the sound of running water. There must have been a stream or brook back there.

He started walking down the path towards the sound of the water. For some reason there was suddenly a very morbid and disturbing thought that was crossing his mind. The gurgling sound coming from the source of the water reminded him of the sound that emanated from a man's throat that had been recently slashed, gurgling and sucking for air, but no smell of blood. He couldn't tell where this feeling was coming from. Was it some vestige of a spirit whose Earthly form had been murdered in battle here, or was he tripping into somebody else's nightmare? He felt a struggle and heard cries for help. He saw flashes of a knight's armor being pierced by a double-bladed axe, the force of the blow knocking the knight off his feet, with a trace of blood flowing from his mouth. He looked further into the woods and saw a row of sticks planted in the ground, each one containing a human head as the centerpiece. The stick had been shoved up through the hole in the bottom of the skull. They looked like they had been there for a while, and had started to dry, taking on the appearance of a shrunken head, leathery in appearance. There was dried blood and spittle in the corner of most of the head's mouths, running down the chin, from a mouth wide open with horror, frozen in mid scream/. Some of the heads had colorful ribbons tied around them, and at this point Cloud realized that they were some kind of battle trophy. Drying out in the mid-day air, waiting to be taken home and bragged over around the evening campfire.

The soldiers had better hurry up though, Cloud thought as he looked at the scene, because scavenger crows had begun to pick at the head flesh, it being just in the state of decay to encompass a gourmet meal. Next came a picture of a woman lying on a bed of straw, piled high for comfort, smoke rising from campfires, and ritual green tea laced with a powerful hallucinogen being consumed. The woman has gone willingly after drinking the tea, wrapped in a silver cloak and the comfort of a sacrifice. People standing around have bought privileged tickets paid for in blood. They shiver in the cold of the high Andean mountains, knowing that the weather could change at any minute if the Gods were pissed and they all could die before it was finished. An eternal monument of frozen flesh on the mountain, only is discovered centuries later and resting forever thawed with the stale stench of a metropolitan museum. Raw pieces of putrid flesh, carrion meat, are placed in leather cups secured over the woman's eyes. The crows begin to do their work, at first consuming the morbid flesh, then attacking and eating the eyes underneath it. The birds are shooed away when their task before it's finished and herbs are placed in the sockets where the woman's eyes used to be. She is then led into a tent to stay and recover for the next few days, the whole thing being timed with the phases of the moon and the woman's menstrual cycle.

The woman then gets a promotion to become the high priestess of the tribe. She has her eyes plucked out to develop the inner vision. Being left without the distraction of all the visual images, she is reborn into the light of the tribe's collective soul, a disabled representative so to speak. She is able to see with much more clarity and much farther than any Eagle. The boundaries of time are stripped away just like the flesh around her eyes. She prophesizes about the deadly future and corn is stored away for the rough years ahead.

The Chieftain has a headache and rotting teeth from eating too much corn.

The bountiful harvest fills the belly but kills the head. The infection roars up into the Chieftain's head and fills it with paranoid delusions. The people panic and raid the food stores, rushing towards oblivion like lemmings to the sea. Success breeds failure and the people die, leaving a legacy behind for the Saturday morning tourists viewing the bones in some far distant future. The Chieftain lies in the tomb of the glass display case on a bed of shells, mouth open wide showing the rotten teeth that killed him. Ironically once the body has died the decay in the teeth stops and the Chief's choppers will probably last forever. The modern day Shaman dances around the display case spitting blood on the Plexiglas. Tourists cover the eyes of their children, not wanting them to see the past wrapped up in the future. The archeologist laughs outside as he carelessly digs up another body, pissing off the spirits that will curse and haunt him. The land lies violated and weeping from the huge bulldozer holes and the whole thing collapses under lack of funding. The burial mounds are plowed under and new high-rise apartments are built over them with ghosts in the basement, haunting the washers and dryers.

The blind priestess stares at Cloud for just a fleeting moment, leaving him to wander if it ever happened at all. There was a man now, bathed in blue light and wearing a green cloak. He was standing behind the cottage, right by the path that led back into the woods. He motioned to Cloud to follow him. The man was old and somewhat stooped over, leaning on some kind of wooden staff. His brow was heavily furrowed, but seemed to shine with an ethereal light. Cloud followed him back into the woods, almost mesmerized by his presence. After walking a short ways, they came upon a small thatched hut. An old oak tree stands just a few feet from it. In a circle around the tree, the grass had been worn away like someone had sat under the tree for some time, thirty years on and off in a Buddha sort of way. Listen to the sound of the grass growing, Grasshopper.

The old Druid in the green cloak sat down heavily next to the oak tree. He made a strange sign with the fingers of his right hand and mumbled a few words in an ancient language. He motioned Cloud to sit down across from him. A warm breeze ruffled the leaves of the tree and Cloud noticed that the very leaves of the tree had writing on them. A strange script that was unfathomable to him, like straight sticks with diagonal slashes on them. The old man motioned for Cloud to sit down across from him. Cloud sat and gazed into the old man's eyes. They were the deepest blue that he had ever seen and as intense as the strongest wave. The man's voice was as deep as the most profound rumblings of the most powerful volcano. It seemed that all of nature was encompassed inside him, or maybe that image came from his understanding of it.

The Druid asked if Cloud had any idea of what was happening to him. Cloud replied that he thought he had died, but after that it seemed that he was caught up in some strange and uncontrollable dream. The Druid replied that Cloud's soul had been fragmented, broken into the thousand little pieces that were his past lives. His was a special case. Usually you gathered wisdom during your various incarnations here on Earth. Put the little pieces of your soul together, life by life until you were complete and able to see the big picture.

But in Cloud's case some kind of big bang had scattered the o pieces of the puzzle through time and it was up to him to find out what the event was and then piece it all back together before he could move on. "In your culture, or I should say in the one that you are presently in, you would seek out a Shaman, who would, after ingesting some plants, try to retrieve your soul for you." "Un- fortunately, you were dumped into my lap and I really can't help you at this time." The Druid began chanting again in his rumbling timber before Cloud could even get out a single word. The air began to take on that shimmering quality again just like before when Clod moved around his past lives like a browser in an antique mall.

It seemed like just a few seconds, but an eternity had passed. Cloud was lying on what seemed to be wet marble. There was a sound not too far away of people chanting and water splashing. He could hear the sound of soft crying over all the commotion. He looked around to see what appeared to be about a hundred people splashing themselves in the river's dirty brown water. Some stood up afterwards and prayed by the river's edge. The people were all brown, bald-headed and dressed in fabrics that were loosely wrapped around their bodies and bunched up at the butt. He looked down and realized that he was wearing the same type of clothing. He wondered how spirit could be transformed into cloth, but then again maybe this was all taking place in his own mind, the last gasp of some dying brain tissue resurrecting an image that he had seen in National Geographic years ago when he was a kid in school.

Truth was he wasn't sure whether he was alive or dead or somewhere in between. It WAS like he was shattered into a thousand little pieces of broken glass, then tossed into a molten furnace only to have the damn thing explode, fracturing him again only now the pieces had lost all their sharpness. He looked out once again at the people washing themselves in the river and glanced around at the temples and buildings of the old city. He moved stiffly towards the murmuring sounds he had heard when he first arrived and thought of how much he needed a drink. He thought how there wasn't supposed to be any hunger or thirst in the afterlife. So many people who had purported to be there and came back had it wrong; it was nothing like they had said it was at least so far. He looked off into the distance and saw a small gathering of people standing around a large bonfire. Some of them were crouched down in monkey posture, knees pushed up firmly against their cheeks. Some just stood there and stared blankly at the fire, while others sat in lotus positions and wept, rocking back and forth. He gravitated a little closer and could feel the searing heat from the fire. He realized then what he had been looking at; it was a funeral pyre, blazing brightly and consuming the mortal remains of an unfortunate Hindu. He watched in amazement as one of the onlookers~ reached right into the fire and pulled something out of the flames.

At first he didn't recognize what it was, then realized it was a human bone of some sort. Trembling, he walked forward a few more steps until he was standing right behind the group of mourners. No one seemed to notice that he was there. He watched as the man wrapped the smoldering hipbone in a silver piece of cloth and ran down towards the river, where he dipped the blackened piece of bone into the muddy water. After it had cooled, he walked slowly back towards the fire as the others watched solemnly. He then placed the bone on a tasseled small golden pillow and the rest of the crowd walked up to it, kissing their fingers and then lightly touching the bone. He would later find out that this was the custom, preserving a symbol of the dead woman that was being burned. Physical evidence that life had once issued forth through that pelvis, her son having the honor of sanctifying the bone by dunking it in the sacred Ganges.

After awhile the funeral blaze began to die down and it was starting to get dark. One by one the family of the deceased started to wander off, eventually leaving the body alone, ashes resting as a public monument until the next wind or flood carried them away to become part of the muddy silt of the river. At one time the bodies were just dumped into the river causing great outbreaks of dysentery and cholera, but now they were at least sterilized somewhat by the heat of the pyre.

Cloud thought he should probably leave now even though he had no idea where he was to go, or even why he was here and what lesson was learned from all of this. But something made him stay and stare at the dwindling embers of the fire. It seemed that something was about to happen, he could feel the astral remains of hairs popping up on his non-existent neck. Then he turned and noticed what it was. There was a group of about four men who he really hadn't noticed standing over to the side. One of them started advancing as the others watched. They looked fearsome, ornaments glinting through pierced flesh, nostrils flaring, a wild fury watching from behind bloodshot eyes. Cloud quickly scrambled behind one of the buildings and watched. People scattered out of the way of the advancing tribesman, running out of fear more than respect. One of the passersby whispered under his breath the name AGORI, said in a voice like he did not want them to hear. The tribesman walked right up to the smoldering fire and hunched down like a monkey. When the fire had first reached its apex of heat, it seared the dead woman's watery corpse, sealing in the juices like a plump steak thrown on a thousand degree griddle. The water inside her started to boil and eventually she exploded, bits of seared flesh not yet burned to charcoal flew in all directions. Stray dogs had consumed most of it, but there were a few pieces right on the periphery of the flame. The tribesman put both of his arms behind his back and in one swift motion thrust his face down in the fire, expertly snagging the piece of roasted flesh.

He rocked back from the fire, resting on his haunches and chewed. Chewed slowly and methodically, ingesting the body as well as the soul. The other tribesmen joined him at the fire, watching intently. They shook their heads in a knowing manner as he swallowed the last mouthful of flesh. He sat there for a while with a grimace on his face, possessed. He began to rock back and forth, and then stood up, looking faint. The others helped him slowly walk away to their vantage point where they had set up camp. The Agori believed that by consuming the flesh of the deceased they could take a shortcut so to speak, around the morass of constantly re-incarnating their lives until they got it right. To the men of the Agori, not many of them left, cutting short your re-incarnations does have an effect on your level of extinction, had started their own little fire and now huddled around it. They pulled out pipes filled with wondrous herb and started to smoke. Cloud watched for a few moments as they started to dance and then walked off into the heart of the great city.

The city had a patina about it, a raw edge that was so bizarre that it had a dreamlike quality. There was a smell of poverty mixed with an acrid odor of industrial waste. Children with swollen bellies and deep-set, hungry eyes peered out from dark hallways. Human waste collected in the cracks of crumbling sidewalks. Heavy perfume of opium seeped through the doors of dimly lit dens, curling around the food money in the pockets of deformed beggars; death and disease, disease and death. The death face smiling on the face of the Tarot Card, happy to be at home again next to the burning tower. Young women sold into white slavery, forced into Bukakke shows with infected sailors willing to pay the price. A snake slithers along the slimy cobblestone, tongue sniffing the air, green eyes glinting. A man in a white turban, missing its jewel, scurries along after the snake, carrying a sodden wicker basket. Young boy climbs up the rope trick and sits on the thin wire, seemingly suspended in mid-air, the wire cutting deep into tender buttocks, blood dripping on the audience positioned below. The leper pushes himself along on a wooden platform atop rusty wheels, his knuckles scarred and bleeding, his body dying one nerve at a time. It started as a tiny black spot on his left foot, not painful at all and barely noticeable. He went on about his business of the opium pipe, sucking out the last flowery essence of life itself. And then the infection started, red swollen skin from red to green to black, then finally gone, and all the while he still didn't take notice. Broken potato chip sticking out of rotted head flesh.

If only the flies had come in time to save him, but they arrived too late. Flies looking to lay their eggs in an infected open wound. The maggots, the babies, scurrying to do their job, eating the pus along with all the bacteria, growing fatter by the minute. And all they leave behind is a tickly feeling. All of life survives and thrives on death. The food chain has no heart or feelings, no greater purpose. It's all a matter of being at the right place at the right time.

The ultimate king of the chain selecting a mad cow's steak at the supermarket, false sense of assurance glows in his well-fed belly. Not so in the swollen belly of a starving child. He takes a more direct approach. But still looks out from under the flood with brown eyes, bloodshot and filled with hope. Too late he gets his ration of white rice, plump from the cooking, but he would have preferred the maggots from the open wound, more protein you see. What appeal has the flowery speech of romance and politics falling on a million deaf ears? The flow of gas all started with the dinosaurs, eating two tons of plants per day and realizing a hurricane of wind issuing forth from an open rectum. It was curling caveman's hair and finally dwindling down to a carrot's worth for a present-day vegetarian, reaching for his bottle of Beano. The snake continues on his journey, hissing at an unfriendly cat. The mark from the stun gun burns two fang marks into the protesters flesh. He comes out of his convulsions laughing at the policeman, much calmer than before.

The snake slithers on, over the fallen body of the leper and up into the belly of the pregnant woman, spitting on the child within.

The aborted fetus chases the snake DOWN THE ALLEY, SPLASHING IN THE RIVER OF PISS. The snake has the advantage in this particular situation. The snake, on the run, rounds the corner then stops. It erects itself, Cobra Hood flashing, eyes fixed on the man standing in front of it.

The man stares back into the snake's eyes, and in a moment of recognition, wants to embrace the viper. Kiss it on the mouth and suck out the poison. But it's too late the snake is gone. The man picks up the egg the snake has left behind and puts it in his pocket. Later he will examine it more closely in front of mankind's dimly lit candle. Hold it in his long fingernails, not allowing it to touch his fingertips. Over the city a new day is dawning, and somewhere, in one of the clouds, a rainbow is struggling to form, trying with all its might to reach the ground.

Chapter 6

The rainbow coalition had been dissolved. "Hot times, summer in the city ....." Cloud was being gripped by a fear that was more intense than he had ever felt before. It felt as if his very being was being smothered in a thousand wet blankets and moldy ones at that. The circuits of his astral brain were being flooded with hundreds of images all at once. It was the ultimate cosmic panic attack. Sounds screamed into his lungs, which had become a vacuum filled with despair. He was suffocating in his own bad Karma. Ghastly demons seemed to float just below his eyelids, two pronged devils and Voodoo dicks pounded at his asshole. Worms crawled out of his nose and crawled straight for his eyes. His flesh was burning hot and felt as if it was being peeled off inch by inch with a dull razor. A drug dealer, his face smeared with white powder, sawed at his neck with a machete, cutting through tendon and bone until at last it was free and dropped it into a boiling pot. He was stirred around and around in the fecund scum, bumping into an assortment of rotted animals. A crown of thorns was placed on his head and he was elected king of the black kettle. He felt a sharp knife cut deep into his back, slowly cutting out his spine. It was then shoved into the ground, tailbone first, along with others to become part of someone's backyard fence. At times the spirit in his head would be ripped out, leaving it dull and lifeless, and sent on some gruesome mission, growing fangs and ripping out innocent throat-flesh. The rest of the time as he sat cooking in the foul liquid, he was assaulted by horrific images of his past lives, thrown up on a celestial movie screen for all the demons in the universe to see. Gangsters broke innocent knees with aluminum baseball bats created specifically for the job. Victims squirming against the ropes as pounds and pounds of Ex-Lax was forced down their throats, and then hit with the bats when they shit all over themselves. Car bombs exploded, hurling severed arms and legs in the air, if only the remote control had been used. Young boys in prison raped by gangs, then assaulted with mop stick handles until they died from internal bleeding. Mental patients locked up in rubber rooms with their own personal demons, then placed in shocking metal helmets and left convulsing on the floor. Finally taken to the Cuckoo's Nest to be given an ice pick lobotomy. Ice pick shoved in through the eye and upwards to violate the frontal lobe of the brain and destroy the ability to think and the patient becomes calm. Later on drugs would do the trick, and they were a lot less messy. Stone age man, the village witch- doctor, sits poised with his rock blade, the master trepanner sawing through the skull to let out the evil demons. Later it would become a new age fashion trend, only this time to let the universe in. Babies born without any openings, no mouth, nose, ears or anus, filling with shit until they explode. Water baby with huge balloon shaped water filled head, drain out all the fluid and there is nothing left. Dante never had it so good.

Fortunately for Cloud, even hell had its limits. That Christian concept of eternal damnation had blown out of the collective subconscious of most rational people long ago; even the Pope had admitted that there was no physical place of Hell, complete with fire and brimstone. Hell was that cold place in your soul that starts to throb with frostbite when you are alone and in pain, the absence of love.

It was hot and Cloud was sweating profusely. He was surrounded by green everywhere he looked and his skin itched. He was running and something was flying and flopping in front of him. There were shouts and voices and whistles coming at him from all directions. The bird, a sort of turkey looking thing had been mortally wounded and laid gasping it0s few remaining breaths in front of his feet. It took him a few moments to catch his breath and realize what he was doing as the others caught up with him. They were all slapping him on his sweaty back and congratulating him on the successful hunt. As they turned away to talk among themselves, he took a few moments to observe his surroundings and himself. He was definitely in the jungle and he was totally naked except for some kind of ribbon thing tied around his penis to keep it sticking up and a sack on his back fashioned out of some plant leaves. He was carrying a spear in his right hand. It was tipped with red and he realized that he had luckily speared the bird as he startled it hiding in the undergrowth. He guessed that this meant that he would eat tonight, but he also knew that he would have to share it with his family, which was quite large, and any of the old people of the village. It was meager pickings indeed. A thought then flashed into his mind about how the women were at home growing a plant that was tubular and starchy, like some sort of maize. It was rubbed up against a rough rock and then ground into a sort of lumpy flour that was set out in the sun to dry. Then it was used to make a flat-tasting kind of pancake cooked over an open fire. This along with the occasional piece of meat and a few nuts and berries was the staple of his diet. He noticed that his lip felt strange and when he tried to speak, drool ran down his chin. He brought his fingertips up to his face and realized that there was a large hole just below his bottom lip that ran all the way to his chin. In it was stuck a large piece of bamboo that hung down a couple of inches below the chin so it was about six inches in length altogether. When he tried to speak, his words came out in a mumble (all the men in the village sounded the same) and his bottom lip jutted out so far that it filled with water every time it rained. During the rainy season, none of the men had to drink water; all they had to do was swallow. He remembered that when he was just a child of four or five, someone had jammed a searing hot stick through his lower lip and then shoved a monkey bone into the resulting hole. It had hurt for sometime and he remembered his mother instructing him to clean it out daily so it wouldn't get infected.

Cloud was jolted out of his daydream by one of the other hunters jabbing him forcefully in the ribs and telling him the hunting group was moving out and heading home. They were all tired and thirsty and horny for their women. Of course the first thing that they would do however, when they got back to the village, was to jump into their favorite hammock, smoke a little pipe, and relate to the rest of the tribe all the marvelous adventures that they had had on their hunting expedition. After that they would pass out from exhaustion and it might be several days before they got around to visiting the women.

This was pretty much what happened with the others, but Cloud stopped for a few seconds on the return trip and picked a couple of small white wildflowers and secretly hid them in the plant-sack that was carrying the bird, which by the way, was starting to smell a little ripe from the moisture and the heat. If anyone saw the flowers and questioned him about them, he would tell them that the flowers were there to compliment the meat and keep it fresh. In reality the flowers were for his partner, Wiesha, whom he was deeply in love with but dare not share it with the rest of the group, as she was already promised to a more important and respected hunter in the tribe.

Cloud silently slipped out of his hammock after relating his small role in securing the game for the village. The small fires in front of the grass huts had not been tended to and smoke hung lazily in the moisture-laden air. Cloud went to his hiding place and retrieved the white flowers. Most of the village was asleep, but in front of a few of the huts there was a rope with a stick hanging off of it and sounds of sexual activity going on inside. His tribe was a polygamous one, most of the men sharing more than one wife, and the easily identifiable stick signaled to the other husbands that the stick bearer was using one of his turns to have a go at the wife.

Most of the women were circumcised when they reached puberty and had their first menses. Part of the clitoris was removed to dull any sexual pleasure they may get from their husbands. No one knew why this was done, but the custom remained with the elders even though some of the younger women had put up a fight when it was done. They had gotten used to another custom and missed the pleasure. They rubbed honey all over their sexual parts and then would sit, baking in the hot sun, letting the ants have a tickling, pinching time masturbating them. All this fun ended with the responsibility of marriage and childbearing. Cloud stood in front of Wiesha's dwelling. He dropped the flowers just inside of her blanket-covered door.

As he started to leave, there was a stirring from within the hut. He moved aside the blanket and went inside. Her father was sleeping in his hammock, passed out from the rigors of the hunt and the party thereafter. Her mother was curled up next to the smoky fire beside him. Weisha stood naked before Cloud. Most of the women in the village had large breasts that sagged from the lack of a wonder bra and suckling children. Weisha's breasts were smaller and definitely did not have any sag action going on. Her face also had smaller features than most, which was a sign if beauty and an added feature. No wonder she went to the best hunter in the village.

She had been promised to be married in a few days and her father had received quite a large dowry of meat and animal skins. The tribe was not a very ornate one, and except for the witchdoctor, no one wore many bangles and beads. Money was the same as food, your wealth was judged by the girth of your belly. When it swelled up to where you could no longer run, it was time for retirement, and the few that survived to really old age, started losing weight and became skinny again. This was called using up your retirement before you died.

Weisha was also a certified virgin, having just squatted before the elder village women for a very through examination. Her value as a bride would be greatly diminished if her cherry had been popped. If the women found that there was something amiss during the examination, as a matter of fact, they would each take a small piece of fruit that resembled a cherry and pop it between their fingers, then throw it at the woman in disgust. This would signal to the rest of the village that the father was trying to pawn off damaged property. He would then be ridiculed in front of his peers. Every once in awhile right before the marriage, the father would conduct his own cursory examination, m~ much to the distaste of the daughter.

Cloud could wait no longer. The feeling came upon him like a tidal wave. As he sank into her, something strange was happening. He suddenly became part superhuman, part animal. As he stared into her wide-open eyes, he could see all the way to the depths of her soul and realize who she really was. Her DNA was laid bare like an unraveling carpet, strands and fibers exposed for all to see, but only he could see how they were woven. Pools and eddies of emotion would swell up inside him, only to disappear in the whirlpool of who he was and had been. She became animal, egg, male and female, all the things that she had ever been, but still they remained together. Together as they had always been, throughout their past lives. Suddenly they were both back at the big bang, compressing and condensing into that spot of pure light that started it all. They were unstoppable, transforming into the pure spirit that was God, or at least part of him. Slowly they regained their physical form. Cloud rolled off of her, kissing her lightly on her sweaty cheek.

He looked around and absorbed the quiet of the room. Then he looked up into the raging eyes of her father. He tried to reach out for Weisha. But it was too late, the father was too swift and too much of the hunter stalking his prey. The spear made a popping sound as it pierced the flesh. Cloud felt a searing pain. There was a moment of silence and a moment of panic, but then everything seemed to slow down. Gentle breezes as the spear rained down again and again.

The last thing he remembered was the bright red blood on the spear and the gurgling sound coming from his throat. Floating over the rocks, washed down to be adrift in the sea.

Chapter 7

Cloud was floating away peacefully, adrift in the Sargasso Sea of the soul when suddenly he was yanked out of the ethereal waters like a sturgeon caught on a hook. He was back in the hut, floating over his mangled body. The man who had killed him was gone but the love of his life sat next to him, weeping softly. There was a hushed murmur of voices outside the hut as one by one the blanket was thrown aside and the startled villagers peered inside, some of them gasping in horror and turning their faces away. The Shaman arrived and motioned to some of the other men to begin making the funeral arrangements. Most of the blood was cleaned up and a fresh blanket was laid out underneath him. The men, under the Shaman's watchful eye, then folded Cloud's body up into a fetal position, his head thrown back and his knees brought up to where they were touching his chin. Ropes were tied around his feet and his wrists, his legs and arms slightly apart. A wooden chair frame was then placed underneath him and he was tied to it. The men then took him outside and rubbed his body with special herbs. They forced salt water through his mouth and filled his stomach with it. After dressing him and decorating his body with some after death tattooing, they propped his body up in front of the hut and built a smoky fire under the chair. Cloud was being slow smoked like a prime piece of beef brisket. The Shaman would come to him several times a day and blow tobacco smoke into his mouth in the belief that this would also help dry out the body.

This went on for several months and Cloud did dry out, losing more than 90% of his body weight. His internal organs became dried, wispy remnants of their former watery selves and his brain was reduced to the size of an orange peel. Finally, after months had passed, a special but-plug made of straw was placed in his anus, and all the other bodily cavities were filled with one thing or another; eyes, ears, nose, mouth, right down to the urethral hole at the tip of his penis. The herbs that had been rubbed on his body contained secret potent insecticides to keep away the worms and other nastiness that would have eaten him if given the chance. He was then placed in a carved wooden casket that looked like a giant walnut that was cut in half.

Cloud had to wait around patiently floating over his body while all this was taking place. For some reason try as he might, he couldn't leave. It was the tie that binds. He was thinking that maybe this had something to do with the magical workings of the Shaman, or was it just to keep this particular aspect of his spirit from haunting the guy that had killed him/ Cloud didn't care, he wasnat out to extract revenge, he had seen a few of his past lives and none of them had turned out very happily and he just wanted to move on. It was just another day another dollar, another life to muddle through and not really learn anything at all. What was the friggin' point anyway?

Cloud was finally able to summon up enough energy to appear to the Medicine Man that had done the mummification and convince him to let him go from this particular time and place. It was the magic after all that was keeping him here. Cloud was back "up there" or back inside himself, he wasn't sure which. His surroundings were relatively peaceful, but he still carried heaviness, like his matrix was covered with some kind of melted lead, a fishing weight that was about to be anchored with bait and thrown into the ocean. Suddenly$ there was a voice in his head, hell there always seemed to be voices, his melon was a very crowded apartment building with all kinds of noisy neighbors. He was aware that he was sitting somewhere and there was a large group of people around him. The voice drifted over the ether. It was humming, a chant of some kind. He was sitting in an auditorium. The audience around him was chanting also, some kind of "Ohm..." type of hymn. He looked at the woman sitting next to him and realized he was gently holding her hand. Her eyes were closed and she was humming softly. She was an older woman, late forties, a little bottom heavy, but her face was cute and relaxed. He looked forward up on the stage in front of him. There was an individual sitting on the floor of the stage, cross-legged in the lotus position. Flowers and burning incense surrounded him, and there were rose petals scattered all around him on the stage floor. A soft light seemed to diffuse around him and it was hard to tell where it was coming from. Cloud looked at the man more closely. He was thin and not too tall sitting there on the stage. He was bearded with long kind of scraggly hair that seemed to shoot out in all directions, thin dreadlocks, some of them braided. As he held up his hands and gestured, Cloud realized that the man's fingers were very long and the nails untrimmed. He didn't seem like the kind of person though that would keep them untrimmed. The hands were smooth and had not labored long in the field. They moved in a soft almost flowing and graceful manner. But the face ..... Oh the face, that was a hard one to figure out. He seemed at first glance to be a man in his early thirties, but them the face would change, almost in an instant. One moment it was much older, then young and lively, male then female, timeless and ageless.

The Punjabi asked everyone in the audience how long they thought they had been meditating and the general response was "only a few minutes." They were then told that they had been transported through space and time for almost forty minutes. Most were shocked and some didn't believe it. Cloud did. It seemed that forty minutes was a mere fraction of a millisecond compared to the journeys that he had just embarked and returned from. The woman sitting next to him interupped his thoughts. "This was nice," she said.

Are you ready to go?" Maybe we can get one of his tapes on the way out." Cloud looked at her, but even though it seemed that they were good friends or even intimate, Cloud couldn't seem to remember her name. Usually in his soul travels or memories, he could just watch parts of his former lives or whatever it was as an impartial observer, but this time it seemed different. Now he was thrown right into the middle of a relationship situation were it seemed that people were familiar with who he was, at least in this lifetime, but he was at a distinct disadvantage because parts of his memory seemed to be missing, almost like he was in a car accident and took a bump on the noggin that caused him to have amnesia. The woman sitting next to him looked familiar, but it was like she was just a little out of his own place and time. He guessed that he would have to face this little life orgasm and deal with the situation as it presented itself. "Yeah." he replied to the woman sitting next to him. "Let's go look at the tapes." He figured that this would give him a little extra time to collect his thoughts and survey his surroundings, as he was still a little dizzy and disorientated.

They walked up to the table in the dimly lit auditorium where there was flowers set out on the table and some burning incense next to a few books and a stack of tapes and CD's. The Guru was shown on the front of the tapes and books standing on the top of a mountain, with wispy wind-swept clouds in the background. They bought one of the tapes and then went outside the auditorium where Cloud discovered ~hat they were at a botanical garden of some kind. The woman sitting next to him wanted to walk around and take in some of the scenery so they walked around for a while. It was a bright and pleasant summer day. They walked through the English walking garden and then through an oriental rock garden where the sand surrounding the rocks and flowers had been properly and ceremonially raked.. The woman sitting next to him (this was as good a thing to call her as any, since a name for her simply would no materialize) asked him if he remembered coming here the year before and watching the Japanese Tea Ceremony that took place on a small island out in the lagoon where she was pointing. He replied sure even 6hough he didn't have the foggiest notion of what she was talking about. They came out of the oriental garden and walked past an open area that contained a small stage. She asked him about the Taiko Drummers they had watched there. He still didn't specifically remember, but there was a few images floating in his confused brain. Young men and women dressed in Karate uniforms pounding furiously on huge drums and dancing around as they did it. Somehow he knew that the drumming had originated as a form of practice for self-defense. Sitting on the grass they had watched the troupe hailing from San Francisco, get all hot and sweaty in the warm September air, feeling the energy from the group spread out from the stage and into the audience and then into the Earth under their butts and legs. He didn't remember the event as much as he felt the results of it. They then walked through a huge Geodesic Dome that had a whole lot of tropical plants and trees in it. There was a place in the middle of it where you could walk underneath a moving stream that had a glass bottom. You couldn't see very much though in the way of fish and plant life because the glass was covered with algae. They stopped for a hot dog at the Coney stand and then started walking towards where they had parked the car. "Oh such a perfect day, feed animals at the zoo, then maybe a movie too and then home ...." Cloud felt happier than he had ever felt in his most recent past life and all the voyages through hell he had recently taken. Maybe this was the reason for all the suffering...hope springs eternal in the human heart. It was the only thing that has permanence through the ages. Hell was just forty days of torture and then it was over, or so it seemed, as long as you believe and don't lose faith. If you let the demons wrap their arms around you and you embrace them, then you're stuck there forever. They meandered along taking in the sights and smelling the tree dust in the air. There was a little wooden bridge in front of them holding some people who were looking over the bridge into the water below. They were feeding the goldfish. The fish were huge and fat, lazy and stupid. Overfeed by the tourists they spent their entire lives, mouths gasping and wide-open just above the surface of the muddy water. They were waiting for a handout, hoping that the tourists didn't run out of change used to feed the little coin box that contained the food. Twenty-five cents got you half a handful. The fish however, had some competition for the food. Ducks and a couple of swans from a nearby lake had discovered the secret; that they had a taste for the fish food also.

Rumor had it among the ducks that the stuff was poison, and what duck in his right mind would want to hang around a bunch of lazy fish? But it was easy pickings once you developed a taste for it. The ducks and swans, being bigger and certainly more aggressive, muscled the poor goldfish out of the way and took all the food. There seemed to be plenty to go around however, and the fish, having a brain less than half the size of a walnut didn't mind. They had developed their own kind of symbiotic relationship.

Cloud and they Woman Who Was Sitting Next To Him fed the fish for a while and then decided to leave the garden and head home. They had ridden in her car evidently and she dropped him off at his apartment. They shared a tender kiss and agreed to call each other. She got in her car and drove off. As he watched her go he realized that he didn't have her phone number and still had no idea who she even was.

The Woman Who Was Sitting Next To Him seemed to be very much into the "New Age" stuff that was gaining in popularity at the time. They smoked a lot of weed, wrote streams of consciousness poetry, meditated until it hurt and made love frequently barefoot in the grass until it hurt too. They hung with a group of friends where sandals, beards, beads, and tie-dye T-Shirts were the order of the day, and Spirituality and religion. Weird Religions; Wicca, the Eastern beliefs, right on up to Voodoo; smoking cigars, spitting rum and ripping chickens to pieces. One friend had a list of some 23 different religions written in a notebook with brief descriptions of each.

At the start of each new day, he would toss dice on a Quija board to decide which religion he would become for that day. He had a little box of ornaments pursuant to each one and would adorn himself accordingly. There was also an Indian Shaman who very closely resembled Billy Jack from the movie of the same name, and who was also an expert in Kung Fu and Tai Chi. Cloud was particularly attracted to this individual, but the Shaman seemed to try to keep a respectable distance from Cloud. Cloud wasn't quite sure if it was because he sensed that Cloud was in reality a spirit manifesting himself through several life experiences or not, but then that was REALLY what we all were doing wasn't it?

Maybe it was because of Cloud's closeness with the spirit world or maybe not, but Cloud took to all this stuff like a fish to the water. He soon became proficient at several of them, but without the board and the dice. One day the Woman Who Was Sitting Next To Him and Cloud decided to take a little trip a couple of states away to a place called camp Russfield. It was located in a little town out side of a rather large city and was the last refuge of the "Spiritualist Movement." A movement that had peaked in the 20's with the advent of rich people going to see mediums and digging up long dead relatives. There was all kinds of stage tricks and elaborate equipment involved, and at the time the movement became so large that it attracted the respect of a number of distinguished scientists and even Harry Houdini.

Harry had an open mind at first, but then became disillusioned when he discovered that most of it was just fooling the senses and slight of hand, at which of course, he was the master. He had WANTED to believe in an afterlife and still clung to a minute amount of hope right up to his death, stating that if there was anyone in the universe that could escape the other world and come back, it was he. But getting out of there must have proven more difficult than escaping from a milk can, because, despite many rumors involving him AND Elvis, no one really heard from him with the exception of maybe a couple of private conversations that he did not want made public.

Cloud and The Woman Who Sat Next To Him arrived at the Camp about 6:30 in the afternoon. The place looked like any other sleepy little midwestern town: Rows of little white houses and picket fences, flowers in boxes gracing the front porches. There was an American flag draped lazily in a few of the front yards. There was a rusty old sign at the entranceway that read: "Welcome to Camp Russfield." A postman waved at the couple as they were passing and they noticed that he was wearing some kind of odd-looking amulet around his neck. They pulled upside a very large burned-out building on their left. There was faded police tape still around it and part of the building had collapsed in on itself. The windows reminded Cloud of sad angry eyes wide open with flame smudges for eyebrows. The place definitely had a spirit about it that Cloud instantly connected to. It was a brick, wood, mortar, and stone's cry for help. They got back in the car after a few moments' reflection and proceeded slowly back up the dusty gravel road. There was a restaurant on the right with a closed sign on it and up ahead a kind of country general store that doubled as a post office. They stopped in and asked directions to the hotel they were to be staying at. The place was very quiet, some- thing they noticed about the whole town so far. As they were driving in they noticed several people just sitting under trees praying and meditating. Others just strolled around, looking like they were lost deep in thought. The lady behind the counter at the store was very old, but she also looked very calm and peaceful. She told them that there was two hotels, both further up the road, neither had air-conditioning and one of them was even lacking running water and electricity. She told them about the story of Camp Russfield; how it was built on what originally was sacred Indian burial ground. This intrigued Cloud and made his eyebrows twitch. Maybe that was the reason he was thrown in here, to meet some of the ancestors, it was about time. The lady continued, telling them how at the turn of the century two sisters had lived on the property. She told them how

103

the two sisters would channel the spirits of the recently dead of the town and then pictures of these people would mysteriously appear as a powdery type of painting on blank canvas. The sisters would then conduct a séance with the family members and sell the painting to them as keepsakes of the experience.

The place had reached it's heyday back in the 1920's when spirituality and spiritualism was all the rage, with the European intellectuals as well as a few distinguished scientists in the states who were hell bent on proving the existence of the afterlife in a scientific manner. Most of theses attempts had failed, of course, and when a number of the spiritualists and mediums were exposed as elaborate fakes by the likes of Houdini, ET. All, the place kind of deteriorated, kept alive only by a few hard core believers in the faith that had turned it into a belief system instead of a parlor game.

All 40 of the little houses that made up the town were quaint and well kept, and a small sign hung on the doors or the windows proclaiming what type of psychic, spiritualist, or medium dwelled within. Each had a specialty and a modality of operating in their contact with the spirit world. Some used index cards and candles, reading the smudge marks left by the flame, some used tarot cards and tin horns positioned in the ear to listen to murmurings issuing from the underworld. Some just fell into an automatic trance and established a direct link.

Cloud and the Woman Sitting Next to Him were sitting in the dinghy though clean and well-kept hotel; the Broken Spirit Hotel, that is. Cloud pulled the plastic cap off the end of the syringe and filled it with clear fluid from the vial that was sitting on the bed next to h~m. He pierced his finger and squeezed a drop out onto the machine.

He looked at the readout on the face of the machine...meaningless numbers that meant life or death to him...but wait a minute...wasn't he already dead? There were things about these physical embodiments that he still didn't understand...hell, he really didn't understand any of what was happening to him, all this past life business. He certainly was sitting here in what felt to be the flesh right now and somehow he had the feeling that this was an important incarnation and he would probably have to physically die to get out of it. He grabbed the filled syringe and injected it into his stomach. He was rapidly running out of places to put the damn stuff and scar tissue had developed under his skin that at times made it impossible for the fluid to go in. Sometimes he would have to stick himself several times to get the stuff to work. He had found out that he was diabetic when the Woman Sitting Next To Him reminded him that he was late for his next shot. He also had to watch what he ate and would sometimes feel faint and pass out when his blood sugar would fall too low. The Woman Who Was Sitting Next To Him would then take out a syringe full of Glycogen and inject him with it to restore his brain to consciousness It was like a shot to control the disease and another to reverse the affects of the treatment. Cloud thought that he probably would die from this, but who knew, maybe a truck would run over him instead. And his eyesight was messed up, The Woman .... told him that he had several eye surgeries to try to reverse an internal bleeding complication that could have made him go blind. He vaguely remembered painfully getting shot in the eye with a laser, a burning hot blinding flash that seared off the bleeding vessels. Blind for several days, eyes bleeding like red dye being dropped in a bottle of clear fluid with an eye- dropper and slowly diffusing, unstill the blood clouds in Cloud's eyes obscured all but the brightest sunlight. He remembered the blindness now, the horrifying feeling of entrapment and fear, tinged in the background by a newfound sense of calm and a heightening of the other senses, touch, smell, and hear. Of course all the blood testing had scarred his fingers so terribly that he wasn't sensitive enough to read Braille, so he had to rely on audio books. The Woman...had been a great help to him during these lonely moments. Being constantly at his side and reading to him, even describing to him what was on the television tube. Finally after a couple of weeks the blood had drained enough for him to make out shapes and gradually got better and better until he could see well enough again to do everyday activities. The surgery however, had cost him almost all of his peripheral vision, but he considered it a small price to pay.

One thing about the Camp was that it was peaceful. Cloud felt a kinship with the place, spending long hours walking the trail alone and with The Woman .... Maybe it WAS the spirits of the long-dead Indians making some kind of connection with him. It was rumored that at one end of the compound, there was a small patch of forest that was haunted by the spirit of an 8-year-old child that had become lost and died there.

One day Cloud was walking along near the area that he thought everyone was talking about and decided to see for himself. Hell, he thought he was already dead and certainly had recently lost some of his fear of the unknown after all that he had been through. There was a small pat h leading into the woods that had mostly been overgrown with weeds. He brushed aside some of the overgrowth and proceeded. Everything seemed pretty normal, it was a hot summer day and Cloud wiped the sweat from his brow. About 10 minutes along he came upon a small stream overlaid with rocks. Most of the stream had dried up. Suddenly he sensed a presence and heard a small voice saying something. Suddenly he froze, unable to move...it was like there was an invisible barrier looming in front of him. He struggled furiously, not really appreciating being held hostage by an 8 year old or whatever this thing was that had a grip on him. Then the voice spoke...."You are Apache, aren't you?" "You ARE Apache ..... "The voice said again, haltingly. "What are you talking about?" Cloud replied. There was a rustling among the trees, but Cloud felt no wind moving them. "You've come to save me! The voice proclaimed. Suddenly Cloud felt a gentle wind in his face, followed by an overwhelming stench that almost made him vomit. He had not smelled anything so vile in his entire lifetime.

He heard the laughter of a small boy, but could not as yet see anything. Ha Ha Ha Ha! Got ya!" The voice said. Cloud wiped the ethereal shit from his face realizing the ghost boy had farted on him.

Standing around on a hot afternoon smelling ghost farts was not Cloud's idea of a pleasant afternoon. He shouted into the trees, "Listen young man, that's enough!" "Show yourself" He felt a tickling sensation in the crack of his ass and turned around; more laughter, but no presence. Suddenly Cloud could make out a little shimmering among the leaves of the old oak tree that he was standing in front of.

He had to move his eyes back and forth like he was dreaming... asleep in the rapid part of REM, to keep up with the vibration level of the ghost, but he could finally make out the image of a small Indian boy, floating half way up in midair. The ghost-boy looked at him with an amused smile on his face. He had the largest brown eyes that Cloud could ever remember seeing and a very small nose and thick lips. For a few seconds, the ghost just floated there, shimmering.

Cloud watched him closely. It seemed that the boy was drinking in some of Cloud's very life force the stare was so intense. Finally the child spoke: "Father!" he exclaimed. "You've finally come to bury me!" Cloud froze. The Ghost-Child was emanating alternating purple waves of hatred and love. The feeling was so intense that Cloud couldn't move, sounds, feelings and even smells broken down into basic vibrations. Cloud felt that he had fallen off of a ship somewhere in a vast ocean and the seawater was rapidly filling his lungs. He tried to think of what his Grandfather would have done. Blast this Ghost with his new found power and send him back to hell, or try to save him by moving him toward the light? But there wasn't any light. It was all gloom in this dark wood of error. A thought suddenly occurred to him. The presence before him was a young boy who's tragic life-end cried out for comfort, but the many years of suffering that, which didn't even have a cause, had turned the boy into a Guardian Demon. Cloud could sense that the boy, even though frail and literally white as a ghost, out powered him. You could not overpower a demon or even run away, you had to sneak around him, distract and run. Cloud didn't know if this came from one of his own spirit guides or if it was something that he had learned on his own, but it didn't matter where it came from, he only knew that it was true knowledge and he had to act on it or he would be stuck here in the woods forever trying to put this child to rest and reading him a bedtime story wasn't going to do the trick. Cloud thought harder than he had ever thought in his life or lives. He stared at the ground, trying to make it open, trying to manifest a grave. After several seconds of this there was a faint swirling of green on the ground, almost like the grass had started to grow and intertwine upon itself. It looked watery like seaweed with electricity floating on top of it. Slow the green quicksand opened like a parting of the waves. It got deeper and deeper and blacker. The child presence looked down at the grave that was forming. The big brown eyes then looked up at Cloud. "Father, this will bring me peace?" The voice sounded scared, weak and little. Cloud cast his eyes aside and said "Yes I will." The boy floated over to get a closer look. It looked almost like he was breaking up. The atom spaces were getting larger, dissolving back to the source. The boy's feet came up into the air in front of him and eventually he was lying vertically, looking almost asleep just inches above the grave opening. Cloud was watching him intently as the child demon lowered himself. There was a slight hint of red around the child's face. Cloud felt the watery grip loosen. It was like the water was getting more shallow and the long distance swimmer just about had his feet on the beach after crossing the channel. Cloud started to slowly walk away from the prostrate ghost, trying like the Indians to let his feet develop eyes and show him the way. He glanced back just in time to see that the red glow around the boy's face was getting larger and brighter. The boy was slowly turning his head in Cloud's direction. Cloud could see that the light was shining from the demon eyes, the one that he had awakened. Cloud noticed that it seemed like the boy was being sucked down into the grave, the boy's body was almost entirely inside it now. Suddenly Cloud's ears were assaulted by a voice that was so deep it seemed to shake the shallow Earth around him. "YOU CANNOT LEAVE ME!" The voice rumbled. There was a pause…."PLEASE!" It seemed to Cloud that during that hesitation there was another significant weakening of the power that was holding him here.

He didn't know which direction to head but he started to run with all his might. Cloud closed his eyes tightly, not caring if he ran into a tree or not. It was like all the flesh on his bones had been stripped away and he was some kind of puppet who had broken his strings and had to pull on his own tendons and ligaments to move his simple wooden joints. He saw a glimpse of light up ahead through the trees and just beyond that the creek with the small wooden bridge over it. His feet made a final tap tapping sound on the planks as he crossed into daylight. He was tired and breathing heavily. He could see the houses of the Psychic town up ahead and slowed down. He walked on the dusty road past the little grocery store and the post office back to the run down hotel where The Woman......... was waiting for him. Cloud was pouring sweat and he sat downstairs in a moldy overstuffed chair. All the windows were open and a gentle breeze blew through them. The lace curtains ruffled softly. The air from outside seemed to be deliciously cooler as it reached the inside without the benefits of air-conditioning. He sat there for awhile and looked at some of the paintings on the wall. They were some of the "spirit drawings" from the museum. The paint seemed to almost be made out of powder that had settled on the paintings. They were portraits of the dead, channeled there by the sisters at the turn of the century. Cloud got up out of his seat and walked over to one of them to get a closer look. He was drawn to it and couldn't seem to stop staring at it no matter how hard he tried. It was a portrait of a little boy, about the age of five, dressed in a white night gown. His hair was scattered and coarse and he looked pale even for a black and white photograph. His dark eyes caught Cloud's. He seemed to be staring right through him. Cloud felt a chill creep it's way up his spine. Once again for the second time that day he felt as if he was trapped in the spider's web, unable to move, about to be consumed. All the liquid life force literally sucked right out of him. He felt dry already. He tried to walk away from the painting. It took considerable effort, but he was able to move to the side for a few steps. He looked back towards the image. The eyes appeared to have moved. The little boy was still watching him from his death trip. Cloud tried moving around the room at different angles to the picture. It made no difference; the eyes were still upon him. Cloud noticed that there was a small faded 8x5 card taped to the wall besides the painting. He got closer and squinted his eyes to read it. It told a small description about the boy. What age he had died and his family name. The card stated that the boy had died from diabetes at the age of five. Slipping into a coma before the day that insulin was discovered. He was suffering from the same affliction that plagued Cloud and had made him enter the dark world of total blindness. Cloud wiped the sweat from his forehead and hurried up to his room. The Woman .....was there, sitting in a Victorian chair dressed in her night gown, even though it was well past noon, reading a book by the open window. She looked at Cloud as he entered the room. He looked a mess, muddy and disheveled from his ghostly encounters. As she looked at him her mouth open just slightly and their eyes locked from across the room. Cloud said nothing as he ran to embrace her. His love and passion for her had never been stronger and he felt that some of it was coming from outside himself, beyond his control. He grabbed at her like a drowning man reaching for a life raft. The motion of time seemed to stand still. He fell on top of her and raised himself just long enough to pull the nightgown up and over her head. She said nothing, just looked at him with a wild stare. Whatever this energy was it possessed them both now. They made love for what seemed like hours, with a fervent energy that neither was used to.

Cloud awoke about eight hours later with the sun on his face and the smell of freshly mown grass both screaming in through the open window. He rarely slept more than a few hours at a time because of his medical condition. Sometimes his blood sugar would take a dip during the night and he would wake up and literally fall to the floor when he tried to get up. Face down with an imprint of his shoe pressed into his forehead. If he was lucky he would be able to crawl to the place where he kept his Glucagon syringe that was filled with the life giving syrup. Other times he was so mentally confused that he would crawl-walk to the refrigerator and try to figure out how to get the damned thing open, his sugar starved brain reduced to only it's autonomic functions. These episodes left him paranoid, never going anywhere without candy and an alarm clock that was set at three-hour intervals so he could get up and check his blood sugar. Diabetes was never far from his mind. He thought about how it had been a scourge to the American Indians. The white man's diet that was rich in fats and carbohydrates probably was to blame. He remembered that it had gotten much worse over the past few years. The last time he had visited the reservation, his aunt had been in the hospital, hooked up to a dialysis machine. Her kidneys had suffered the onslaught of a lifetime of uncontrolled blood sugar, finally giving out and causing her to literally swell up like a balloon. The kidney ward had some twenty machines that were constantly in use. Sometimes people had to wait hours to get hooked up and sometimes the hospital would run low on filtering supplies. Some of the patients hooked up to the machines were asleep and other just prayed or read books and magazines. The machines made a clicking and whirling sound as they pumped the waste blood out and through the filter to rid the bodies of the toxins that they had accumulated over the past few days. All the patients had looks of hopeless resignation on their faces. In this part of the country transplants were mostly out of the question and the dismal small hope for any kind of a normal life combined with hypertension and the chronic alcoholism that ran rampant among the Indians made most of them throw in the towel and die early.

Cloud rubbed his eyes and moved his head, trying to adjust the blood that normally floated in his field of vision. The laser that he had on his eyes had stopped most of the bleeding that had caused him to go blind but he still had residual clots of the stuff that would float in his field of vision for years to come. He instinctively reached over to the Woman That Was Usually Lying Next To Him, but felt nothing but clammy sheets. He got up and walked around the room then put his clothes on and went downstairs. It was a beautiful day. The sun was warm and the grass smelled sweet. He asked an old woman that was sitting outside of the old hotel if she had seen The Woman. She replied that she had not, but had only been sitting there for a short period of time. Cloud walked around the gardens for about thirty minutes looking for The Woman. He visited the cafeteria and bought himself a cup of coffee. His stomach was starting to rumble and he knew that he would have to take his injection and have breakfast soon. It always pissed The Woman off when he ate without her although he had tried to explain on many occasions that it wasn't out of rudeness but rather a medical necessity. Cloud finished his coffee and walked back to the Hotel. He thought that maybe she was there waiting for him. As he entered the room he noticed the small sheet of yellow paper that was on the nightstand next to the bed. The note was scrawled on flowered paper in her usual flowing script, but this time the letters were a little shaky, kind of nervous looking. The note started out saying how much that she had loved him and how much the last night when their respective passions had exploded, meant to her. Then the script got a little shakier as she explained in the next paragraph why she was leaving. She felt that there was something deep within him that resembled love but that she would never be able to find it. There was also the problem of the passion.; the physical side. She felt that Cloud was embarrassed by sex. Guilty. She hadn't known what spirit visited them last night, or how it happened, but one thing that she was sure of was that she wanted more of it, a lot more. The other thing that she was sure of, and it had taken several years to find this out, was that she wasn't going to find it with him. She laid a lot of the blame on herself. She felt that she was too heavy and unattractive to Cloud. She warned him not to look for her, that it was all somehow better this way. Cloud finished reading the letter and looked up at the cracked ceiling in the faded room. A thought from his childhood raced in front of his eyes. He had spent long hours sick with a fever and had looked at the cracks in the ceiling of the old house that he had grown up in. Watched as the cracks formed tracings to the old ceiling light fixture that had one time probably been brass but was now a dark and muddy brown. It was the last thing that he looked at as he faded off into a fevered and troubled sleep. He remembered reciting the prayer that his Grandmother had taught him. "Now I lay me down to sleep, I pray the Lord my soul to keep. If I should die before I wake I pray the Lord my soul to take." Suddenly the old hotel room looked an awful lot like that room In his childhood and he felt just as alone and uncomfortable. But back then the pain had mostly been physical and he lay in bed dreaming of when he would be able to get up and play again. This time he wasn't sure. It seemed as if the world had stopped just past the door. Just past the open window.

Chapter 8

Cloud was falling back into the void; starry, starry night, deep purple cloudless space still containing color. It was a long fall through what seemed like a boundless eternity of space. AND time. But then again there were the same thing weren't they? Cloud was face down on the ground. A ground that was hard and rough to the touch. He lifted his face a few inches from the ground and realized that it wasn't Earth that he was grounded to after all, but rather stone, old gray stone that had been weathered by the pull of centuries. The position that he was in was unusual. Prostrate, he was face down with his forehead pressed against the stone floor, his hands turned upwards, and his back arched. It was almost as if he was looking for something and had his hands reaching out for a magnifying glass. Contact lenses? He suddenly realized that he was in some kind of a room. It was dark and large, there was definitely a feeling of space, a feeling that the room went on and on and had many times been filled with echoes. He could still hear the ghostly imprints…of chanting. A low soft vibrating murmur that resonated off the crystals buried deep within the rock. Slowly thoughts crept back into an empty brain. Cloud realized that he had been crouching in this position for a long time. His back, forehead, and knees hurt. He attempted to get up and it was not without some difficulty. Then he reached a certain point and his body seemed to flow into a Seiza position. His back was straight and he rested his weight on top of his heels, his feet tucked neatly underneath him. As his vision came back to him in the dark cavern he realized that he was staring at a very large pair of stone feet. His eyes slowly scanned upwards at the statue that was sitting in front of him. The statue was fairly large, about twice Cloud's size. Carved robes of gray stone covered the figure. There were carved beads around the wrists of the statue and also draped around it's neck. But it was the face that impressed Cloud. Oriental in its anatomy, the face had a very serene look about it; small lips, bridged by a rather large nose that was flattened at the bottom and high cheekbones, bounded by heavily lidded eyes and a low forehead. The statues had no marble hair but rather a cap of some sort covering a bald stone head. The surface of the cap was pebbled with bumps that reminded Cloud of grapes for some reason. The expression on the statue's face seemed very serene and well…Buddha like. Hell it WAS a Buddha of some sort, but it certainly didn't look like the small little grinning Rosewood ones that you would rub the fat belly for good luck down at the local five and dime. Cloud looked down and realized that he was dressed in some kind of robe also. Not quite as flowing as the statue's and white. His feet were bare and his head was covered with some kind of headdress. The cap was also white and appeared to be tied into some sort of knot. The knot looked like a braid that framed his face and made him look like he had horns, large white floppy horns that drooped down both sides of his face like sideburns. Cloud suddenly felt very thirsty and sick. He retched with dry heaves and he felt sweat try to pop out onto his forehead, but none came. He felt cool and dry. He brought his right hand up and touched his face. It felt cool but thick and almost leathery, like he had spent many years out in the sun. Deep wrinkles were etched into his forehead and his cheeks felt very hollow. He looked down at his hands and they looked…well …..DEAD! His fingernails were dark blue and brittle and he almost though for a moment that he was wearing a very tight pair of leather gloves. He could see the faint outlines of veins under the opaque skin and could almost make out the outlines of bone. WHAT THE HELL WAS GOING ON HERE??!!

There was a voice. A voice that was at first small and tinny, but at the same time rich and re-assuring like it was being spoken through a horn of plenty. "Hoc Theiu!" it said. "Master, please allow me to help you to your feet." The voice was spoken in a strange dialect, but it was one that Cloud naturally seemed to understand. Cloud felt very dry and weak, like he had sweated gallons on a hot summer day and then had tried to run the length of a football field. He struggled to his feet and looked over at the person that was assisting him. The figure was dressed in a white robe; his head was shaven, not a follicle of hair on his face and head except a faint outline of eyebrow. The man's skin glowed faintly in the candlelight and reminded Cloud of a smiling, yet concerned, yellow moon. "Master, allow me to get your cane." The man said as he let go of Cloud and scurried across the room, his feet taking very small steps and making scratching sounds on the stone floor like a rat scurrying for cover. The man handed Cloud a walking stick that was rough-hewn and had a small wooden knob on top. Cloud tried to take a few steps and was rewarded for his efforts with great pain as a wave of nausea overtook him. Cloud started to sink to the floor as the aide spoke once more. "Remember your vows Master!" the man said quietly. Grey images began to flood into Cloud's mind and they brought with them the comfort of a misty morning's rain. The pain and sickness slowly faded to the point of practically not existing at all. It was replaced by a low hum that almost sounded like a chant to Cloud. Somehow he realized that he had caused this and was somewhat amazed at his own powers. His rubber band-like legs began to move on their own accord as he walked slowly ahead towards the light at the end of the tunnel. "Sometimes you get like this and I have to remind you of your great mission." The man that was walking beside him whispered. Cloud slowly turned his head towards the voice. "And what mission might that be?" Cloud asked, his voice as dry and cracked as centuries old rice paper. "To become a Buddha!" the voice answered.

The man guided Cloud through what seemed to be miles of corridors through the maze of the centuries old Monastery. They finally arrived at cloud's room, which was small, musty, and damp with the morning's dew. The lesser Monk poured Cloud a small amount of red-colored liquid from a ceramic jar that was perched on the small table next to Cloud's straw mattress. There was a small statue of the Buddha sitting in the corner of the room surrounded by flowers. The man sat Cloud down in front of it, Cloud's legs seemed to naturally flow into the full Lotus position. "Calm yourself now Master." The man said. "Meditate." The Monk then left in a rustle of Saffron robes. Cloud sat in front of the statue and closed his eyes trying to get in touch with the pain that was pulsating through his body in waves. He tried to bring back the humming chant that superceded all thoughts and brought him into the river, the flow of the Tao. He had to empty his mind of all thoughts and dip into the well of No Thing ness that brought him back to the void. Instead thoughts kept advancing like enemies to the front and images of a child; a child hungry, cold and crying. There was then an experience of floating, flying almost as the child was picked up and comforted. There was a strange scent that Cloud wasn't really familiar with, but he recognized it as a Mother scent, warm and comforting. He looked up from his arm cradle into the eyes, the eyes that seemed so big and round. He had seen similar eyes before, but he could not remember where or when. A nipple was placed into his mouth, but it too was not what he was accustomed to. It tasted cold and plastic, but he sucked anyway and the milk was warm and sweet. His tiny hand reached out but landed on unfamiliar territory. Instead of the soft feel of his Mother's breast, he felt the hard surface of the bottle, smooth and unforgiving. But it didn't matter as his hunger overtook him and he fed voraciously for almost twenty minutes. Finally sucking air into his full belly, he was upended and tapped gently on his back. The resulting burp was such a relief that he closed his eyes and began to gently fall asleep. The last words that he heard was his Mother's voice saying "Get the car, we're taking this baby home."

Baby Cloud slept in the car most of the way back to the hotel. George, his newly adopted father had been stationed in Japan right after the war. He was in the Army stationed as a diplomat trying to help heal the massive wound made when little Fat Boy landed and the Nuclear Age began in earnest. George shuffled papers working with the Red Cross and the military trying to get medical aid and supplies to the thousands of children who were maimed or horribly burned when the blasts went off and ended the war saving thousands of casualties in the process, not to mention the civilized world. He was pretty high up in the paper shuffling biz and was allowed to send for his wife Susie about a month before he was to go back home to Nebraska in the states. It was shortly after Susie arrived that the couple reached an agreement to adopt the child that they both had wanted all their married lives. Now in their thirties, he was ready to retire from the horror of the military and the war and live on his pretty fat pension while Susie maintained the position of house maker or rather homemaker was the term that they preferred to use. It had taken quite sometime to negotiate the adoption, but then George was after all in the paper shuffling business and he pulled strings like they were attached directly to the heart. Now the big day had finally arrived and they were to take the new baby home for a test drive and prop him up right nest to the new Oldsmobile and the frost-free Kenmore refrigerator. The new family stood on the tarmac of the Air Force base that still had fighter planes parked on it ready to take off at a moment's notice. They looked at the shiny silver prop plane that would start them on their long journey back to the States. Susie held on to Baby Cloud so tightly that he could barely breathe. All that Cloud could make out in his fuzzy field of vision was the underside of Susie's nose. He tried to concentrate on the smells instead. Of all his senses these seemed to be the most primordial and also the sharpest. His Mother's was a friendly smell except when she tried to cover it up with that smelly bath powder that made Cloud wheeze and cough. His Father's smell was usually tinged with the acrid smell of pipe tobacco. When things got too confusing Cloud would sometimes take a whiff of his own familiar scent just to re-assure himself that he was still there. His scent was constantly changing from the sweet smell of flesh to the pungent ammonia smell of urine, bitter smell of new shit, and the sour smell of burped rancid milk. These odors seemed to get the attention of his parents as well, especially his Mother who would fuss and turn her face into a frown when Cloud messed his diapers, sometimes to the point of making him cry. The airport contained a lot of assaults on the senses for Baby Cloud. There was the dirty smell of gasoline and the terrific wind tunnel whoosh of the fighter planes landing and taking off. Somehow he managed to nod off during the midst of all of it and slept soundly during the 16-hour flight back to the States. The last thing that Cloud remembered was the pressure pop in his ears as the plane landed in Holton Nebraska.

"Stay away from that sewing machine!" His Mother yelled. Cloud didn't seem to notice as he pushed his entire body weight down on the metal footplate that operated the old Singer Sewing Machine. There was an old floral colored bedspread that was thrown over the top of the machine and Cloud, now the glorious age of three, loved to crawl underneath the spread. Then he would push on the big push pedal plate causing the large spin wheel to move which in turn caused the needle to move up and down on the top of the machine. Once he had gotten his little finger pinched in the flywheel and his fingernail turned several shades of yellow, then purple, and then fell off. His Mother had forbidden him from ever playing underneath the machine again, but that just caused him to sneak there whenever he could. There was something about the word No that a child of his age just couldn't understand. It was like the void. It did exist, but then again didn't. So when he was told NO! Don't play with that, the only words that registered were the ..."play with that! Part. And Cloud always tried to do what his parents told him to especially when there was a NO! in front of this because that caused then to get really excited and pay a whole lot more attention to him. Even to the point of slapping him on his behind, which he enjoyed tremendously. His parents decided that he needed a more worthwhile and constructive mechanical diversion and since Christmas time was rapidly approaching, they bought him a little red mechanical car with foot pedals. Susie had argued for the Little Red Wagon, but George insisted on the car. It was a guy type of thing and after all Baby Cloud WAS his son. It was something that George had read in Harper's Magazine that infants with make believe cars somehow grew up to be better drivers. When he got a little older, George would buy him the plastic dashboard complete with workable speedometer that was hanging on the wall behind the meat counter down and Moyer's Grocery Store. Until that time though, Baby Cloud would have to be happy with the little red car and the toy metal fire truck.

It was Christmas time and outside the wind hummed against the windows and Nebraska snow was piling up outside. There was a tinsel Christmas Tree in the corner of the living room that changed color every few seconds thanks to a flood light with a multi-colored reflector in front of it. Baby Cloud, who was now getting old enough not to have to sleep with his parents anymore, would gaze at the changing tree long minutes before he finally fell asleep. Sometimes his parents would find him stretched out in front of the thing looking almost as if he was worshipping it, prostrate on the floor with his arms stretched out in front of him. What a peculiar baby, they sometimes thought.

George and Suzie's Aunt thought that the Baby wasn't "quite right" in some other ways also. Clarice was kind of the Psychic of the family, rumored to know when the phone is about to ring and who was calling. She was a born-again Christian, attending services regularly at the Antioch Baptist Church. She more or less hinted one time that the port wine birth mark on Baby Cloud's forehead was somehow the mark of the Devil. The dot was only the size of a small pea, but it was right in the center of the child's forehead almost like that mark that you see on women over in India. Clarice would offer to give the child a bath just so she could look for new signs of Satan, but she never found any. She also confided to some of the people at the Church that she objected to George bringing back a "nigger baby" from overseas. To the rest of the family she just sighed and said that these things sort of just happen because of the war. To Baby Cloud, Aunt

Clarice was naturally repulsive, reeking of an unnatural scent of cheap perfume and Geritol. She had a green and white wicker purse that held snotty old lace handkerchiefs and fractured remnants of Chiclets chewing gum. The other thing that the baby hated was The Aunt's propensity to grab a hold of the baby's cheeks and squeeze the ever-living hell out of them. When she did this she made some kind of clucking sound like an old rooster getting his hook on for the last time. Sometimes The Aunt would get too close when she was squeezing and Baby Cloud would extract his revenge. He would reach up quickly and hook his fat stubby little fingers into her nose and pull. This would make the Aunt scream and run for the bathroom to flush out her nose. She had read somewhere that children were the carriers of all kinds of nasty cold viruses and all manner of other nasty things and Baby Cloud, being foreign, who knew what he brought along with him. She was also convinced that the baby played with himself when nobody was looking because sometimes his fingers would have that sort of "musty smell" about them. She was firmly convinced that masterbation was the root of all evil and would not only cause warts to spring out all over your hands, but also land you straight into what she liked to call the "crazy house." When baby sitting she checked the covers over the baby frequently for "bulges" that would indicate foul play going on. She would then wake the baby up by shaking him and demanding to see his hands. She looked at them disgustedly, imagining that there was hair growing all over them. Overall she had considered sex to be really disgusting too, even with her late husband. God only put the sex urge in people so that they would procreate." She was fond of saying. "Otherwise why would they even think of doing such as nasty thing?" The couple had twin beds in separate room all through their some forty years of marriage. About once a month he came to her closed and locked bedroom door and asked for permission. Sometimes he got it and sometimes not. One of the determining factors was whether or not he had whiskey on his breath. The Aunt abhorred drinking and smoking and even chewing tobacco, all habits that she considered as filthy and disgusting as getting poked. Her husband worked in a shoe factory and once a month he got stinkingly plastered at the Union Meeting. It was at this time he was his horniest but usually too drunk to even get it up. This was a great relief to the Aunt because he was a big man and could get his way if he wanted, but usually he just gave up and went back to his room, passing out on the bed. He then would stay in bed all day Saturday, nursing his hangover.

The Aunt was determined to save Baby Cloud's soul so she got up early on Sunday and dressed him in his finest outfits and took the bus across town to the little storefront Church that she attended. The Church was small and Baptist in nature. They arrived promptly at nine O'clock (if the bus was on time) and Cloud would sit through an hour of Sunday school. The teacher, an older woman named Mrs. Benwell always wore a paisley dress and had a mole on her chin with hair growing out of it. She handed all the students little tracts with colorful pictures of a cartoon Jesus on them. Sometimes they showed Him walking around in an ancient setting and sometimes he was the doorman at a hotel or a garage attendant. He was always faced with making right or wrong moral decisions. Even though Cloud was now only about four years old, he read through them and quickly discarded them, asking for more. "That will have to wait for next week!" Mrs. Benwell told him. She also would catch him reading the Bibles and hymnbooks that were kept for the adults in little wooden slots behind the pews. Mrs. Benwell told Cloud that they were for the adults and he would have to read all the pamphlets in Sunday school first, but finally gave up and told the Aunt that she should get Cloud his very own "adult" Bible.

One day Cloud was exploring around in his Aunt's closet. He loved rolling around with the shoes that she kept on the floor, inhaling the smell of the perfume on the dresses. It made him feel safe and warm. After he was finished, he would rearrange the boxes of shoes and the dresses that he had disturbed as best he could. He was certain that his Aunt knew that he spent time playing in there, but so far she hadn't said anything. One day Cloud discovered his Aunt's terrible little secret that was hidden in the small closet. When he opened one of the shoeboxes he discovered that the box contained no shoes. Instead it was full of Catholic propaganda; booklets from the Knights of Columbus and the like. There was even a small Catholic Bible. Cloud didn't know what all of this meant. He just assumed it was more stuff like he had already seen in Sunday school. For the other Church members to find out would have been worse than them finding a box full of nasty pictures. Could it be that The Aunt was a closet Catholic? Cloud put all the propaganda back into the box where he found it. The Aunt didn't say anything to him about it, but he noticed that the box was gone the next time that he opened the closet door and took a peek.

Aunt Clarice's husband Lawrence was a shoe worker who sat on an old wood bench all day "tacking" shoes. Before the days of glued on soles, everything was put together by hand and after the leather was cut and fitted for the tops of the shoes, they were put on a machine and the soles were tacked into place. Then they went on down the assembly line where the tacks were removed and the soles were permanently sewn into place. Sometimes the tacks were left in and over a period of time they could wear through the shoe and into the person's foot. It was always the first thing that he checked when he went to buy a pair of shoes.

On Saturday mornings Lawrence would wake little Cloud up early and they would walk together down to the Farmer's Market that was about twenty city blocks from their house. Lawrence had a folding metal basket on wheels that he would carefully fit a piece of cardboard into the bottom of so none of the fruits and vegetables would spill out on the return trip. On the way down to the market he would pretty much let Cloud do all the pulling of the empty cart. As he got a little older he was allowed to try and pull the thing back home when it was loaded with groceries. The only time that he had trouble was when they had to pull the cart up a hill or up one of the street curbs. Cloud would get stuck and put both of his hands on the handle and pull with all his might, but Lawrence usually had to step in and save the day.

The market itself was very old, built in the late 1700's. It was also very large, taking nearly an hour to navigate all through it. There was a cluster of old brick buildings at the center that lacked heating and air conditioning, with open-air stalls heading off in all directions right outside of them. Behind the stalls was a place where the truck farmers could pull up and unload their wares. Inside the first building was a store that sold live pets, including edible ones like chickens. As you moved further in there was a popcorn vendor who would fill you up a cardboard cone of corn and pour a freshly melted secret butter mixture over it until it soaked through the cardboard all over your pants. Next came a bakery and donut shop that sold the best lemon rolls that were ever created and glazed donuts with a yellow custard filling that were so greasy that they usually soaked their way through the brown paper bag they came in before you could get them home. After making the rounds of the bakery, you usually went to the "Will Doctor." The Will Doctor was an old fashioned butcher shop where you could actually buy the hog whole or maybe just the head, or they would "doctor" it up for you anyway you liked it. The place was also known for its' fresh sausage that was made right there on the premises.

As they walked through the market, Lawrence would make a zigzag pattern from one side of the place to the other, checking out the produce stalls. Each truck farmer had his stuff piled in the shape of a pyramid, at least all the round fruits and vegetables anyway. Then a small stick would be jammed down into the center of the produce. Atop the stick was a brown paper bag announcing the price. Sometimes towards the end of the day there would be a slash through the price made with a magic marker. Of course in the fine tradition of open air markets across the world, everything was debatable. Lawrence had this skill down to a tee. Lawrence would reach into his pocket and pull out his pocketknife if there was a suspicious peach or apple. His contention was that some of the farmers kept their produce in "cold storage" and that affected the freshness. He would ceremoniously cut open the fruit and examine the inside closely. If the inside was soggy or there were any brown spots, he would toss the thing right back at the vendor and wouldn't buy it at any price. If the fruit or vegetable looked ok then he would take a bite out of it and announce his verdict. Then he would say that it tasted ok but was way overpriced. The haggling would then start in earnest. Lawrence would usually walk away with a pretty good bargain. In the case of a large object like a melon, Lawrence had a different test. He would first thump the melon holding his ear close to it and then scrape a little of the skin off that was underneath. Sometimes he would smell it. Most of the purchases were under a dollar and Lawrence kept one of those leather coin holders that was folded into the shape of a star in his pocket right next to his pocket knife and the little silver can of chewing tobacco. He would squeeze the thing with his left hand to open it and then poke through the change with his right index finger. Sometimes he would remove a coin that was painted red or smashed by a car and hold it up in the air, looking intensely at it. Then he would shake his head like he was offended that someone would try to deface American currency.

On one particular Saturday morning Cloud kept saying how much he would like to have some watermelon. Cloud loved watermelon and fried chicken and that, along with his dark skin color, made his aunt and uncle sometimes worry that he had some Black blood running through him. Being foreign was bad enough, but being mulatto was a little more than the two guardians could handle. Lawrence finally gave in to Clod's whining about the watermelon, but he made a stipulation. Cloud could pick out his own melon as long as he followed his uncle's guidelines for establishing freshness, but he had to pull the basket all the way home with the melon in it. Cloud quickly agreed and ran over to the watermelon stand. He picked out the biggest one that he could find after thumping on it and scratching the underside. Lawrence helped him take all the brown paper bags out of the cart so the melon could be placed on the bottom. The wheels on the cart creaked as Cloud tried to pull it. It would barely move. Lawrence suggested that they get a smaller melon. Cloud refused, saying that this was the one that he wanted.

Cloud managed to get the cart most of the way home. The only time that he had trouble was when he had to lift the thing over the sidewalk curbs. Lawrence gave him a little help then. He didn't consider it cheating. The hardest thing to do after they got the melon home was to wait. Wait for the large orb to cool on the bottom shelf of the refrigerator. There were two things to remember about watermelons: one was to never eat the thing warm, two was to never eat the white part next to the rind, that would make you get indigestion. The next day right after Cloud's usual lunch of brown and serve sausage and Campbel's vegetable soup, Cloud was ready to dig into the melon. There were two acceptable ways to go about this, and it all depended on how you sliced it. You could slice the melon into wedges and eat it with your hands and get the sticky juice all over yourself, or the preferable method was to keep the slices round and eat it with a knife and a fork. Then the only thing that you had to worry about was to get the juice-laden plate over to the trashcan without spilling it. Eating watermelon was definitely labor intensive. One thing that Lawrence insisted on was never to leave the watermelon juice and rinds in the trash overnight because that would attract roaches. And the last thing in the world that you wanted to have in your house was a roach. Those filthy vermin were reserved for the poorer families of color that lived around the block and were a sure sign of a dirty and ill kept house. The only place where bugs were acceptable was down in the basement. Remember to turn on the light before you entered the dark and musty place because otherwise you would step on the water bugs and they would sound like popcorn under your feet. The exoskeletons would shatter and the bugs would leak out this mysterious white substance that was hard to get up off of the concrete floor. Most houses on the block had a snapping turtle or two in the basement who never ate the lettuce that was set out for them, but helped rid the basement of critters by eating all the insects. Sometimes there were hushed whispers of a possible rat in the basement. This would spur Lawrence to get out his pellet gun and sit in ambush for the poor varmint. A few hours later Lawrence would either give up and wait until the next day or emerge triumphant, holding the rat up by the tail for everyone to see.

The very same pellet gun was used on the pigeons that inhabited the eaves of the house. The pigeons would sit on the metal gutters that surrounded the roof of the house and position themselves the wrong way, their bird-asses hanging out into the air. Then they would shit, sometimes every few minutes. Long white stripes tinged with green of the material ran down the walls of the old house. Lawrence pretty much left the birds alone until the fateful day when he was walking in the back yard and felt something wet land on the top of his bald head. He made the mistake of looking up and got an eye full of bird shit. Ever since that time he took up bird shooting as his hobby when he wasn't going after the rats. He would spend a few hours each day that he had off from the factory perched on the windowsill of his bedroom window, shooting at the "nuisance birds," as he called them. Sometimes he would just wing then bird. Then he would go down to where the bird was laying on the ground and either stop it to death or twist its' neck. He had a special pair of rubber gloves just for that purpose, as he was convinced that they carried every communicable disease in the book.

Cloud got up out of bed and attacked the watermelon that he had struggled to get home with a vengeance. He slurped it down, spitting out the seeds in all directions. He even slurped up the seedy juice that was left on the plate. By the time he could eat no more of the thirty-pound or so melon, his stomach was as tight and thumpable as the melon was. He also sloshed a little bit when he walked. After a couple of hours Cloud began to develop a little green tinge around the gills so to speak. He was urinating every thirty minutes from all that water and the diuretic effects of the melon. Then it began to strike him in another arena; the back door. He ran for the upstairs bathroom hoping that his cheeks wouldn't fail. He remembered the incident a few years ago when he had an accident in his pants and he hid the soiled underwear in one of the dresser drawers. When the dried, smelly and pasty clothes were discovered several weeks later, things got a little hot and heavy.

Cloud was discovered in his bed, moaning and groaning. His Aunt gave him a mixture of castor oil and paregoric. That really did the trick.

Cloud survived with his Aunt and Uncle until he was about fourteen or so, that's when he moved to the other side of the tracks, so to speak.

It was a hot day in July. The kind of day where everything was still and sticky, a heaviness that the bright sun vainly tried to cut through. Cloud woke up just as the first rays of the morning sun pushed their way through the torn curtains on his bedroom window. A tall, dark and skinny kid with coarse black hair that hung down in bangs, he rubbed the pasty sleep from his eyes and looked down at the thin sheet that covered him. It was already getting hot and he moved his feet back and forth, trying to free them. There was a bulge about waist high, signaling his morning wood. He reached a hand down into familiar territory and found that his manhood was stuck to his underwear. The events of last night slowly filtered through. As he had often done before, making sure that his Aunt didn't notice any movement; he had grabbed hold of himself and slowly rubbed his member right under the head with his middle finger. He would then become erect and savor the experience until he fell asleep. Last night something strange happened though, he felt a contraction about halfway through and a warm, pleasurable fluid spurted out. Cloud had no idea what was happening, and at first when he saw the white sticky substance he thought that he might have an infection. He squeezed it, looking at the pee hole, but nothing else came out. He felt warm and fuzzy after that and then very quickly went to sleep. This morning the old familiar urge was back again and he encircled his hand around it and tugged up and down a few times. Once again there was an eruption and his body shook a little. He was a little confused and alarmed, but was more concerned that someone might discover the mess that he had made on the bed. He quickly got up and folded up the sheet and stuffed it into his dresser drawer, then went quietly into the bathroom and washed himself off. After getting dressed and brushing his teeth, he remembered that he now had a job. He was spending the summer with his cousins and their parents. They lived in a little white house across from the horseracing track and the parents took care of horses for a living. They contracted out to the owners of the thoroughbreds for stable space and to train what they hoped would be future champion racers.

Cloud hurried down to the stable, went into the tack room and pulled out his little red wheelbarrow. He went in to the first horse stall on the left and opened the wooden door. Inside the door was a strap made of canvas that kept the horse in the stall when the door was open. He moved the feed bucket aside and looked at the enormous creature inside. Cloud both feared and loved the horses. Most of them were pretty well behaved, but a couple would try to bite or kick you when you entered the stall to try to clean it. The first horse was a dappled gray mare named Polly. She was gentle and moved out of the way of the pitchfork that Cloud held in his hands. He would take the pitchfork and move the straw around looking for wet spots or clumps of horseshit. Then he would scoop up the soiled straw and put it in the wheelbarrow. When it was filled he carried it out to the compost heap and would dump it there. Then he would return to the stable and repeat the process. When all the stall had been cleaned out, he would go to the fresh pile of straw that was right outside the door to the stable and fill up the wheelbarrow. Then he would lay down the fresh straw in the stalls. After he was finished doing that he would go back to the tack room and fill up the feed buckets with grain from several large burlap sacks. After feeding then horses, sometimes he would brush them, smoothing out the dust from their coats and brushing out the manes. Once in awhile his cousin's father would let him take out one of the gentler horses and exercise him a bit. This usually meant walking him around the paddock, but occasionally he got to ride one of them a little ways up the road.

After that he was free for most of the rest of the day, or at least until suppertime. Today Cloud went to his favorite spot: the little creek that separated the barns and stables from the racetrack. He would walk for what seemed like miles along the creek, imagining that he was on some adventure in the jungle, or a soldier fighting in some far away place. He had a small machete that he used to slash at the overgrowth along the way. He would get all hot and sweaty and sometimes be covered in mosquito bites and poison ivy when he got back home, but the adventure was worth the risk. He would get covered with calamine lotion and the next morning he would pick at the itch that was still underneath the pink liquid until the stuff came off like a scab.

Cloud came to a small group of rocks that made a ripple in the center of the stream. The water was so low that you could easily walk across. He took the machete and was poking around in the sandy soil, when he saw what he thought was another rock poking up just below the surface. He dug down a little ways and discovered that the rock was really made out of bone. Cloud kept digging and soon unearthed a human skull. He washed the dirt off of the thing and stared at it, not really knowing what to make of it.

Holding the skull on his lap and staring intently at it, Cloud began to feel a strange sensation. The bony edges of the eye sockets seemed to take on a softer, blurry around the edges look. Clod blinked his eyes and looked at the skull again. The porous bone seemed to be shifting, forming some kind of skin over it. Red splotches appeared over the jagged teeth and seemed to be forming themselves into lips. Cloud felt the heat come up from the water in the creek and he felt woozy. He cupped some of the water flowing over the rocks into his hand and splashed it onto his face. He felt feverish and hot. Rubbing his eyes with a muddy hand he looked down at his lap and into his own face. The face on the skull was older, but he could definitely recognize it as his own. He bent over to have a closer look and slipped off of the rock that he was sitting on and fell into the creek. His blood had thickened and was now pounding in his ears, making a great sound like a freight train plowing through the night. Face down in the creek; he made his last attempt to gurgle a breath. The snake slithered out from behind him and went on its merry way; the danger from this much larger creature was past. Cloud's body would not be found for a number of years, still holding the skull.

Chapter 9

Through all of the incarnations or re-incarnations that Cloud had went through, he still was the drunken cigar store Indian lying on the cardboard box in the warehouse. Since that was his present life, all of his previous lives seemed to have been built on it. His soul, spirit, energy body was spinning rapidly, jerked back occasionally by the silver thread. Once again he was going through the process, but this time it seemed to be more like a dream. Maybe the dream was a little slice of heaven.

Cloud was standing in a beautiful, sculpted garden. There was a fountain directly in front of him, and the soothing sound of the splashing water seemed to sooth some of the energy that was still whirling around inside of him. Around the base of the fountain were the most incredible flowers that he had ever seen. But they were not just candy for the eyes, but the smell was sweeter than anything that he had ever experienced. There was also a strange humming sound coming from the flowers. It wasn't really a sound, but more like a vibration that seemed to match his own. For some strange reason he felt like dancing. Light on his feet, he started moving around the fountain of life. He expected at any moment to look down in then water and see a thousand shiny copper pennies looking back at him. When he looked he saw that the bottom of the pool was covered with small white pebbles. Somehow he knew that these pebbles were the cremated remains of some of the world's great masters. All of the pebbles were a brilliant white in color, but it wasn't because they were old, or bleached by the sun, but rather it was a reflection of their purity.

A sudden impulse to get one of the stones came over Cloud. He reached out his hand and plunged it into the water. The stones seemed to be only a few inches from the surface, but every time he tried to reach them, they seemed to move farther away. There seemed to be voices whispering over the humming sound of the flowers: *The dharma teachings are intrinsically pure, I am intrinsically pure…the dharma teachings are intrinsically pure, I am intrinsically pure….* The whispering voices became softer and faster, closer to his ears. Finally he could stand it no longer and moved away from the fountain. He walked around the garden for a little while until he came to a gravel road that was leading away from the garden. There was an arched gateway that he went through before he came to the edge of what looked like a forest. He stood looking at the path that led way through the woods when he heard a voice. The voice was that of a young child, maybe six or seven years old. "Come on Dad!" The voice exclaimed. "It's time to go home." Cloud turned and looked at the boy. He was small and tan and wasn't wearing a shirt. There was a big smile on his face and he looked up at Cloud in eager anticipation. Cloud felt a deep emotion tug at the center of his chest as he reached down and hugged the boy. He knew exactly what to do and took off running down the path with the boy following close behind.

The forest was a magical place and Cloud seemed to know everything about it. He pointed out strange and exotic looking plants to his young son and explained how they grew. There was every so often a strange electric creature that shifted in shape, almost like a ball of energy, before vanishing into thin air, leaving behind a crisp and a crackle. There was no sky at the top of the forest. It just seemed to end at the top of the trees. Or maybe the canopy was so thick that it blotted out any sight of the sky. The place seemed to be lit by a soft glow that illuminated everything without revealing where it was coming from. Soaking in the sights and smells, Cloud seemed to be energized and more alive than he had ever felt before. Cloud was wearing some kind of straw sandals that were fixed to his feet by a strap between his toes. Several times he looked down and tried to kick them off of his feet. They seemed to be slowing him down a little. But a few steps later they would magically reappear. It was during one of these between times when he was standing there barefoot that Cloud noticed a small puddle of water on the path. It almost seemed that someone else had been there before and left a footprint in the soft, sandy soil. Cloud placed his foot into the puddle and pressed his toes down into the mud. It was one of the most pleasurable feelings that he had ever felt. Cloud looked up and spied what appeared to be a huge fallen log directly in his path. The tree was about the size of a redwood, you could almost drive car through it. A soft rain had begun to fall as Cloud tried to get a look inside the log. A small stream of water was flowing over his feet and into the hollowed out trunk of the tree. He turned and told his son to follow him. Cloud ran full speed toward the entrance to the log and did a belly flop right when he got to the tree. It was almost like being on a waterslide at an amusement park. Cloud shot through the log like a stuntman shot out of a cannon with his son in close pursuit. His will seemed to be forming everything around him. He was making up the forest as he went along and felt incredibly enabled. The water ride through the log seemed to go on forever. Perhaps it was because for the first time in all his lives, Cloud felt truly happy and didn't want it to stop.

The two finally reached the end of the tree tunnel and both lay on the ground laughing. The boy sprang into Cloud's arms and Cloud felt that this miniature human was a new and fresher version of himself, one that didn't reek of metabolized whiskey and stale cigar smoke. The two were standing in front of a huge wooden door that seemed to spring out of nowhere. The whole forest seemed to be surrounded by a log fence that snaked off into the distance. Cloud told the boy that if he thought that the waterslide was something, then watch what he was about to do next. The only problem was that Cloud had no clue as to what he was about to do but he would make it up as he went along. He told the boy to stand where he was as Cloud went over to the oaken door cracked it open a little and peered outside. What he saw was the most spectacular sight he had ever witnessed. The night sky was a deep purple with varying hues of darker purple storm clouds whirling about like breath from a God. A few stray drops of rain caused the bare tree branches to shine and glow into the darkness. There was no source of light but that which came from within. Light wasn't needed to see, just thought and being. Cloud motioned for the boy to come over and take a look. The boy stared at the sky with his eyes open in wide wonder. Then Cloud whispered to him to keep watching and he waved his hand up at the turbulent sky. The clouds rolled away, replaced by a midnight sky that was peppered with brilliant stars that seemed to dance and twinkle across the heavens. Cloud then snapped his fingers and the light darkness gave way to the beautiful sunshine of a bright summer's afternoon. The sky was a powder blue with fluffy white wisps of clouds that assumed fanciful shapes at the mere suggestion of a thought. Cloud then thought that it was time for the grand finale. Once more he turned the sky into a dark magenta, only this time it was graced by a glowing full moon that was so bright that it almost hurt the eyes to look at it. Then with another snap of his fingers a sliver of a crescent moon appeared to be chiseled into the full one. Then, as magically as it had appeared the scene around Cloud began to fade. Soon it would disappear and this recess in Cloud's spiritual journey would be over. A great sadness gripped him as he clutched at his son one last time. He knew that he would never see him again unless he had the power to summon him from within. For a moment he regretted the entire experience, but then the old expression that it was better to have loved and lost than never love at all entered his consciousness. Cloud felt himself get a little lighter with the fading scenery and knew that he would be resting in the darkness for awhile. It was time to re-enter the primordial soup for a rest.

Chapter 11

"Life is but a dream...sha boom sha boom. Life is but a dream...sha boom sha boom...sweetheart."

Cloud's astral body landed into the corpse that was sitting at the table with a thud. There was an annoying stench that assaulted his nostrils as he realized that he was face down in some kind of puddle. The stench was a combination of sour wine, beer soaked wood and vomit. His vision had a bleary red tinge to it as he struggled to open his eyes and lift his head. There was a gnawing pain in his stomach mixed with hunger and his head felt like a ripe watermelon that was getting ready to bust. "It must have been one hell of a party he thought to himself." His vision was getting a little better as he rubbed his swollen eyes and looked out at the table that was before him. He was in some kind of huge banquet hall and the table seemed to stretch on forever, at least within the confines of the room. There was a dead vulturized carcass of some kind of bird in the center of the table and fancy gold wine goblets strewn all over the place. He looked down the row of oak table chairs that lined the table on either side of him and noticed that a couple of them were still occupied by the tenants from obviously the night before. He looked up and around the hall. It was huge but sparsely decorated. A couple of massive doors stood at one end closed by a huge log that didn't have a lot of finish on it. At any time he expected Grendel to burst through the door in a sea of blinding light and either devour him or rip his arm off. A smell of wood smoke lingered in the air and mixed with the other odors and yet there was something foreign about it. Something smelled almost like wire insulation overheating or plastic burning, but if this place was somewhere in the Middle Ages, that wouldn't be possible would it?

Cloud wondered what possible past life he was living now. He thought that he had already visited this period of time. Was there something that he had missed the first time around?

"Would there be something else that you require, sire?" The voice came from out of nowhere and startled Cloud. He turned in his chair to face a small man about five feet tall, dressed in some plain brown cloth from head to toe. He was ca slight fellow with dark liquid eyes and a haircut that was befitting of a Monk's tonsure or Moe from the Three Stooges. A sparse beard spotted itself across his chin, abruptly stopping when it got to a colony of old acne scars.

"What is this place?" Cloud asked, reaching up to scratch his own face and discovering that he was wearing a thick beard himself. "Why, it's the great dining hall. " The fellow replied, looking puzzled. Cloud stared back at him with no reply. "There was a party here last night, and it must have been quite the party by the looks of things, you were invited and I guess that you had a good time, by the looks of you." The small man said as he scurried about, righting wine goblets and wiping off dishes. Cloud told the servant that he didn't remember much about last night's activities. "It's ok." The man replied. "Maybe later I can show you around the castle a bit, but right now I have to get this mess cleaned up or the Master will really be pissed." He then wrapped what he had scraped together into a pile in the center of the huge wood table in the somewhat stained tablecloth and walked away, struggling not to drop anything.

Cloud decided not to wait for the man's return but rather try to check the place out himself. After all he must be some kind of guest here and they wouldn't try to stop an honored guest from being impressed by the grander of the Master's castle now would they? Cloud decided to check out the outside first. He needed a little fresh air. He was dizzy when he got up from the table and his stomach felt like it was still full of food from the night before. At least if he threw up outside he would spare the poor servant from having to clean up the banquet table again. As he was walking toward the huge wooden door, Cloud got a glimpse of what he was wearing. He looked like Hagar the Horrible from the comic strips. There was no two-horned helmet on his head, there very well might have been one, but it probably fell off during last night's celebration. His very large stomach was covered by a shirt made out of some kind of animal skin, turned so the fur was on the outside. The situation with his pants is that they were just the opposite, the fur was on the inside, making him sweat and want to scratch his balls. There was a belt tied around his ample waist, but no belt loops to keep the thing in place, so he was constantly adjusting it as he walked. His socks were dirty and they looked like they were made out of lamb's wool tied around his calves way to tight. He thought that they were probably cutting off the circulation in his legs. He tried to loosen them, but they were tied in some kind of foreign knot that refused to budge. His feet ended in leather sandals that again appeared to be too tight. Boy these people must have been very afraid that they would lose some of their clothing when they were running or fighting, Cloud thought to himself.

After struggling to get the door open, Cloud found himself in a very nice sculpted garden. The owner of the castle must be very wealthy indeed. There was a statue of some Greek God standing at the end of the garden. Cloud walked a little ways down the path that snaked it's way though the surroundings and turned back to look at the house, or rather castle. And that's exactly what it was. It appeared to be pretty old, it had that rounded brick, weathered look that Cloud had seen in pictures. He really didn't have much to base his impression on because he had never actually seen one in person.

Cloud was walking down the path when he heard the sound of horse's hoofs on the gravel behind him. He turned just in time to see what appeared to be a knight in shining armor sitting on a valiant steed behind him. The knight looked rather quixotic, a little rumpled and out of place in time. The knight struggled to lift his visor. When he was able to release his face, it appeared to be one of a man in his fifties, with that sun etched look of someone who had either worked in the fields of who had too much time to lazy around on his yacht. Cloud quickly decided that in the case at hand the latter was the case. The knight pulled a sword out of a scabbard that was attached to his waist. The thing looked as if it had at one time been a letter opener and didn't look very intimidating. He pointed the thing at Cloud.

"Are you a guest here or what?" "State your business and be quick about it!" The knight said. About halfway through the presentation, his visor clamped shut down over his face and muffled the last of his words. Suddenly there was a ringing sound that seemed to echo around inside the knight's armor. "Just a minute." The knight said impatiently. He took off his gauntlets and fumbled around with what appeared to be a latch in his armor near his left hip. Cloud was surprised when the man pulled a cell phone out of a pocket concealed under the tin and began talking on it. Something was not right about this whole scenario. Cloud thought to himself. The knight finished talking on the phone, the sword resting on his lap the whole time. "Never mind." The knight said. "You must be a guest, you came from the castle." "Brunch will be served in the East courtyard in about thirty minutes. See you there." The knight kicked his seemingly sluggish horse in the side and the horse took off in a gallop, almost throwing Sir Whatever off in the process.

Cloud just stood there for a few moments trying to figure out what was going on. It was as if he had everything figured out; the whole reincarnation thing, sent back in time to sort out his past lives. Now past present and future all seemed to be mixed together and confused. Or maybe that was the next lesson. There was no past and future, just the now. Most people, as they lead their lives of silent desperation, only focus on what they think is the past and the future without realizing that it's all the same. But we have to compartmentalize everything. He had no idea what compartment this was, but everything so far seemed rather pleasant, so he would play along. He looked up in the sky and determined which way was East, and headed for the courtyard.

He came to a clearing in the sculpted forest and saw the courtyard. It was a large grassy area surrounded by stone arches that were granite pink in color. In the center of the courtyard was a large fountain and along side that stood a large table that stretched the whole length. These people sure seemed to be focused on the feast. He walked over to the table and sat down, nodding to several people that seemed to recognize him along then way. The settings on the table were unusual, at first they seemed to all be carved out of some type of wood, even the utensils and the wine goblets. After picking up one of the plates, Cloud realized that they were instead made out of a hard plastic. Everything seemed to be made out of this same material, even the castle. Maybe this was some kind of retro-future where everyone decided to recreate the past using only modern materials. Serving wenches started bringing out the food, plate after plate. There was a lot of fresh fruit and vegetables and mounds of freshly baked bread. The knight that Cloud had bumped into earlier had taken off his helmet and was sitting at the head of the table. Some of the other people sitting at the table also wore armor while others were dressed in either leather (or maybe it was the plastic again, it was hard to tell) or a kind of material that looked like coarse cloth. The knight stood up and proposed a toast. The wooden goblets were filled with some kind of orange sparkling wine. Cloud drank from the glass and it was some of the sweetest liquid that he had ever consumed. It didn't taste alcoholic strong, but when it reached the back of his throat, he literally saw stars, bright flashes of light zoomed across his field of vision. He felt a little light headed and dizzy. The next course was arriving at the table. Holders made out of the same plastic material had been placed in front of each of the guests. Then a steaming plate of what looked like ostrich eggs was brought out and one of the eggs was placed in each one of the holders. Everyone bowed their heads briefly before turning to the knight at the head of the table. He reached out and brought the egg closer to his plate. Reaching out, he seemed to be caressing the shell, moving from the bottom to the top with his fingers. Then he reached out and picked up an instrument that had been sitting by the side of the plate. It looked like a fork of some kind with the tines sharpened. He took the fork and began piercing the shell of the egg. Carefully working his way all around the egg until the shell was cracked in half. He then lifted up the egg and its holder and placed it in the center of his plate. Reaching out, he grabbed the top of the shell and pulled it off. Cloud was watching this intently and felt a little wave of nausea hit him in the pit of the stomach when he saw what happened next. Inside the egg was what looked like a fully developed bird fetus that had been par boiled. Yellow streaks of egg yolk ran down the side of the cup and onto the plate. The knight picked up the cup and dumped the rest of the contents of the egg out onto the plate. The scrawny bird lay there in a viscous puddle of blood and yolk as the knight picked up the thing with his bare hands and took a very large bite out of it. Some of the liquid ran down his chin and he promptly wiped the gooey mess out of his beard stubble with the white napkin that was laying next to the plate. The rest of the guests took this as their cue and there was the loud cracking of eggshells resonating everywhere. Cloud just sat there and stared as everyone stuffed the bloody birds into their mouths, blood guts and feather.

Then everyone seemed to stop chewing at the same time, looked up from their plates and stared at Cloud. He was the only one who wasn't eating. He looked at all the people watching him, their faces in varying states of smeary. Some had looks of disappointment while others seemed right on the verge of being angry. Since they were all armed, Cloud figured that he had better give the half raw bird fetus a try. Following what the others had done, he cracked open the egg and dumped it out onto his plate. Holding the creature by what looked like the beginnings of a beak, with its legs dangling in front of him, he lowered the thing into his mouth and bit down…hard. He figured that the hard bite might distract his thoughts from what he was doing. Everything came warm and fluid into Cloud's mouth and he halfway expected to toss his cookies right there on the table, but the end result surprised him. Not bad, not bad at all. The more he chewed the better the thing tasted. Cloud found he was chewing faster, then reaching out and literally devouring the rest of the half eaten bird sitting on the plate. It wasn't just good it was incredible! It was the best thing that he had ever eaten. As he swallowed, the meat and juices seemed to infuse him with the warmest most wonderful feeling that he had ever experienced. He was hooked. He had to have another egg. He motioned for one of the serving wenches to come over to where he was sitting at the table. He asked her if he could get another egg. The smile that on her face quickly eroded to a look of fear. "Oh no!" She whispered to him. "There can only be one egg." Looking somewhat embarrassed, she quickly turned away and walked over to a tray that held a wine pitcher and began filling everyone's cup. Cloud turned to the man who was sitting next to him and asked him why you could only get one of the absolutely delicious eggs. He wondered aloud if they were that expensive. At that point he would have given everything that he had to experience another egg. The man stared at him in what appeared to be semi shock. "One egg is all that anyone ever gets, period!" You can never have another one, it would kill you and the person who gave it to you." He quickly turned away from Cloud and resumed drinking then wine. Cloud couldn't figure it out. He felt that he was going to lose his mind if he couldn't get his hands on another egg. It wasn't just that the thing tasted better than anything else; there was something more that made the egg so appealing. It was almost like tasting life for the first time. The egg not only made you feel good, but also filled a need inside you. The nearest feeling that Cloud could equate it to was the warm fuzzy that you got after having a little warm milk and then being tucked away by your Mom on a cold winter's day. After eating the egg, everything seemed right with the world, everything seemed to be in the right place. Or maybe YOU were in the right place.

One of the serving wenches then came around to all the places that were set and placed a small napkin next to everyone's plate. On the napkin was a very small light brown wafer. One by one, as everyone took the wafer up and placed it in their mouths, they quickly fell asleep. Some appeared to be out dead cold while others snored softly. The man sitting next to Cloud told him to make sure and eat the wafer when it was his turn. "You have to sleep after you eat the egg." The man said.

Cloud didn't feel all that sleepy, more of a feeling of being satisfied and content. Like he had just had a delicious meal, some fine wine, and a back rub all combined. Everyone at the table was either asleep where they had sat or had wandered off to snooze in the grass or on one of the benches in the garden. Cloud could feel the wooden bench tremble underneath him and for a brief second he thought that there was an earthquake going on or a strong wind rocking him. Then he realized that the rumbling was in his stomach, accompanied by hunger pains like he had never experienced before. He stared at the wafer that was next to his plate and didn't even think about eating it, he knew that the tiny wafer would do nothing to quench his hunger. He had to have another egg, that was all there to it, end of discussion. He got up and slowly made his way back to the castle, trying not to wake any of the other guests, but they all appeared to be dead or at least dead to the world. He found his way through the massive front hall and into the kitchen. The small butler was scurrying about, finishing up with the dishes. Cloud asked him about the egg. "Oh, you mean the Egg of Life." The little man said. "The egg carries within it the very essence of life, washed down with the milk of human kindness and the wash cloth of compassion." The man said. Cloud asked him where the eggs came from. The man replied that he didn't really know, just that the owner of the castle went to great lengths to get them and sometimes had to risk his life in the hunt. And each guest was allowed only one. Cloud asked him if there were any more of the eggs in the castle. The man shook his head and said that even if there was, he was certainly not allowed to give them out. Something came over Cloud. It was as if someone had smashed him in the face with concrete and his eyes as well as his thinking process were glazed over. The little serving man stared at him intently as he moved over towards the sink and the very large carving knife that it contained. Cloud grabbed the knife and lunged towards the smaller man, pinning him against the table. "I want another egg!" Cloud screamed into the man's face. The little man was shaking and making a sound that was somewhat akin to that of a kitten who had been caught out in the rain. "Give me the egg or I swear I'll kill you!" Cloud screamed. The little man reached for a brass ring that was attached to his belt. Several strange looking keys were fastened to it. The man pointed to the correct key and told Cloud that the eggs were in the locked cupboard next to the rather modern looking refrigerator that was in the opposite side of the kitchen. Clod relaxed his grip on the man's neck and turned towards the cupboard. As he was walking away he suddenly turned and backhanded the man across his face. A trickle of blood ran out of the corner of the little man's mouth. He gurgled a little as he spoke; "You didn't eat the wafer did you?' The man asked, his breath coming out in small gasps. "The wafer is sort of a protection against all the effects of the egg!" "You can't do one without the other." Cloud ignored what the man was saying, he was totally focused on getting the egg out of the cupboard. He was wired up and so hungry he could hardly move, but at the same time he felt better than he had ever felt in his entire life. As he fumbled the key into the lock, his hands shaking violently, he was finally able to get the damned door to open. Inside the cupboard lay one last solitary egg. It was such a sight for Cloud's eyes that the thing seemed to take on an otherworldly glow. Cloud grabbed it out of its stand and smashed it onto the corner of the table. The egg was raw, and the creature inside of the egg was still moving! Cloud didn't care, the sight and the smell of the egg was far too much for him to handle. He tore at the egg, biting the head off of the creature like some sideshow geek, and sucking down all of the yolk in one huge gasp. The shattered fragments of eggshell fell out of his hands and onto the floor. Cloud stumbled out of the kitchen and into the huge receiving hall and collapsed onto a pile of skins that had been lain by the fireplace. The great hall was spinning around in front of him, but he felt incredible; more alive than he had ever thought possible. He sank down into the skins and very quickly fell asleep. He dreamed of God. It was a bright and sunny day, the kind that sometimes comes in the early spring and gives you a glimpse of the glory days ahead. Patches of clouds peppered the baby blue sky and the air was sweet with the smell of the first grass of the season. Cloud was walking along when he saw a huge church on the top of a hill. It's spires seemed to reach all the way to heaven and the red front door was welcoming and open. Above the church was a golden throne on which God sat. Cloud was beginning to make his way into the church to pray when suddenly a giant turd fell from the heavens, smashing through the roof of the church, shattering it and causing the walls to collapse.

The next morning the guests and the owner of the castle found Cloud's body lying still and breathless on the skins. They buried him in an unmarked grave right before the feast began.

Chapter 12

Cloud woke up to find himself standing outside in the pouring rain, soaking wet, smack dab in the middle of the worst lightening storm that he had ever seen. He looked up at the bolts of energy sweeping across the purple/black sky. His hair was standing on end and he felt like the energy was trying to crawl up his spine like a snake. He was wearing a brown hooded robe that felt not only like it was several sizes too large but also weighed a ton from being soaked from the rain. His arms were stretched out in both directions and in his right hand he held a long wooden staff. He was mumbling some words that were foreign to him: "Anail nathrock uthvas bethud…." A giant blazing white finger of God complete with knuckle flicking blasted down from the heavens so close to him that it almost knocked him off of his feet. He wasn't quite sure what he was out here doing, but one thing that he knew for certain was that he had to get out of this weather or be killed. To make matters worse a circle of trees surrounded him and one of them appeared to burning with a green flame! He was in the middle of a frickin' forest in the middle of a huge lightening storm and he had no idea how he had gotten there. It was dark and he didn't seem to have any source of light with him and he certainly didn't have time to look through his rain-drenched cloak to see if it contained a candle. It was during one of the intense flashes of light that he was able to make out the dark outline of a horse standing underneath one of the trees. The horse had a strange looking saddle on his back so he must belong to somebody and Cloud was amazed that he hadn't bolted from all this bad weather. Cloud didn't even remember if he could ride a horse or not or whether it belonged to him, but given the circumstances he might as well give it a shot.

The horse was a coal black stallion and it didn't seem that he was all too happy about the entire situation himself. His eyes held a mixture of fury and fear, wide open against the night which was blacker than he was. He looked like he had been driven hard, the sweat mixed with rain running down his side, his tail erect. Cloud approached him cautiously, afraid that he would run away though he could see that the horse was tied loosely around the tree. Cloud started whistling; a shrill sound not unlike that of a bird on a sunny morning that was dwarfed by all the thunder, but the horse seemed to hear...and respond. In a flash the animal broke away from the tree and was headed right at Cloud, nostrils flaring and hoofs punching at the air. Cloud thought about running but held firm. The horse stopped mere inches from him and seemed to be awaiting his command. Cloud looked down at his own feet and was surprised that he wasn't wearing any shoes. He was equally surprised when he absently brought his hand up to his face and discovered that he had a beard. A rather long one at that. Cloud could feel the wet Earth squishing between his toes as he lifted up his leg and tried to find the stirrup. His leg felt stiff and there was pain in his knee as well as in his back. The stirrups were slippery, but he was finally able to mount the horse, even though at one point he was afraid that he was going to slip off the thing and land on the ground on the others side. As soon as Cloud's old bony butt hit the saddle the horse was off and running. It seemed like he was hell bent and determined to outrun the storm. Either that or hell bent on getting them both into hell faster than anyone thought possible. The horse made his way through the woods like ball lightening was following them. He must have an antenna sticking out of his head, but Cloud didn't see any. In a matter of about ten minutes the beast stopped in a clearing that. The ground seemed to swell in front of them and start reaching for the sky. They were at the bottom of a pretty steep hill and on the top was the castle.

Cloud could make out that there was a small, rocky path that seemed to wind its way up to where the building sat. He urged the stallion to start making the climb and the horse didn't seem to mind. He dug his hoofs into the slippery rock and flexing the huge muscles that sat atop his forelegs, began to climb. In a matter of a few minutes they reached the top. Cloud dismounted and stood looking up at the "castle." The wind and rain had eased up a little and he could make out more clearly what he was looking at. The "castle" was more like a cave that had been built up with flat shaped rocks precisely piled one on top of another, forming a dolman-like entrance. There was a large oak door with rusty iron hinges guarding the entrance. Cloud felt around in the pockets of his robe and found a very large skeleton key. He inserted it into the lock and turned the key. The rainwater that had soaked through the metal helped him turn the key, but normally it would have taken two hands. Inside the door was a tunnel that was a couple of feet higher than Cloud's head that led further into the abode. It was very dark. There were a few torches scattered about hanging from the walls, but he didn't have anything to light them with. He walked right into a small outcropping that protruded from one of the walls, banging his head. He cursed and then said out loud: "I wish that there was some light!" As soon as he finished speaking, a series of sparks ignited right above all of the torches and they burst into flame. Cloud wondered how he had done that as he walked further down the tunnel. There was another arch and then he came to what he guessed was the great room of the cave/castle. There was a huge fireplace at one end of the room that was made out of stone with a square hole at the back that led somewhere. Cloud looked at it, wishing that he had a fire to warm himself and dry off his clothes. He focused on the wood in the fireplace wishing that it would light just like the torches in the hallway. Nothing happened. After a few minutes right before he was ready to turn away and explore the rest of the place, he muttered: "Light! Damn you!" That must have been the right spell, because a few minutes later there was a nice cozy fire. Cloud took off his sodden robe and hung it on a metal hook by the fireplace. He hadn't noticed, but he guessed that the spell had lit up the rest of the room, as there was an assortment of oil lamps, torches and candles burning.

The room was large but it was sparsely furnished. There was a large wood table across the room from the fireplace that seemed to hold an assortment of scientific instruments and some parchment paper with some strange writing on it. Above the table hung a strange glass globe that was painted cobalt blue. There was a hole at the top of the glass and inside sat a black candle. Cloud said the word to light the candle and the room was filled with a strange glow. The white undergarment that he was wearing was glowing in the black light. "How strange." He thought to himself. Underneath the wood table he spied a handmade wooden box that was covered with some strange symbols. From his limited knowledge of such things, they appeared to be runes. He unlatched the box and opened it. Inside there was a green cloth, also covered with symbols, but they were different than the ones that were on the box. The cloth felt heavy when he picked it up and took it out of its container. Inside there was an assortment of Magical tools. The first thing that he noticed was a golden scythe. Curved like the shape of a gold half moon, razor-sharp and inlaid with rubies that sparkled in the quivering candlelight. He picked it up and held it out in front of him. A spark of red light seemed to appear on one of the jewels that graced the white handle. Then the glow shot out like a beam of energy that connected with the other two rubies that adorned the bottom of the blade and the finally, on up to the one that was on the point of the blade. He slowly moved the thing around in the air and instead of leaving a shadow or trail, the reflection just hung there in midair. After what seemed like a few moments it dissipated leaving a crackling residue. Cloud sat the scythe down on top of the table and reached back into the box. The next thing that he discovered was an ornate knife that looked like it was very old. The knife was so sharp that the slightest touch on the blade would have drawn blood. The hilt was also encrusted with jewels, but these were the clearest blue sapphires in contrast to the rubies on the sickle. When Cloud waved the knife in the air, you could see it cutting through like the air was water. Energy ripples were created on each side of the knife and they too lingered for a few seconds after the action was completed. The next object to come out of the box appeared at first glance to be a bull horn of some type. As Cloud held the horn in his hand he noticed that something strange was happening. There was a warm swirling sensation that began in his solar plexus and spread through his groin. He quickly put the horn down on the table as he realized that he was becoming sexually excited! It gave new meaning to the word "horny." The next thing that Cloud found while rummaging through the wood box was a large beautiful sea shell or conch. He looked at the shell and imagined the creature who once inhabited it. He felt sad for some reason and tears began to flow down his cheeks. He quickly sat the shell down on the table next to the horn. The next item he found was a medium sized crystal. The crystal was a bluish purple in color and as he held it, it seemed to vibrate, changing frequency every few seconds.

Cloud looked at the arrangement he had made of the items on the table. The knife was sitting in the East, the horn in the South, the shell in the West and the crystal was in the North. The sickle was smack dab in the middle of the other Magical tools. Cloud had no idea why he had arranged the items the way he had, but he knew that was the way they were supposed to be.

The Tools called to him from the table to use them, but Cloud turned away. Maybe later. He had some more exploring to do of this new/old life. He wandered around the room noticing that there were a couple of small rooms at the back of the great hall that looked like they were used as living quarters. There was a large piece of stone that seemed to glide open on unseen hinges that had ice growing out of the stone wall. There was a hook shaped tool hanging on the wall that was used to chip away at the ice when it was time to be used. The cubby hole had a few spare food items on the shelf: a gourd that contained some kind of milk, a brownish piece of meat wrapped in paper, and some hard, crumbly cheese. There was a wooden cupboard that had a few eating utensils in it as well as some dried fruits and vegetables. On the opposite side of the room was a table that held an assortment of cooking herbs and a few live plants that seemed to be nourished by some glowing crystals that were embedded into the wall. In the other room was a simple cot covered by a fur blanket. There was a night table sitting next to it that held a single candle.

Cloud walked back into the great room and spied a bookshelf over by the fireplace. The shelf was huge, carved into the stone and taking up most of that side. There were hand-sewn binders that appeared to be made out of some kind of skin, books that looked to be very old, their pages yellow and crumbling, and some rolls of papyrus that were by all intents and purposes even older than the books. Another table sat in front of the shelf. On it was an old globe of the world and some brass looking instruments that he wasn't quite sure of their purpose. Clod noticed that if he opened one of the books that on first glance the scribbling made absolutely no sense to him, but if he really concentrated for a few minutes on the material he started to understand it. The only problem was that the understanding seemed to give him a huge headache that dissipated when he closed the book. Maybe his brain was already too full to take on any more knowledge, but he knew that he needed it. Next to the bookcase there was a slab of stone that seemed to have been placed into the wall. Cloud touched it and tried to pull it out. It stood firm, very much belonging to the stone. He could barely get his fingers into the crack. Cloud stepped back and focused on it. After a few minutes his head started hurting again and there was a strange humming sound in his ears, but something strange began to happen. The thin stone slab began coming out of the wall! Cloud stepped back and watched as the stone moved out and then sideways by itself, revealing a small opening. Cloud grabbed one of the torches off of the wall and squeezed through the opening. He was standing at the mouth of a small tunnel that seemed to stretch far back into the mountain. About a hundred yards in, the tunnel branched off in several directions. The other passageways were dark, but there was a strange glow coming from the end of one of them. The opening was very small and Cloud had to bend over and crawl through it, holding the torch by the side of his face and almost catching his beard on fire. The walls of the tunnel were moist and warm, the rock felt fuzzy and slippery and somehow familiar. Cloud made it through the rite of passage and into the room. When he stood up he realized where all the light was coming from: the room was filled with some of the most beautiful crystals that he had ever seen!

The crystals in the walls were every hue of the rainbow, from brilliant diamond to crimson purple. There was a palpable amount of energy flowing from them and Cloud felt better than he had ever felt before in his lives. He reached out his hand to touch them and to his amazement, his hand went right inside of the rock! It took quite a force of will to withdraw his hand. When he looked at it all the wrinkles had disappeared! He felt that his grip had become so powerful that he could have crushed the rock if he had so desired. For a brief moment he thought about trying to walk into the wall and encase his whole body in the energy, but something told him not to do it. In the center of the crystal room sat a very large piece of quartz. Cloud settled his robes and sat down in front of it. As he peered into the crystal it seemed that he could see all of his past lives broken up like facets. All the emotion, pain and suffering as well as the happiness were contained with in the rock. The scenes would change as he moved his glance around the crystal. In the center was the visual story of how each of his lives had ended. It was like staring into the sun or looking upon the face of God; just too much for one mortal to bear. It almost seemed that Cloud was getting an overdose of the energy. He struggled to get to his feet, feeling confused by all of the energy. He knew that he had to leave immediately or stay in this place for the rest of eternity. It was a tempting idea. He somehow knew that being a part of the crystal as the crystal was a part of him, would give him access to all of the different dimensions and turn him into what all intents and purposes was a God. Maybe that was his destiny, but he also knew that he had things to do in this lifetime and important lessons to learn from the others.

Cloud forced himself to retreat from the crystal room, back through the tunnel and into the great room. The cave was beginning to feel rather stuffy. He needed to get outside to ground himself in the Earth. He rolled away the stone and saw the black stallion outside still tied to a tree. He must remember to feed him. Or maybe he was a magical horse that didn't need food. Cloud had felt while he was in the crystal room that all this that surrounded him, the castle, the horse, the books and crystals, everything, was really a manifestation of himself. He was the creator, the uncreated one. Cloud walked a ways down the path and back into the forest. The place seemed to be filled with strange and magical creatures that he had never seen before. Snakes writhed around trees and howls and screeches assaulted his ears. An arm-like branch hung low out of an old oak tree. Cloud grabbed hold of it and hoisted himself up onto the branch. There was a bright full moon overhead that lit up the forest in black light: To sleep perchance to dream. The Goddess never sleeps, but when she blinks she dreams. Cloud lay on the branch for six moons and a change of season before the wolves awoke him with their mad poetry.

When Cloud did awake, he found that it was in the middle of the summer, the birds were singing and he heard the fish jumping in a small stream that was flowing nearby. Cloud was a little moldy from lying in one place (on the tree) for so long. He noticed that there was a little loose bark clinging to the exposed parts of his skin that he had to peel off. His beard had grown longer and coarser during his sleep. He felt refreshed and as full of life as the Nature that surrounded him. He was however, just a little stiff from the lack of movement, and getting off of the tree branch and walking around took a considerable effort. He found his walking staff that was sitting next to the tree. It was long and crooked, carved out of birch, with an eagle's head at the top. Since it looked like a cross between a snake and an eagle, he affectionately named it Sneagle. He called to Sneagle and the stick immediately came to him. He rubbed its head like an old friend and started walking towards the sound of the brook. When he cleared the forest and came upon the stream, he noticed that an interesting thing was happening. In an area where the stream widened a bit and made somewhat of a turn, grew a hazelnut tree. Every so often, as Cloud watched, the tree would ceremoniously drop a nut. As soon as the nut hit the water, a salmon would bob his head above the water and snatch it up. Cloud removed his robe and jumped into the water, trying to grab the fish with his hands. The fish was on to him and turned directions at the last moment and swam away. It seemed to Cloud that when you thought that you were powerful and smart, you could always find someone smarter than you were.

Finally, it was the blind ambition and determination to get a hazelnut that was the fish's undoing. One of the hazelnuts dropped into the water and the fish headed straight for it, oblivious to the fact that Cloud was waiting for him. The fish swallowed the nut just as Cloud grabbed him behind the gills. The salmon was really too exhausted to put up much of a fight. He thought about finning Cloud, but then decided against it. Cloud looked the fish in the eyes and asked him if it was all right if he ate him. The fish replied that he was at the end of his life and since Cloud seemed like a fine wizard, he would rather be eaten by him than die and rot in the water. Cloud promised him a swift end and cut off his head and cleaned him without further ado. Cloud looked around for some dry wood and started a fire. He cooked the fish to a tender state and broke off a tiny piece and put it into his mouth. The fish tasted sweet and delicate and as soon as Cloud swallowed him his perceptions of the world began to change. After all this was the salmon of knowledge who had just swallowed one of the nuts of wisdom. Cloud could then see the true nature of all things that were in Nature. He could see how the tree was connected to the other plants around it and to the birds that perched on top of it. He could see how the clouds in the sky played a part in keeping the stream flowing. How the wind rustling through the trees helped the seeds, and so on and so on. Most importantly however, he could see how he fit in with all of the rest. He could see the web and marvel at the spider that created it; the delicacy in which it brought its legs together and fixed a tear in the web. There would be some to come along and fear the spider, spray him dead and then wonder why the web was unraveling. Unfortunately by eating the web the usurper would gain a temporary sense of power sitting in his marble house, smoking a cigar and dreaming of the crude. Then he would put on long flowing robes of white while the Earth starved and turned black and dream of his Father banishing all the Evil in the world. Pulling the dictator out of the spider hole by his long beard.

Cloud closed his eyes and blinked several times, breaking the spell. Seeing the web of life and the connectedness of all things meant that you saw the future as well. Cloud suddenly knew everything about everything and that meant what was back at the castle as well.

As Cloud walked back to his humble abode it seemed that the whole world was talking to him. He was quite delirious and quite mad with delight. The trees spoke as well as the butterfly perched on the flower who by the way was abuzz with gossip about the bees. "The birds were singing so happily, playfully, joyfully watching me…" Cloud finally had to concentrate on closing his ear flaps, the pointy ones, to try to shut out some of the noise. Then he heard a strange clicking sound and something that resembled a low moan. It seemed to be coming from just over his right shoulder, but it also seemed to be coming from everywhere all at once. He perceived footsteps behind him, but when he turned there was no one there. Then he noticed something looking out at him from the shadows underneath a fallen and rotted log. As he looked into the log, he could tell that a little of the noise was coming from there. He noticed that it was getting on towards evening and that the sun was starting to set. The rumble and moan of the night was getting louder as he watched the shadows lengthen and slowly advance. He felt a little less good than he had before, a little nervous and apprehensive.

Then he realized what had been going on. Eating the salmon of knowledge had given him the ability to see, feel and communicate with all living things, but he could now also see that death was everywhere also. Interwoven into the very fabric of life itself. But life, being alive and not yet experiencing death was blissfully unaware of its existence! Some of the more advanced forms of life knew about the existence of death, but only thought that it applied to what was being eaten, and it couldn't happen to them. Cloud felt like he was being thrown out of the Garden of Eden like the very first Adam. Why did he have to pay this price? Why did he have to have knowledge of all things and the termination of their existence? It was almost too much to bear. He looked around and saw the shadow starting to cover everything. Birth, aging, pain, death birth, aging, pain, death; On and on in an endless cycle that was bound to come to an end. There was a small bird sitting on a branch in a tree just over his head and he watched as the shadow finished covering the bird and the bird was no longer there, just a bunch of dusty feathers sitting on the ground. But then he saw where the bird had come from and there was a bright glowing orb that had taken its place. Out of the orb sprang a new bird. It glowed with the freshness of new life, but the shadow was around it too and starting to move ever closer and closer. So this was the nature of things, something that he had known all along but had never realized.

Cloud walked back to the castle, closing the huge door behind him to ward off the advancing night. He willed the fire to start, the flames to leap higher and higher, but he still felt very cold.

The very next morning Cloud was hard at work in what you could probably call his laboratory. Even though he had knowledge of all things, there was something that he didn't have, something that he had been working on for a very long time and hadn't made very much progress. And that was the secret to immortality. Well, from his own personal experiences he knew that the soul was immortal in a way: the whole procreation thing and re-incarnation. He wanted to be able to extend life indefinitely. Of course he knew that was statistically impossible. Even if you could live forever, and forever would end when the Earth and the stars ended, eventually an accident would catch up with your immortal body, or someone would kill you. But finding the alchemy solution to physical aging, or the fountain of youth, so to speak, would at least give you a fair head start, and heck, with a little luck and precaution, who knows what might happen. He knew that slowing down the metabolism was the key. Get rid of those nasty free radicals that burned out the cell altogether. He was intrigued by the stories he had heard about the Breatharians that lived in the East. Mystic yogis that stayed in caves and in addition to a glass of juice every once in awhile, they were able to gain sustenance from breathing the air alone. Yeah they looked a little anorexic, but it was told that they lived for an incredibly long period of time. Cloud had another idea: attack the problem from a different perspective. Find an elixir that got rid of your perception of time. Then living one more moment would seem like an eternity. The only problem with this theory was you would have to find a way to step out of that perception and move about, or else what would be the point? These thought exercises usually would get him trapped in his own mental maze and could keep him at his desk staring at a candle flame for hours, so he had to be careful.

Cloud walked over to a marble pedestal that sat by the bookcases. Perched on top of the pedestal was a rather large black bird, a stuffed crow to be exact. A small bronze plaque on the front of the column read "Samwell Greedyguts. Cloud looked at the bird and said its name. Suddenly the bird sprang to life in a cloud of dusty feathers. "Akkkk!" The bird tilted his head and looked at Cloud out of an eye that appeared to be made of glass. "It's about time! What took you so long!?" The bird exclaimed. Cloud folded his arms in front of him and looked at the bird with a puzzled expression on his face. The bird took a few cautionary flaps with his jet black wings, moved his beak up and down a few times, and said: "I'll be right back!" With that he promptly flew out of the room. A few minutes later he returned.

"Whew!" He said. "What a relief. Do you know how hard it is for a bird to hold it in for that long a time?" "What's it been, a couple of hundred years?"

"OK, what's for dinner?" The bird swallowed chard as he spoke, trying to clear the marble dust from his throat. "Oh never mind, I'll get it myself." He then flew off towards the kitchen.

Suddenly the whole castle shook. Loose rocks fell from the ceiling, candle fell off of the tables and a huge ball of flame circled in black sooty smoke poured down the outside tunnel and into the room. Cloud covered his face with the sleeve of his robe and crouched down near the floor. Samwell came flying back into the room, a strip of what looked like rotted rat hanging from his beak. The bird tilted his head back and quickly swallowed the meat, landing on his marble perch in the process. Then he spoke in a high croaky voice: "He's back and he sounds pissed!" Cloud said: "Who's back?" "You'll see soon enough." The bird replied.

Cloud decided to see for himself when the dust had finally settled. Grabbing his staff, he cautiously went through the tunnel to the outside. There he was so taken aback by what he saw that he dropped the staff and almost fell over. As soon as he saw the creature that was standing before him he knew what and who it was. The memories came rushing back into his brain like a flood on the Tigris River.

"Draconius!" Cloud whispered under his breath. Standing before him was the largest and nastiest looking dragon that Cloud had ever seen. It was the only one that he HAD ever seen so he really didn't really have anything to compare it to. But he knew that as dragons go, this one was no baby. The thing was probably several hundred feet tall and just about as long. His serpent-like body was covered in green to brownish scales with a few either fallen or knocked off here and there. His eyes were large, ominous and cat-like. One of them was closed with a deep scar running from side to side of it. The thing's mouth was partially open, revealing pointy dagger teeth, a few of them cracked and broken. Smoke that smelled like a rotting corpse at a barbecue trailed out of the corners of his mouth and was immediately sucked back up into his flared nostrils.

The dragon spoke in a voice that was so loud and so deep that it almost shattered Cloud's eardrums. "So! I finally get to meet my creator!" The dragon bellowed. GOODBYE! With that the dragon took a very deep breath and exhaled a ball of flame in Cloud's direction. There was nothing that he could do. There was immense pain at first as the heat stripped away his flesh. The last thing that he remembered was the image of a Buddhist monk dousing himself with gasoline and striking a match. Somehow each of their lives and deaths had somehow become intertwined for a brief second out of time and eternity. The monk was still sitting in a meditation pose, perfectly balanced, after all the flesh and organs had been burnt away. Cloud, on the other hand, was back between lives, given pause to reflect on whether anything that had just happened to him was at all real. Of course the thing to remember is that there is really no "real" to begin with. This is that and that is this. There is just the universe and where we think we are in it.

Chapter 13

Cloud woke up in bed with the smell of sex about him. He looked over at the woman who was lying next to him, sleeping. She was young and brown with nice curves, spiky hair and full lips. Cloud was naked and uncovered while the woman had the satin sheets folded around her like she was a present that was starting to come unwrapped. He noticed that he was cold and his mouth was dry. As he folded his arms around himself, rubbing up and down with his hands in an attempt to get the circulation going, he noticed that there were bumps up and down near his elbows. He could see the "tracks" there from the needles used to inject the heroin. He wondered if some of the chills that he was feeling were from withdrawal. He put both elbows up closer to his face to get a closer inspection. None of the bumps appeared to be fresh. Maybe he had used the drugs in the past and had given them up. He could think about that later, right now he needed to get a drink of water and go to the bathroom. There was a brown silk robe that had been thrown on the floor next to the bed the previous evening and he reached over and picked it up and wrapped it around himself. Stumbling over some shoes on the floor, he made his way out of the room and found the bathroom. There was no cup to drink from so he turned on the tap and sucked some water out of it. After a few seconds the water turned hot and almost burned his mouth. "Damn!" He said to himself. Turning off the faucet he slid over to the toilet and opened his robe to relieve himself. He was a little shocked and pleased at what he saw.

Cloud walked back to the bedroom and lay back down beside the woman. She was just starting to sir out of her sleep and she reached over and put her arms around him. Snuggling up close to his face, she whispered "baby" into his ear. Cloud thought about going back to sleep for a moment and then decided, what the hell, he might as well check out the new rather "ample" equipment.

The past, present and future are one. The past hides in dreams, and then we wake up and dream about the future. We can never be happy realizing our dreams, for like life the secret is in the process. We think that we are a single entity, a solid, a whole that is apart and surrounded by a concept that we call "reality." In truth the thing that we don't even realize is that everything, we, the world around us, the universe, are all processes. Nothing exists, just the process, the method, the going on and the madness. The universe creates itself from the uncreated and then starts to decay. Negative entropy, chaos, baby. The only defense that we have lies between our legs. Shoot the world and create some more hopeless and sordid tissue that you will have to guard, protect and nourish until it starts to rot and the smell becomes more than even you, who is in the midst of professing love, can bear. Then you hope that you have inspired enough fear and joy into the process that it will turn around and return the favor. Wrap those fleshy arms around you in your moment of pain and death that your last gasp will be short and sweet. At least the creation process feels good, sometimes, though you might regret what comes after. There's got to be a morning after closer to the sky because sooner or later we perceive the passage of time. The end is always there and sooner or later all of our history is just a black speck of carbon, flicked away into space by a giant dirty fingernail.

Cloud got up out of bed and put his robe back on, pushing his still erect manhood down between his legs. She was back asleep and by the way she had grasped at him through the fog, he wondered what she/they had taken the night before. As he walked into the dimly lit kitchen and looked around for the coffee pot, he noticed that wherever he was living was not exactly the Park Avenue. He felt something warm and wet squish between his bare toes and looked down to see that he had ended the brief life of a giant cockroach. Arching up the front of his foot he limped back into the bathroom and wiped off the mess with a piece of toilet paper. He then turned on the hot water faucet and lifted up his foot to wash off the residue. Making a stop back in the bedroom to find his slippers under the bed, he shuffled back to the kitchen and looked in the cabinets for the coffee. All he found was a jar of instant. He must have been a busy man. He poured some rusty water into an old beat up saucepan and placed it on the stove. He turned on the gas to the burner and went to sit down at the table. After a couple of moments he noticed that there was a strange smell in the room. Realizing that it was the smell of gas he quickly went over and turned off the burner. There was a box of wooden kitchen matches on top of the stove and he used one of them to light the thing. As soon as his finger was a couple of inches from the burner the gas exploded into a miniature ball of flame that singed his fingers. With a curse he went to the sink and ran a little cold water over them. His hands were pretty callused and the thick skin protected him from having any blisters. He went back to the table. It was a large wood table, probably made out of oak. It looked like it had been painted over at one time with white paint. It was old and creaky. Useless old. Useless old was something that had outlived its usefulness but was too young to be considered an antique. The table was littered with an incredible amount of items, cans of food, both opened and closed. The open ones looked like they had been there for some time. A few had roaches crawling out of them and forks welded to the bottom of the cans by a dried sticky residue of food. The table was also littered with what looked like bills and old newspapers. In the middle of all the mess Cloud spied something that was shiny. It was a mirror. There were several lines etched down the center of the mirror and they were filled with a white powder. Out of instinct Cloud picked up the mirror and held it up close to his face. He rolled up one of the letters stating that he was way overdue on his credit card payments and placed the end at the start of the powder line. He put the end of the makeshift straw into the left nostril of his nose. Placing his finger over the right one he inhaled deeply. It was like someone had shot an amber current of electricity through his brain. His body shook a little as he closed his eyes and wiped his nose.

Cloud finished the other two lines on the mirror and stumbled back into the bedroom to find Kiesha just starting to come out of her revelry. She noticed the white powder still clinging to his moustache. "Aw, baby. I hope you didn't use up the last of it! You uptight motherfucker!" She said, her speech a little slurred from the narcotics induced sleep. Cloud said nothing in reply, but instead hurled himself on top of her with a fury. She struggled to get out from under him, claiming that she had to go to the bathroom. Cloud grabbed both sides of her head and forced his lips down onto hers, turning her loud protests into a muffle. Her skin was hot and sticky, sweet and salty all at the same time. She was like bittersweet chocolate melting beneath him. He licked up the sweat, tasted her and bit her with his teeth. He entered her with an erection that no Viagra pill could induce, throwing her legs up into the air and riding her so hard that the bedsprings almost broke in protest. After he was finally finished Cloud rolled over in bed, exhausted but still snapping with nervous energy like he was a broken power line. Kiesha slapped him hard on the side of his face, calling him a bastard and then getting up and put on her robe. Cloud heard the flush of the toilet and then heard her rummaging around in the kitchen looking for the coke. "Fuck!" he heard her yell a couple of times. This made him smile. After all these bitches were all about getting over on a brother and he wasn't about to let that happen. A few moments later he heard the sound of glass breaking and knew that he would be down at the dollar store buying a new mirror. She came back into the bedroom a few minutes later in a somewhat better mood, her mouth smelling of cheap wine and the musty after smell of a cigarette. Cloud was starting to come down a little, softening up a little as he went. He motioned for Kiesha to hand him the bottle of Gallo and he took a deep swig. That seemed to calm him down even more and steady his shaking hands.

Cloud got up out of bed despite Kiesha's protests and questions about whether or not there was enough money to get any more powder. Cloud told her that he wasn't in the business of supporting her habits and that she should try to go out and work of sell her stuff on the street it didn't matter to him. He pulled on his silks and a Nike hooded sweat, took one of her cigarettes from the pack on the nightstand and walked out. He had a little business to take care of this morning. It probably wouldn't net him anymore than about two hundred dollars, but what the hell, that was better than the zero he had in his pocket at the present time. Things had been rough in the dealing business lately as the bust that had come down that netted his partner left him scrambling to find another supplier. Now was the time to pause and regroup and settle a little on some old business that he had let slide in more prosperous times.

A few moments later Cloud pulled up in front of the old buff brick apartment building with the rusty fire escape stairs in the back that hadn't been used for years. Even though he didn't drive he knew that Armand would be home. Armand worked as a waiter at the local steakhouse and pretty much stayed in his apartment the rest of the time. He was tall and thin and looked a little bit like Michael Jackson before the surgery. He was about as gay as a well used cucumber, speaking with a lisp and waving his hands around in the air when he spoke. Armand was in his late forties and had grown up in the French Quarter in New Orleans. He had went to New York seeking his fame and fortune on the Great White Way, and although he had landed a few bit parts by selectively sleeping with one of the producers, the tastes changed and he was booted out. His boyfriend, Lance was about twenty years old, blond and beach boy like, with a drug habit and a case of HIV he had picked up from a shared needle. Armand tested negative after he found out and hated to have to use a condom all the time, but he was madly in love with the younger man and would make any and all sacrifices that were required.

A couple of months prior Armand's young blond lover had gotten in trouble. He broke into the house of a couple of senior citizens down the street and got caught when he tripped and fell face first on the way out, landing on the concrete steps, his pockets loaded with fake jewelry and silver. He was now facing a few months of shock time down at the local prison where the "exit only" that he had needled into his ass would have no meaning. He had bought drugs from Cloud a few weeks prior and failed to make good on the transaction. Armand was struggling to make ends meet, he had just invested all of his money not only supporting his boyfriend's drug habit, but also in getting some more gold in his mouth to impress him. He called it his "gold blow" when he would take his young lover into his mouth and let his prick slide along on the smooth metal, and his boyfriend liked it almost as much as the metal studs in his tongue. There was an eviction notice posted on his door from the sheriff and a cut off notice from the electric company in his mailbox. He made about sixty dollars a day at the steakhouse and he was too old to suck dick for a living and his anal cavity had become big enough to drive a tractor through, so it wasn't of much use. Armand was aware of the money that his boyfriend owed Cloud and had tried to pay him off a little at a time, giving him twenty dollars one time and fifty dollars another.

Armand had just curled up on the couch, fixing himself a hot cup of tea and turning on the television set. Cloud got out of his car and lobbed a brick through Armand's front window to get his attention. Cloud stood and watched as the man inside screamed and turned out the lights. Cloud was concerned that he might call the police but he had visited him the prior week and politely threatened him and at the time he didn't notice that Armand had a phone. Cloud hurriedly went inside of the apartment building and stood a few feet to the side of the door so Armand couldn't see him if he peeked out. Sure enough, after a couple of minutes the door opened up a little, held only in place by the thin "security" chain. Cloud moved in front of the door, smiled at the man inside and put his twelve-inch boot to the task. The chain broke away easily, sending the man standing behind it sailing to the floor. Cloud picked Armand up by the collar and threw him onto the couch. He smacked Armand loudly across the cheek. Then, unexpectedly, Armand threw himself forward, wrapping his arms around Cloud's ass and burying his head into his crotch, sobbing. Cloud grabbed hold of Armand's ears and pulled his face away a few inches, and then he unzipped his pants.

After he finished, Cloud took what little money that Armand had in his wallet, about fifty bucks, and then left, telling him that he had one week to come up with the rest of the money that his boyfriend owed him.

Cloud had been on the 'Down Low' for about a year now. He wasn't sure why he, like a lot of other brothers, had embraced a gay lifestyle. He wasn't really attracted to men, as a matter of fact; at times their bodies disgusted him. But laying a brother down and having his way with him was an ego boost and a power trip that he had become accustomed to when he had spent some time in prison. In there it was either do or be done. And he had preferred to be on the giving end instead of the receiving and had gained a reputation as being quite the cocksman.

Cloud got back into his car with an itch in his groin. He hadn't the chance to wash himself off after Armand had serviced him and who knew what his spit contained, how bad his teeth were and when the last time was that he brushed them. All this human contact in one morning, first with Kiesha and then Armand had left him with a powerful thirst to get high in one way or another. He didn't have much money, but it was enough to get him a bottle and a couple of lines, or maybe a rock to smoke. Rock was a whole lot cheaper, but it was like Chinese food, you wanted more shortly after you consumed it. The neighborhood was middle class, older homes that were ranch in style with some newer construction on the periphery. Most of the residents were retired factory workers who displayed American Flags somewhere on their property and would never guess that the new neighbors were evil drug pushers. Cloud had found that in recent years the image of a pusher had changed from that of a rapping inner city dude with a lot of gold and a BMW to that of a more middle class genre. It was an easy way for the ex-businessman to make a little extra money in these tough economic times. The man that he was going to see was small potatoes, selling maybe a couple of thousand dollars worth a week. The guy's name was Ralph, believe it or not, and he lived in the two story white house with his two daughters. He had lost his job during a downsizing a couple of years ago and as luck would have it, his wife was killed and he was injured in a car crash shortly there after. Things got tough and he went on a drinking spree and started intensifying the coke habit that he had started when the corporate onus was running high and the money was flowing like the wine at the corporate parties. When he was laid off a friend of a friend recommended that if he started "selling" he could get free drugs a little or a lot of spending money. Ralph had never been a lawbreaker, but by his view he really didn't have a choice in the matter if he wanted to continue owning the house and feeding his daughters.

Ralph's daughters were six and nine years old respectively. The younger had reddish hair and pigtails and freckles and her father had teased her about looking like Wendy the hamburger girl. The older daughter was nine and was kind of at that awkward age, all legs and arms, skinny, but with the potential to blossom. As a matter of fact, Blossom was her nickname. She had long brown hair that unlike her sister, she refused to sit and have braided. She was a tomboy that liked to run around and roll on the grass and get dirty playing ball, but also liked to sing and dance at school. She was a big fan of the Wizard of Oz and could keep up with Judy Garland through all of the yellow brick road songs without missing a note.

Cloud pulled up in front of the house and walked to the door unannounced. Usually he would call before showing up to make a deal, but this was a Saturday morning and he was in a hurry, and anyway he was sure that Ralph had nothing better to do and would be glad to see him. Ralph basically had been a mess since the accident. He wore the emotional scars on his face as well as the physical ones on his body. He was a small man, only about five foot eight and a hundred and fifty ponds. He wore his greasy hair in a comb over and his ears stuck out too far on the sides. His eyes were set fairly close together and his nose had grown a little too large and bumpy. The most distinguishing feature about him though was his chin. It was weak to begin with and sort of contrasted with his large neck and Adam's apple. His lips were small and his teeth were crooked and this sort of put the bottom part of his face out of alignment. Add to that the fact that his chin had been broken in the accident as well as his leg and it looked like the bottom of his face was a ball of crushed aluminum foil. His leg had been fractured and was held together with pins and caused him a great deal of pain and had also caused him to be addicted to painkillers. When he walked he drew his face into a painful scowl that was like pulling the top closed on a duffel bag. He sort of rolled along, one side of him a lot longer than the other.

Through it all though he had taken care of his two daughters and tried desperately to keep them from harm, playing both roles of a Mother and Father with the help of a friendly neighbor or two. They would watch them when his whole life situation became unbearable and he would drink, snort and pill himself into oblivion.

Cloud stood at Ralph's door and pressed the doorbell. After waiting several minutes he knocked on the door. No one came to the door. Getting a little upset, Cloud knocked harder, almost breaking the small glass window in the door. After waiting a few more minutes he walked around to the back yard. Looking over the fence he noticed that the kid's play set and some of the toys were still outside. As Cloud turned to go back to his car he was confronted by one of the neighbors who asked him if he was with the Police. Cloud answered no, that he was just a friend who was looking for him. The neighbor was an older man with thick glasses and a paunch. He was the type who would sit out on the porch in his underwear on a hot summer day, sipping a beer and watch the person next-door struggle to get his lawn mower up the hill. The man told Cloud that the Police had been here earlier and had arrested Ralph. They had asked him to watch his two daughters, who were inside of his house at this very moment watching TV. He wasn't sure when Ralph would get home, but it looked like the arrest was a pretty big deal. The back door of Ralph's house had been busted out and it looked like the S.W.A.T. team had been called. The man couldn't understand why all of this had happened to Ralph, he seemed like a really nice man who cared deeply about his daughters.

As Cloud was talking to the neighbor, one of the daughters, Blossom came out onto the porch and asked if she could get a drink of water for her and her sister out of the refrigerator. She looked at Cloud with a faint hint of recognition and a little fear. Then she smiled and brushed her long brown hair back from her forehead. Cloud couldn't help but feel a little tug at his groin area. The girl gave off a fresh scent and in some countries she would be considered almost ready for marriage. Cloud quickly dismissed the thought, he had enough problems to deal with besides adding a statuary rape charge to the mess. For a moment he wondered if the drugs had begun to affect his judgment. He had sex with both men and women and now he was thinking about children. What would come next dogs and horses?

Down at the police station, two detectives were questioning Ralph. One's name was Sam and the other, who looked a little like Robert Culp from the old I Spy television series. His hair was perfectly combed and he wore tan shorts and a white sleeve white polo shirt underneath his blue jacket that had POLICE emblazoned across the back. In a word he looked just like a movie Dick and he was studying for his PhD, which everyone who knew or worked with him, stood for Pretty Huge Dick. Of course this was really a misconception as he was in reality another part of the anatomy: an asshole.

They were playing the old Good Cop Bad Cop game with Ralph, which surprisingly still worked after all these years. There was something about being "under the lights" so to speak, that would make even the hardest criminal seek out a kindred spirit, or at least someone who was seemingly willing to lend a sympathetic ear. And Ralph was no hardened criminal, just a poor smuck who was down on his luck and trying to provide for his daughters.

The Bad Cop told Ralph about all the dire consequences that he was facing: huge fines and hard prison time, where the animals that inhabited the place would tear up the asshole of a cripple like himself like they were using a wrecking ball. The Good Cop told Ralph that on the other hand there was an easy way out of this mess. All he had to do was co-operate and tell them the name of the guy that he got his dope from. They were, after all after the big fish and not some little Guppy like himself. When the droplets of sweat stopped flowing down Ralph's forehead, he agreed. He told them that the man who supplied him was a Mexican by the name of Alverez who lived on the West Side of town. It was rumored that he was a pretty big fish who had several hundred smaller dealers working for him. He was directly supplied by one of the cartels down in South America. Ralph was a little scared of the Mexican, but the Police promised that there was no way that he could find out who ratted on him. As Ralph was being led out of the interrogation room, the Good Cop guy stopped him by the door; "Oh by the way." He said. "There is one more small thing….we need you to make a phone call to the Mexican."

"You're such a lovely audience, we'd like to take you home with us, we'd like to take you home…"

There was quite a gathering of government personnel around Ralph as he made the call to the Mexican. They had to let him us his cell phone because the Mexican had the luxury of caller ID and wouldn't accept any calls from an unidentified number. But first they had to charge up the phone's battery and since the charger was at Ralph's house, one of the detectives had to make the trip there and then break into his car. While he was getting the car's door open he filled out a report noting the license plate number and the registration number just in case they wanted to seize the thing later because it was involved in a drug bust. Since it was a Ford and not a Mercedes, they'd probably let him keep it unless one of the officers wanted it for one of their teenage sons or daughters. One thing that they neglected to tell Ralph was that they would more than likely take his house away from him. It would be sold at government auction and since the bank had a lien on it, he would be responsible for paying the thing off anyway. Add that on to the fines, court costs and the cost of retaining a lawyer, and the cop's offer of freedom for Ralph started to look a little green around the edges. Looks like he was going to be interred into the lovely world of a financial prison, probably for the rest of his life.

Ralph was a little bit nervous when he pressed the speed dial on his fully charged cell phone to contact the Mexican. What he got was the answering service, the thick Spanish accent asking him to please leave a "messjaazz" and they would return his call as soon as possible. This involved the whole entourage in Ralph's cell waiting for almost another hour before the cell rang. At least they were kind enough to furnish him some coffee and a Danish. Ralph breathed deeply and talked slowly into the phone. He told the Mexican that business had been better than he had expected and he needed to buy some more coke. Normally this would have set off an alarm in the Mexican's head, because Ralph was usually a small producer and the job he had selling was actually a favor, a kindness of the heart given the two girls and his family situation. It didn't raise an alarm however because the Mexican was being given a blowjob by two horny little sisters that both bore a striking resemblance to Jennifer Lopez. He asked Ralph how much "blow" that he needed and reminded him that he had used up all of his credit and the transaction would have to be in cash. All the cops gathered around nodded their heads in unison as Ralph agreed to the price. As he hung up the phone after making a time to go over to the Mexican's house and pick up the dope, one of the narcotic detectives walked over to him and massaged his shoulders for a brief instant. They all thanked him and then told him that although they enjoyed his company, they now had some urgent business to attend to: busting the bad guy.

A few hours later the whole squad, which included several members of the S.W.A.T. team, were ready to take down the house. They ran down the middle of the street, crawled around the foundation of the house and through the bushes. They even went over the river and through the woods. On the PhD's signal they went at the reinforced front door like Storm Troopers at the castle gate. POLICE! POLICE! Everyone shouted in unison, their nervousness and strain showing in their collective voices. They thundered through the house, expecting and sometimes hoping for the worst, just so they could shoot somebody and kick some ass for the ten o'clock news. To their great disappointment however, all they succeeded in doing was to shake the Mexican out of the J LO sandwich and cause him to shit in his underwear. The girls were questioned and released and the Mexican was hog tied and thrown into the back of a Police cruiser. But not before he wiped his butt and put on a fresh set of silk boxers emblazoned with the name of a major league sports team. A few hours later he had posted bond and was talking to a lawyer dressed in a $1500 suit.

It wasn't hard to figure out that poor Ralph was the one who had turned over and made the Mexican's life a little more interesting. The Mexican looked at the attorney and did his best Al Pacino "Scarface" voice: "Get me a couple of niggers in here now!"

Cloud had just screwed the cap off of the second bottle of Gallo Rose' Wine when he heard the glass in the front door break with a crash and a tinkle. His first thought was that it might be the police. Instead he was grabbed by two of the biggest thugs that he had ever laid eyes on, and he had seen a few. They very quickly escorted him out to the waiting car after checking the house to make sure that there wasn't anybody else home.

Cloud knew that the Mexican had sent them when he recognized the smell of the hair oil that was glistening on the curly locks of the biggest one. The oil was a certain brand of Afro Sheen that hadn't been on the market since the Jerry curls of the seventies. It carried the toxic smell of something like the combination of coconut and Pennzoil, or maybe it was Quaker State. Curls was driving the almost new Lincoln Navigator while his partner Smalls, who was anything but small, weighing in at about four hundred pounds and standing about five foot six. Curls and Smalls had been a team for about five years now, mostly doing strong arm and delivery services for the Mexican. Cloud asked the two what this was all about since he knew that he didn't owe the Mexican any money and hadn't for several years now, not since Curls and Smalls had taken great pleasure in breaking his left leg. At least they had given him a choice of which one that he had wanted broken. They told him that he would find out when the Mexican told him, but they believed that he was going to be offered a "money making opportunity that he wouldn't refuse." Cloud hated how the Mexican and his thugs often used corrupted verses from movies like "The Godfather or their most favorite; "Scarface." They pulled up in front of the Mexican's house. The house was in a bad neighborhood and looked pretty rough on the outside, but had been completely renovated on the inside. A few blocks away there had been a multi-story high rise that the government had built in the sixties and then realized that no one wanted to live there even if they got food stamps and promptly tore it down in the early nineties. The house that the Mexican lived in was pretty much the only one that was left standing on the block. It was a pre-Civil War era mansion that was built up on a hill overlooking what once was a cobblestone street. The street had been paved over so many times that the layers of asphalt had peeled away in large chunks that were perfectly suited for slamming someone in the head with. They were also adjustable in size. All you had to do was throw a chunk that was too large down on any hard surface and it would promptly break in half. The cobblestones however, endured through the ages, made sturdily out of a granite based brick it was almost as if they objected to being covered by puny asphalt and would spit the stuff that they were coated with out every twenty years or so. The house itself had the remnants of a large front porch that at one time had wrapped all the way around the building. The back part of the porch had rotted away and the back yard had been covered with concrete and had become the playground for the hounds from hell. Three nasty Pitbulls lived there that were so mean that even the Mexican refused to invade their turf, unless he intended on shooting one of them, as had happened frequently in the past. The dogs were fed through an opening in the fence and had their vocal cords removed so they would be silent as well as deadly. They were also given a daily ration of red pepper mixed in with their food, the constant pain in their stomachs making them even meaner. In days gone by the family that occupied the house (small time hoodlums from the Middle East) used to sit out there in wicker chairs to escape the sweltering heat. They consumed a lot of alcohol, but they never dealt in any drugs, prostitution and numbers running being their expertise. They had also ran an illegal trucking business where they would bribe the drivers to report the truck as stolen. They would then sell the contents of the truck on the black market and collect on the insurance as well. The FBI had finally put several of the key family members in prison for racketeering and other crimes against humanity.

Now the house was covered with iron. Iron on the windows and iron bars on the doors. The Mexican had also installed video cameras all over the place and would sit and watch them for hours, being high on coke just like Tony Montana. What was left of the housing projects still loomed to the East where the Blacks conducted business. They had reached an uneasy truce with the Mexican. There was a kind of a force field that extended out from the Mexican's house for about a three-block area in all directions. Everyone knew not to cross the boundaries. Another thing was for certain: you never walked the streets, you ran from place to place just as fast as you could. There were still a few small time Lone Rangers that would hit you over the head with a brick and take all of your money to buy drugs, no matter who you were.

The iron door opened with a creak that was badly in need of some WD-40 and he was led down the dark hallway where to the kitchen where the Mexican conducted business. The Mexican was sitting at the table, his eyes bloodshot and a few more wrinkles on his face to match the lines on the mirror that was in front of him. He told Cloud to sit down. He asked him if he knew Ralph. Cloud nodded his head yes. The Mexican explained the situation to him. He knew that Ralph had ratted him out to the Police and he would have to be "taken care" of. He asked Cloud if he knew what that meant. Again he nodded. The Mexican asked Cloud if he wanted to do him a big favor. He couldn't have any of his "niggers" do the job because he was afraid that it might be traced back to him. He offered Cloud ten thousand dollars and agreed to throw in enough coke to keep him lit up like a Christmas tree for well over a year. Though Cloud wanted no part of killing anyone, especially someone like Ralph, he knew that he really didn't have any choice in the matter. The Mexican handed him two envelopes, one with five thousand dollars in it as a down payment and the other contained a small amount of white powder. He told Cloud that he could take the cash now, but he would hold the coke and the other five thousand as an incentive for him to move fast and get the job done. Cloud agreed. The Mexican asked him if he needed a weapon. Cloud shook his head no, he would come up with all that he needed. He didn't want to shoot Ralph for fear that one of the girls might get hit also. The Mexican told him that he could kill all of them as far as he was concerned. "The older one's kinda' cute, you can rape her if you desire." The Mexican said with a grin. "I don't want to rape a nine year old!" Cloud replied. "Oh, then maybe you want to rape Ralph before you off him." The Mexican said, flashing his teeth.

Cloud took the money and lefts, preferring to get a cab back to his apartment rather than be escorted.

The next morning Cloud called down to the precinct station where Ralph was being held to find out how much his bond was. He then called the Mexican and told him about the extra "business" expense. After all how could he kill Ralph if he couldn't afford to get him out of jail? The Mexican told him that he would take care of it that afternoon. Cloud had a plan that would make the whole affair nice and clean and get him off of the hook, both as far as the police were concerned and the Mexican as well. But for this plan to work, timing was everything. Cloud stopped at the local hardware store and bought some tools and a small white emergency candle. He then proceeded to drive to Ralph's house. He figured that he had a couple of hours before Ralph was released from jail, but that would give him plenty of time. Access to the house was easy; Ralph certainly hadn't been very concerned about security, being a drug dealer and all. Cloud broke into the basement, that was the easiest way to get in and it was also the exactly the place in the house that he wanted to be. It didn't take him very long to find the water heater. It was an older type and powered by gas. Perfect! In a couple of minutes he was able to override the shutoff valve and blow out the flame. He could already smell the gas as he broke off about an inch of candle, lit it, and placed it next to the water heater. The plan was to have the basement fill up with gas when Ralph got home and when it reached the flame of the candle, BOOM! No more Ralph and he could collect his money and his drugs and take a nice little vacation. He decided not to take his girlfriend along. With plenty of both money and coke, who needed her anyway. Cloud quickly gathered up the tools that he had bought and went back out the way that he came in. He replaced the piece of plywood that had covered up the hole in the window. Windows covered with plywood were always easier to break in to, you didn't have to worry about the sound of broken glass. All Cloud had to do now was either wait until Ralph came home and blew himself up, or read about it in the newspaper and make sure that he bought a copy for the Mexican. Cloud really wasn't to hot about staying and witnessing the incident, but he decided to risk the prying eyes of the neighbors and make sure that the job was finished, after all he didn't want the Mexican coming after him for messing it up.

Of course Ralph had to late, almost two and a half hours had elapsed before he came pulling up in the driveway. It looked like someone had given him a ride. Cloud realized that the police had probably impounded his car and he was sure he didn't have any money for a cab. The car drove away and Ralph started walking towards his neighbor's house instead of his own. "Damn!" Cloud thought to himself. "He's going to pick up te kids!" Cloud was starting to wonder if this was a good idea after all. A friend who used to be a firefighter had told him about the candle trick, but why hadn't the thing blown up already? He was starting to think that maybe when he broke the candle, he might have messed up the wick, causing it to go out after a few minutes. Cloud watched as the two girls ran out of the neighbor's house towards Ralph. They both rushed into his arms and hugged him. Then they ran into the house as Ralph suddenly turned and went back towards the neighbor's. Cloud watched in horror as a light came on inside the house immediately followed by an even brighter one as the giant fireball rose about two hundred feet up into the air. He watched as Ralph, who had just made it to the front porch ran down the stairs, his shirt on fire. Cloud ran out of his car and jumped on top of Ralph, rolling him over on the ground and putting out the flame.

Cloud left Ralph smoldering on the ground. He could already hear the sirens in the distance and the last thing he wanted was to be questioned by the police. He had been seen by half the neighborhood when he was rolling Ralph on the ground. It didn't matter if he was wanted for questioning, all the evidence was circumstantial and by then he would be out of the country anyway.

Cloud drove over to the Mexican's house to get the rest of the money and the dope. Getting the coke out of the country might present a problem, but he had done it before. He could just sell it before leaving and get some cheaper stuff where he was going. After knocking on the door and waiting for what seemed like forever, the door opened a creak, just enough to reveal the pudgy face of Smalls. The very dim bulb that was Small's brain lit up a tiny fraction when he saw Cloud. "The Mexican is not here, but we have a package to give you." Smalls said. He motioned for Cloud to come inside. This made him feel nervous. These guys were a couple of loose goons and Cloud felt uneasy being in the house with them without the Mexican. Cloud told him that he preferred to just get his stuff and leave. Smalls told him that the Mexican was afraid that after all the narcotics busts, the FBI was keeping an eye on his house, so they didn't want to transact any "business" right out in the open. Cloud had no choice but to follow the fat greaser into the darkened house. He's wished that he had the forethought to bring a weapon along with him, maybe something hidden in his boot, that might escape the pat down that he was given on the way in. He was led into the kitchen where Curls was seated at the table in the chair that was normally reserved for the Mexican.

As soon as Cloud saw that one of the kitchen chairs was missing, he knew that he was in serious trouble. The chair had been moved to the others side of the room and covered with plastic trash bags. This was not a good sign. He immediately lunged at Curls, smashing him in the face and knocking him off of his perch. Smalls threw his considerable bulk on top of Cloud, pushing him on top of the table and almost collapsing it. Cloud was a lot quicker than the fat man, but he was pinned down. Curls threw a right hook, smashing Cloud's nose back into his face. The shock threw him even more off balance and threw a shock wave through his brain. They wrestled him over to the plastic covered chair and tied him to it. Cloud's left eye was covered in blood that had splattered up from his nose and he shook his head from side to side, trying to see. Curls walked over to one of the cabinets and pulled out a shopping bag full of boxes. The boxes all contained different kinds of laxative pills, some were prescription, others were over the counter. In the old days they had used chocolate Ex-Lax, and there was some of that in the bag too. Now a days there were a lot of other alternatives that weren't quite as messy as the chocolate.

Smalls went up behind Cloud and grabbed hold of both of his ears. He felt just below them and pushed as hard as he could where Cloud's jawbone fit into his skull. Cloud felt a sharp pain spread through his sinuses, as his mouth was forced open. Smalls opened one of the boxes of laxatives and filled up his right hand with them. He pushed them into Cloud's open mouth and then slammed it shut. Cloud tried to resist swallowing, but it was no use: it was either swallow or choke, and he couldn't control his reflex. This process was repeated several times. The two men stepped back and looked at Cloud. "Now the fun part begins." One of them said. Curls produced a roll of silver duct tape and ran it around Cloud's face, smashing his lips back into his teeth. Smalls went back into the bedroom and got the baseball bat.

The idea was to force feed Cloud enough laxative pills that he would shit all over himself. Whenever he did though, the two men would take turns hitting him with a baseball bat. Sometimes this process would go on for half the night, or until the victim passed out and they could no longer revive him. Then they would put a bullet in his head and dump him in the river, or in the foundation of a house. It was an old classic gangster trick that the Mexican had read about in a book and decided to try out for himself to see if it worked or not. It did.

Cloud was floating in the shallow grave of his Mother's womb. The deep veins of his umbilical cord pulsed every minute with the energy of his life's blood. He was trapped in its warmth. He moved his newly developed fingers with the rhythm of the heartbeat. He kicked his feet and sucked his thumb. He gazed across time and looked down at his Mother, now eighty years old and curled into a fetal position, lying in the Brookdale Nursing Home.

Chapter 14

"I don't know what it is, but ever since I've gotten older sex seems to be a big problem for me. I must have become more attractive because now everybody wants some. The boy that delivers the groceries, the people that I

play Bingo with, store clerks, the government, friends, family, complete
strangers that I meet on the street…. everybody wants to fuck me!"
Anon. Senior Citizen

Zella's parents were born of good German stock with a little Scots and Irish thrown in for good measure. They came over on the boat with the clothes on their backs, a willingness to work the land, and a few crusts of bread in their pockets. Seeing the far off smokestacks looming on the horizon of the big city, they decided that the American Dream resided there, the dusty and unproductive land being a little too much like home. They came by horseback, food, train, or faded old rusty automobile, any way that they could. They reproduced along the way, dropping the children in a soft piece of grass and then picking them up and moving on after they had hardened a little. The kids were like an egg, fragile at first, but after a few hours in the hot mid day sun they were pretty solid, even if the center was a little rotten. Of course some of them developed cracks and then broke wide open, their shells left to bleach dry out on the plains. One out of every six newborns didn't make the grade.

It was 1925, just a few years before the Great Depression. Zella's father decided to give up his trade of butchering animals and get into the industry of making shoes. He was the best shoemaker who ever stitched a lathe in a factory, singing the songs that the flappers were dancing to while he stitched the leather together. Zella was born in a house with heat supplied by the burning of the direct fossil: coal. The coal smelled and filled the air in the basement in the winter with an acrid scent that tickled the nose and sent rhythms throughout the stomach. She was born with bright red hair, betraying the German side of her heritage. She was the third oldest with two brothers before her and only one sister that made the females two in a row. But then the dynasty ended with one stillborn and the last and youngest brother sharing the bright red hair. Prohibition came into force and Al Capone wasn't to far away in Chicago. After working all day in the factory, father came home and filled up the bathtub with all the ingredients for making Gin. The smell of fermenting alcohol combined with the aroma of coal left little need for the paregoric that was in the medicine cabinet. And it was a good thing that the woman of the house knew how to cook, the smell of neck bones and 'kraught canceling out all of the above.

The Great Depression made things tough for everyone, but Zella's father was able to keep his job at the factory, St. Louis was after all, first in booze, blues and shoes at the time. Zella soon became the workhorse of the five children, at the age of nine delivering homemade pies and cakes that her mother had baked to homes and businesses throughout the neighborhood. At the age of fifteen she lied about her age and got a job at the factory across the street from where they lived, making fifty cents per hour assembling street lamps. She would end up keeping that job for forty-five years.

When she was seventeen Zella started dating the brother of her older brother's girlfriend, Bill. About a year later all four of them went down to get marriage licenses together, creating quite a bit of confusion at the license bureau. Zella's brother Bob and his wife Olive would end up having a tumultuous thirty year marriage but things didn't work out to well for Zella and Bill from the very start. Bill had a drinking problem and started out right away taking things out on his new wife and the baby that had just been born. Bill was a truck driver who spent quite a bit of time on the road and away from home. When he got back from the road, strung out, tired and nasty smelling, the first order of business was to take up where he had left off and smack Zella around a little. For the first few months of their marriage she put up with the beatings, hiding her face at work with a bandana and running back to her parents to drop off the baby. One particular Saturday night Bill came stumbling home from the bar feeling particularly mean. When Zella fought off his advances she was anally raped with a broom handle. This was the straw that literally broke the camel's back and it wasn't from the broom. The following evening Zella told Bill that as soon as he came home drunk enough to pass out he would lose his precious manhood. She told him this as she held the point of a butcher knife to his drunken chest. The threat was taken seriously and Bill left to go back out on the road never to return. Zella never asked for a penny in alimony or child support, preferring to raise her first son and the two that were soon to follow without the benefit of a man around. It would be another thirty years before she would marry again or touch one of the bastard creatures.

One summer day in 1968, Zella met Mack. Mack was a beefy Irish ex-prize fighter that had just been released from Alabama State Prison after doing seven years there for manslaughter. He had slipped the blade of a pocketknife into the belly of a fellow bar patron after the other gent had tried to start a fight. Since the other man was unarmed and promptly bled to death, Mack took the rap. Although officially his name was Clarence, Mack would soon become his moniker, as in Mack the Knife. He probably could have gotten off with a lighter sentence. It was after all his first felony offense, but sneaking out of the prison's horse farm a couple of times and making it West to Arizona to live with an old Indian woman who was fond of bananas didn't help matters much. Time was added and time was spent.

The debt was paid and Mack took his temper and his lack of respect for society back out West, this time to California, to be a stunt double in the movies. It was a tough business and the only job he was able to land was to jump onto a train off of his horse in a John Wayne movie. To supplement his income he worked the rodeos, riding broncos and breaking nearly every bone in his body and getting a steel plate implanted in his head. The damage to his skull was done compliments of the horse's hoof landing squarely on the back of his head and forcing fragments of his skull into the brain. For good measure the horse also crushed a testicle and that was lost to the rodeo life also, but hell he still had one left.

Mack had a passion for dressing in the finest of fashion, even if his wardrobe was a few years behind. He bought second hand suits at the local Goodwill before it was fashionable to do so, but that was all he could afford. He fell in love with Zella the first time he laid eyes on her, when they both were teenagers, but she was with Bill at the time, so he had to wait almost twenty years before anything could happen. Down and out and unable to find any immediate work with horses which was his one and only true love where employment was concerned, Mack got a job at the factory where Zella was employed. They re-introduced themselves and caught up on old news. Zella had always thought that Mack was a nice guy, but she was in no mood for that kind of nonsense after her brief excursion with her ex-husband Bill.

"I smoke old stogies I have found, short and not to big around. I'm a man of means by no means...King of the Road."- Robert Miller

The old Roger Miller song was Mack's favorite because he had lived it, riding in boxcars from one side of the country to the other. Now he had decided to settle down and he was determined to marry Zella despite all of her protestations to the contrary. Zella on the other hand was a little attracted to Mack's non-judgmental kindness and his stories about living on the road did impress a woman who had never really been out of her home state and had worked in a factory for most of her life.

The two finally hooked up and tied the knot. Mack quit his job at the factory and was able to get work as a part-time trainer at the local racetrack. Zella stayed employed at the factory and Mack would get up every morning before tending the horses and take her across the river to her job and then pick her up afterwards. Zella had never learned to drive. The few attempts that she had made both with Mack and her father usually resulted in a fender bender or most of the occupants of the car being thrown up against various parts of the car, as those where the days before seat belts. But somehow everyone survived. Both of the men weren't too quick to offer up their driving instructor skills again, instead preferring to be a taxi.

At the time Zella was raising the last of her three sons, a teenager named Mark. Mark was thirteen years old and had been sickly most all of his life with allergies. He was allergic to everything from the pillows he slept on, to the pollen from the trees, to dogs and cats. He stayed inside most of the time and went into coughing fits when he was exposed that were so severe that sometimes he would convulse. Mack was hell bent and determined to do things with his newly acquired stepson: One was to get the boy to like him at all costs, and secondly, make a man out of him. The first step was fairly easy because the boy desperately needed a father figure in his life and Mack liked to take him out and have fun. Even though money was scarce, within the first few weeks of marrying the boy's Mom, Mack had bought Mark a horse, some boots and a cowboy hat. Of course the boy was scared to death of the huge animal, a Palomino pony that was fifteen years old and stood about fifteen hands high. Mark however, was also determined to not let his newly found Dad down, so he summoned up all the courage that he could muster and rode the horse. The only problem was that after about ten minutes he was on the ground writhing in a spasm from all the horse dander. Mack had a plan and a solution to the allergy problem. He got Mark his first job at the stables cleaning out the stalls. He figured that if the smell of hay and fresh horseshit didn't cure him, then there was no hope. The amazing thing that happened was, it did. The doctor said that maybe it was because Mark was outgrowing his childhood allergies, but never the less, it did work.

Mack had been a semi-professional boxer when he was in his twenties and he had the face to prove it. His nose had been broken many times, but somehow it remained pointy. The only thing was it kind of leaned to the left, though it had nothing to do with his political affiliations. One day while rummaging through the bins at the local Goodwill store looking for a new/used pair of shoes, Mack stumbled upon an old pair of leather boxing gloves. He bought them for two dollars and took them home to show to Mark. Up until that point Mark really didn't have a problem with bullies. Small and skinny he was really no match for them one on one, though he was pretty fast with his fists. His solution to the problem was to put with the harassment until his temper got the best of him and then he would use the element of surprise. He would sneak up behind the bully and take him out with some kind of hard object to the back of the head. One time it was a rock, the other time a piece of pipe and the third time the bully went flying down two flights of stairs at school when he met a very heavy Geography book head on in the face. Mark was usually very well behaved and usually there were no witness's to his foul play. When it came down to his word against the bully's, Mark usually came out on top. Mark's approach was dead sincere and there wasn't any retribution on the bully's part because he was convinced that the brick to the head would happen again and again no matter how many times he kicked Mark's ass.

Mack knew about all of this but had a couple of concerns. He firmly felt that all was fair in love and war, but he was afraid that Mark would accidentally kill someone with the brick treatment. Although he wasn't familiar with the prisons up here in Missouri, he was sure that they wouldn't be much better than the ones in Alabama. So the decision was made to teach Mark how to defend himself.

Mack took Mark out into the back yard and sparred with him. It was basic instruction. He showed Mark how important it was to concentrate on your footwork and take your time, measure out your opponent. He bought Mark a practice bag that hung from the rafters in the basement and encouraged him to use it. After a couple of months, Mack felt that Mark was ready for his first bout, but first he took him down to watch some of the Golden Glove matches. There was a local boxing promoter that Mack knew from Detroit by the name of Johnny Radison. Johnny owned what was known as a rough neck bar in the neighborhood. A rough neck bar was one that if you didn't know at least a few of the people that hung out there, chances were that you would get your ass kicked sometime during the evening. Regular patrons always took a seat or a barstool that was facing the door, just in case someone popped in who was "after them." That way they wouldn't get waylaid from behind.

The Golden Glove matches took place down at a local gym that wasn't that far from the bar and downstairs at the bar Johnny had a complete gym set up complete with a ring. That way the kids could practice there after school and the bar flies could beat each other up with the benefit of the police sticking their noses in. Beating people up was a thankless job, but somebody had to do it.

Mark and Mack sat in the folding metal chairs that were strewn around the backside of the gym and watched two small Black kids who couldn't have been more than ten years old go at it. The kids both wore boxing helmets, but the smaller of the two finally got knocked on his butt. Because of their age, the bouts only lasted a couple of rounds and many didn't even go that long. A few of the older kids did make things a little bit more interesting and by the time the last bout was over, there was blood in the ring. During all the matches, Mack sat and patiently explained to Mark what the boxers were doing right and what they were doing wrong. He told him that this Saturday was the big day, he had talked to the Fathers of a few of the kids in the neighborhood and they were all coming over for an elimination match. Mark could hardly wait.

That Saturday dawned warm and a little humid. The fights were to take place in the morning before it got too hot. About ten o'clock there were about four expectant Fathers gathered around on Mack's front porch and about twelve of the neighborhood kids had shown up. There was a makeshift ring constructed in the front yard using some rope and duct tape. The kids that Mark was scheduled to fight ranged in age from about ten years old to seventeen years old. Mack had accepted all challenges for two reasons: One was that you never refused a challenge for a fight no matter how old the person was or how big. And secondly, he felt that with all of his training, Mark was ready to take on the world.

It was Saturday morning and the bell was about to ring in Round 1. Mark dispatched the first challenger with ease, a deaf and dumb kid named Billy. Billy was pretty tough and mean, but he had co-ordination problems and he found it difficult to land a punch. The second punch that Mark landed on his face left him with a chipped tooth, disorientated and confused. His father threw I the towel. The victory made Mark even more ready and confident to take on the second challenger, a squirrelly little kid named Jimmy. Jimmy was a dirty blonde with two creases at the elbow where his forearm started to bend. He was extremely poor and suffered from a weakness in the bones from lack of vitamin D and had severe gum disease that had made most of his teeth fall out. His family couldn't afford a dentist and the free clinic had been closed. Mark popped him in the mouth after the first few punches were fended off and out came a tooth. The glove leather was well worn and soft and the bloody tooth stuck into the glove. Mark at first tried to shake the thing out of his glove, but then had to suffer a wave of nausea as he walked over and extracted the tooth by rubbing the glove against a tree. The tooth fell to the ground and Jimmy went over and picked it up, putting it into his pocket. There was a fifteen-minute rest period where the adults went inside for beer and the kids sat on the porch steps and drank lemonade. Mark got up and did his best Ali shuffle little aware that he was about to face his biggest challenger. The next fighter in line was a couple of years older than Mark and almost two feet taller. He was thin and didn't have that much upper body strength or even speed, but his reach seemed almost twice as far as Mark's. The round started pretty cautiously, after all Mark had dispatched the first two opponents with ease. The two felt each other out, Mark was kind of afraid of the other boy's reach when the first punch that he threw landed solidly to the body. Mark really didn't have any opportunity to throw any punches at all. Spurred on by his landing the first blow, the tall kid went wild, swinging his long arms at Mark like a Dutch windmill gone out of control. Mark did the best he could, covering up and burying his face in his gloves, trying to find an opening to counter punch just like Mack had taught him. But the punches were just coming too fast. The force of one of them turned Mark a little too much to one side and the next one went wide, landing square on his left kidney. Mark saw stars for the first time in his life without looking up to the sky. His knees went totally limp and he sank down to the ground. The tall boy kept on swinging, landing a punch to Mark's eye and another one that broke his nose. Mack rushed over and pulled the tall kid off of Mark and cited him for un-sportsman like conduct. Mack took Mark inside to the kitchen where his mother gasped in horror when she saw the mess on Mark's face. Mack sat Mark on one of the kitchen chairs and grabbed his bloody nose, forming his fingers into a V and popping Mark's nose back into place. He then went over to the icebox and took out a steak for mark to hold against his black eye to help reduce the swelling. Mark sniffled from all the blood that was just starting to congeal inside his nose, but he did not cry. Mack patted him on his back and rubbed his legs just like a prizefighter and told him that he had done a good job. Mark had never felt prouder in all of his life.

After seeing her son mostly black and blue, Zella put her ample foot down in regards to the Friday night fights, even though Mark didn't seem to mind. Some matches still took place in some of the other kid's basements using the boxing gloves that Mack had bought, and some took place out in the streets without the benefit of the padding that the gloves offered.

Mack had been working at the racetrack while Zella pretty much supported the family by working at the factory. Unbeknownst to the rest of the family, Mack had been squirreling away most of the money that he had been making at the track, tied up with rubber bands and kept in the bottom of an old oil encrusted baseball cap. Down the road from the track was a livery shop called The Tack Room. The tiny shop smelled of soap and leather and Mack soon became fast friends with the old couple that owned the place. He put reins, a horse blanket and an old worn out saddle on layaway. There was a small house situated on the paddock side of the track that was empty that the owners let Mack stay in when the races ran late and he slept over. Sometimes he would bring Mark and his Mom over for the weekend to take in the sights. Zella had always liked to gamble and she took to the track like a sweaty horse out for a midnight run. Mark didn't like to risk the few dollars he got foe an allowance on bets, but he was fascinated watching the people who showed up. There seemed to be a wide cross section of society: young woman whom appeared just a tad loose and their amateur boyfriends who seemed more interested in drinking beer than watching the races. And then there was the professionals, short balding men chewing on the stumps of cigars and intensely studying their racing forms. There was a carnival atmosphere about the place, the vendors selling everything from popcorn and hotdogs to tips on what horse was going to win the next race. They all moved either outside to the track or to the television monitors like a herd of cattle when the scratchy voice of the announcer came over the tin speaker to call post time. The poor people were the ones who headed outside, dragging along their plastic lawn chairs behind them, while the richer folks stayed up in the grand stands and made phone calls to their bookies that placed the bets for them. Mack patiently explained the entire goings on to Mark and sometimes even gave him a couple of dollars to bet on one of the horses. Some of the folks who went to the track had elaborate systems to figure the odds, while others just bet the favorites or because they liked the sound of the name. Mack had become friends with some of the jockeys and always asked them how they and the horse they came in on felt before the race. Things were a little biased as they usually told him that they had the winning nag, even if that wasn't always the case.

Mark got his first job, working as a stable boy when Mack put in a good word with Doc Kane. Doc was a well, retired doctor who owned more racehorses than anyone else in town. During the summer Mark slept in a little room right next to the stalls where some of the saddles and other gear was kept. Across the room from his bunk were three large barrels of grain. One barrel held desert grain that was laced with maple syrup. He awoke hungry most every morning to the smell. His first duty was to feed the dozen or so horses that he was in charge of. The owners had written down what kind of feed, how much and at what time of day they had to be fed. Then came breakfast and the fun work, cleaning out the stalls. Most of the time Mark just moved the horse around in the stall while he scooped through the straw with his pitchfork. He had a bright red little wheelbarrow stationed right outside the stall and he would toss the shit-laden straw over the canvas gate that kept the horse from getting out, into the wheelbarrow. If the horse objected to this and started bumping Mark into the side of the stall, he would then have to put reins on the horse and tie him up outside. A few of the horses would try to bite him as he worked, their long straight front teeth literally ripping his skin like a cheese slicer. Mack had his own solution to this problem; he would simply punch the horse in the nose. This was kind of a signal to the horse to top biting. When Mark tried this however, the horse would simply pull his lips up over his teeth in a snarl and then come after him again.

One day sfter Mark had finished his work, Mack told him that he had a surprise for him. He went into the stable and came out with a rather large pony that he presented to Mark and told him that it was his to keep.

About a year later Mack was at the softball park that was across the street from the house that the family was currently living in, playing ball with Mark. Mark was getting to be a pretty good fielder and hitter, though he was still kind of shy and didn't do very well in a team setting. When he was by himself though or just playing with a few friends he had no trouble keeping up. That night Mark went back to spend the night with his Grandparents. It was a hot, muggy August day and the sun was just acting like it was starting to set. A Lebanese kid that lived next door to Mark's grandparents stopped him on the street and asked him if he would like to go to a special exhibition football game that evening. The game featured the World Champion New York Jets playing the local team that had one of the worst team records in the NFL. The Lebanese, whose parents had gangster roots that grew all the way back to the old country, had gotten the tickets from his Uncle, who was a state senator. Mark replied sure, he would love to go. The two hurried back to the neighbor's house where the senator's limousine was parked, waiting for them. It was the very first football game that Mark had ever been able to go to, even though Mack was a big fan and had promised the boy to take him to one as soon as he was able to come up with enough money. Mark sat at the game, eating hotdogs and drinking soda, just waiting to call Mack in the morning and tell him about the experience.

After Mack had finished throwing the ball around with Mark, he felt tired and went into the house to see what Zella had fixed for dinner.

"It was a hot summer night and the breeze was burning, there was fire drifting over the sands... "-Meatloaf

"Lay lady lay, lay across my big brass bed...stay lady stay, stay with your man awhile.... "-Bob Dylan

Mack and Zella shared the big brass bed. Mack like most everything else in the house had bought the bed from Goodwill Industries, save a buck and help the handicapped, or, as they were called back in the day, the cripples. The bed had a well-worn mattress and a solid frame. The brass headboard was bent in a few places and rusted in a few more, but that just meant that the thing had a little history and a whole lot of romance in it.

The night was like any other, Zella had cooked dinner and then done the ironing, sighing and sipping her bourbon, while Mack watched some television and polished his shoes. It was around twelve o'clock when they finally went to bed. Zella had pinned up her hair and was already asleep while Mack sat on the side of the bed that faced the window and took in a little of the warm summer breeze. He finished smoking the stub of a Pall Mall cigarette. *"Wherever particular people congregate... "* The rumpled red pack of unfiltered cigarettes sat on the nightstand. Mack was wearing his paisley boxer shorts and an undershirt without any sleeves. He lay down on the bed, turned off the light, patted Zella on her behind and went to sleep. Zella, who wasn't all that fond of men in the first place, used to say that one of the things that she liked about Mack was that he was content to pat her on the ass and not want to do anything else to it.

About three o'clock that night Zella became restless. She lay awake and stared at the dimly lit ceiling. Mack stirred a little beside her and then suddenly sat up. He put his hand on his forehead. Zella asked him what was the matter. He replied that his head felt a little funny. Then she heard him say that he loved her as he slumped down in bed, the arm that had been holding his head twisted in an unnatural shape behind his back. Zella ran to the kitchen to call an ambulance, but it was too late. The man she loved brain had collapsed into a mass of bloody jelly, a hemorrhage that had drained the life out of him.

After Mack became a ghost rider in the sky, Zella took Mark and moved in with her brother Bob. Bob was a self-employed mechanic who could fix an automobile with a rubber band and a piece of chewing gum and liked to think of himself as the last of the independents. What this translated into in reality was that he never held a steady job his entire life. Most of the time he fixed cars for the people in the neighborhood out of his garage and never paid any social security or taxes. He was a big strapping brute of a man who wasn't really easy to get along with, especially when he had been drinking. Though he was kind of a secret softie at heart, he certainly liked to talk tough.... And act that way. He was fond of showing complete strangers how he could rip the transmission out of an old clunker and repair it while the thing was balanced on his chest. He also wasn't very fond of going to the doctor or the dentist, preferring to treat himself with a bottle of Jack and a pair of pliers whenever he had a toothache. Fist he would swallow an ample amount of the whiskey and then swish some of it around in his mouth to numb the area and sterilize it, then pull out his own tooth with the pliers. A tea bag or two and some gauze to stop the bleeding and he was back in the shop the very next day. He took pretty much the same approach to the rest of his health. He had a football-sized rupture in his abdomen from trying to lift part of an engine back into a car without the benefit of a hoist. The thing grew steadily over the next thirty years when he refused to have surgery or wear a "bra" as he liked to call the support that the doctor offered him. Walking around with a large part of his intestines on the outside of his body didn't seem to bother him. He told everybody that he would die when he was ready and only then. The devil didn't like him and God thought that he was too much of a pain in the ass to have in heaven.

Bob was married to Olive, who was the sister of Zella's ex-husband Bill. Bob had always had a special fondness for his sister Zel as he called her. She was about the only one in the family who could outwork him and out drink him if the situation called for it.

Bob had come up with this idea to purchase some investment property; some fixer upper property. The house was huge, the bottom floor being a storefront at one time. He would rent out some of the space to his parents, and another floor to his sister and her son and this extra income would pay for the expenses involved with repairs. The house was in pretty rough shape on the outside and even rougher on the inside. The first thing that he did was knock out the large storefront windows and replace them with smaller aluminum ones surrounded by plywood. Bob did most of his construction shopping at a used supply place called Hood's. He tried to cut costs whenever possible, and the grade of plywood that he bought was more for kitchen cabinets than outdoors, and it soon warped the windows into a crazy angle. The house had a large porch at the front of the house that badly needed painting and a large turret at the corner of the place. In back was a rotted wood porch that swayed so much when you walked on it, you definitely felt that it was in imminent danger of collapse. The porch wasn't a priority to Bob since there was more than three ways to get out of the house, so he just roped it off and put a small "Keep Out" sign on it.

Bob had always had a strange sense of design and purpose. He liked to thing of himself as cutting edge. He once had a project where he covered an entire car with purple contact paper. The paper had nice white swirls on it and he had used the same stuff to line his kitchen cabinets and cutlery drawers. The contact paper made perfect sense to him, as it was durable, waterproof, and smelled of plastic, that kind of new car smell. All you had to do was to get all of the bubbles out.

The outside of the house also was in dire need of tuck-pointing. The thing had been built about a hundred years ago out of brick and there were gaps between some of them large enough to park pigeons. Instead of shelling out all that money to fix the bricks, Bob decided to paint the place. He enlisted the help of his nephew who wasn't really a painter, but who had worked for a short while, as a steelworker on one of the bridges downtown and at least wasn't afraid of heights. This was a plus since the building was over three stories tall. The only problem was that the nephew had been fired from the steelworker job because he had a drinking problem and had reported to work drunk and had almost fallen off of the damn bridge. He was however, willing to work for beer and a place to sleep.

Bob had a color scheme for the place. The brick that the house was composed of hadn't been painted, but it was a dull red color, the color of well, brick. Bob had been driving around in the city and had seen a small adobe house that had been painted a sort of salmon color with some of the adobe clay bricks painted a dark shade of red. He thought that this would be perfect for his house. Bob went down to Hoods the very next day and got a steal on a whole load of paint that had expired. Some of the cans were rusty and leaky and some of the paint inside had dried up, but he could discard that and use the rest. Besides most of the paint was a nice neutral color and they would throw in some tint for free. That way Bob could customize the color of his house to exactly match the color of the one that he had seen in the city. The only problem with this scenario was that Bob was slightly color blind and his nephew was slightly drunk. The result after two months of the nephew getting drunk and almost falling off of the ladder was a partially painted pink beast of a house. It didn't help matters that every other brick was painted bright red. The neighborhood kids started calling the place the "candy cane hooker house" and Mark was so embarrassed and at such a tender age, he refused to live there. When his mother told him that they had no money and no choice, he opted to tell everyone at school that he no longer lived there, that he was staying at his uncle's. He would get off of the bus several blocks away from the house and walk the rest of the way, hoping that no one would see him. By the time he had sneaked into his own house, he was almost as red as the pink bricks themselves. It wasn't that he didn't like the place once he got inside. Being sort of a loner who liked to have his own space, the fact that the entire third floor of the house was his made him happy. There were four rooms that had been made out of the converted attic. Mark used one as his bedroom and made one of the other rooms into a study. Putting together some old wobbly bookshelves to store his ample supply of books. Mark spent most of his time either in the attic rooms, sometimes crawling through the spaces between the walls, or in the bowels of the building; the basement. Access to the basement was gained in one of two ways: there was a trap door with steps on the outside, in the back, but that way was dangerous because the door's hinges had long since rusted away and the doors were heavy. There was another trap door in the front hallway just as you came through the door. An old brass handle lay flat against the floor. Mark had to brace his feet and pull with all of his strength to get the thing to open and then hope that he could support the heavy door with his arm as he hurried down the stairs. If he didn't move quick enough he could get wedged and then he would have to call someone to extradite him. His Uncle Bob found an old warped slate pool table at a garage sale and installed it into the basement. Mark spent a considerable amount of time after school learning to shoot pool as best as he could with the warped table and a bent pool stick. When the pink painting cousin wasn't drunk sometimes he would come downstairs and shoot some pool with Mark. Mark liked his cousin but the remarks he often made about Mark's sexuality often made him uncomfortable. He would jokingly refer to Mark as the little pussy of queer who had never been laid. The cousin had spent sometime in prison and would graphically relate to Mark how he had made a little sissy boy like himself his bitch and had done him in the ass. "If you don't do the hole then you do the pole, he was fond of saying." One time when the two were hot and heavy into a game of pool, Mark was concentrating on the shot so hard that his cousin told him to please stop licking his lips, it was getting him excited. Mark told him to shut up and quit talking to him like that and the cousin replied: "Sissy, I could MAKE you suck my dick right now if I wanted to." Mark threw the pool stick across the table and went upstairs. For the rest of the time that he stayed at the pink house he avoided his cousin. It was bad enough that he had to suffer the humiliation of his classmates when they found out where lived without the harassment from his messed up cousin. He contemplated that next time he wouldn't just throw the pool stick across the table, but rather bust it upside his cousin's head. He decided that avoiding him would save them both a lot of trouble.

Mark opened his eyes to the bright sunshine that was pouring through the hospital window. His left arm hurt as he tried to move it. He had fallen asleep in a chair that was by his mother's bed. He looked down at his watch and noticed that he had been there in the room with her for about seven hours. Mark stiffly got up out of the chair and looked down at his mother lying in the small cramped hospital bed. He put his hands on the guardrails and sighed. He was in his forties now and his mom was reaching for her eighties, but at this point he wasn't quite sure if she was going to make it or not. She had lived longer than most everyone else in the family though, Uncle Bob and even the horny drunken cousin were all long gone. He wondered why he had been dreaming about him and the infamous pink house under these circumstances. Mark had moved out of the house when he was eighteen and had moved to Texas, getting a job as a restaurant manager. Zella had continued working at the factory for a total of forty fives years, living alone and retiring with little more than the clothes on her back and social security. She had stopped drinking when she was in her sixties, complaining that the daily whiskey caused her to have a severe pain in her side. The one thing that she couldn't give up though were the cigarettes, and after some fifty years of puffing two packs a day it had finally caught up with her. She had a bad case of emphysema and only had about forty percent of her lung function left. There had been a twenty year gap in their relationship, Mark heading off on a jet plane to Texas and Zella watching the last of her children fly the coup choking back the tears. Mark had called her about once a month and had sent her cards on all the holidays. Zella had been strong and never one to get into gratis showing of affection, but she did have a soft spot for greeting cards. It was the one thing that she had insisted on, calling Mark a few days after the holiday if she didn't get one and keeping all the ones she did get throughout her life in an old cardboard box. Something had happened though these last few years, Mark had returned to St. Louis and had been trying to make up for lost time. She was pretty much the only relative that he had left. His one brother, whom he hadn't talked to for years, had a few children here and about, but they were total strangers to him. He didn't even remember their names. He went through a nasty divorce in Dallas and being tired off the warm weather and palm trees, decided to head North. At times Mark had taken on a few strange directions, first traveling to New Orleans to study Voodoo and then Wicca in Texas. On a trip to New Mexico he had ingested Peyote for the first time and studied American Indian Shamanism, reading all of the Carlos Castenada books that he could get his hands on and playing with rattle snakes. Throughout all of this Zella had kept an amazing open mind for her age. Mark had spent long hours on the phone telling her about his new religions and had even drove to her house a couple of times to do drumming rituals with her a couple of times. She hadn't really understood what they were doing, but she had loved her son very much and played along, even if she had thought that he was a little weird.

A few weeks ago Zella had awoke with an intense pain in her back that forced her to call Mark in the middle of the night. Through all the years that he had known her, she had never sounded so sorrowful. She was out of breath and barely able to speak. He called an ambulance for her and then drove to the emergency room. She lay there on the hospital gurney looking every bit of her eighty years. In the past, even though her body had shown the ravages of time and the years of abuse, there was always a spirit inside that had come through, reflecting in the energy in her eyes.

The only other time that Zella had been in the hospital had been a couple of years prior when she had complained to her good friend Mable that she was a little short of breath. She was diagnosed as having a rhythm disturbance in her heart. She was scheduled to have an angiogram, a procedure where radioactive dye was injected into her arteries, and x-rays were taken. By accident the test revealed that she had a large aneurysm in the descending aorta perched on top of her heart. This was like a balloon on the side of a tire and if it burst from too much pressure she would bleed to death in a matter of minutes. The operation needed to repair it was very risky for a woman of Zella's age and medical condition. She decided to hell with it, she would take her chances and live out the rest of her days as she saw fit. After all it wouldn't really be that bad of a way to go, probably painlessly, silently, in her sleep. The doctors decided to put her on several kinds of medication, to slow down the heart rate and keep her blood thin.

When a heart doesn't beat normally, there is a chance that stagnant blood will pool in its chambers and clots could form. These clots could break off and travel to the brain or the lungs and cause a serious problem. Mark had been out of town when all of this was happening though he called her almost every day when she was in the hospital.

Now he looked down at her lying in the emergency room. Her faded red hair seemed to be plastered into a halo around her face from being on the gurney so long. The drugs that they had given her for pain were finally taking hold and she was groggy, but could respond to questions and talk, even though at times she faded in and out. The cigarettes and whiskey that she had plied her body with so long seemed to have left her with a natural immunity to pain killing drugs, even the opiates. It was the part of her that had maintained control for all of the years on the street that wouldn't let go. No time to relax. Fight to the bitter end. After she was in the emergency room for about ten hours Mark was a little concerned that she hadn't taken her medications. Earlier on in her life Zella had bragged that the only medication that she needed to make it through the day was a cigarette, a Pepsi, and maybe an aspirin or two. When Mark asked the nurse whether or not Zella had taken her medications, the nurse replied that she would check on it. A few minutes later she returned and told him that the paramedics had written down the list of drugs that she was taking but somehow that list had been lost. Mark then drove to his mom's apartment and gathered up the medicine bottles and brought them back to the hospital and gave them to the nurse. He thought that everything was going to be ok. Mark sat in the waiting room clutching his mother's purse. He had retrieved it from the apartment when the hospital asked for her Medicare and insurance card.

Rummaging through her purse in search of the cards made Mark feel a little uncomfortable. Years ago when he was living with her, someone had broken into their apartment and ransacked it, stealing the old television set and about sixty dollars Mark had sequestered away in a metal box secured by a padlock and a bent nail. They had really trashed the place, breaking the lamps and smashing anything that they figured wasn't of any value. Mark had a stack of play money that he used to play Monopoly with laying in his desk drawer, hundreds and fifties, and that must have really freaked them out for a moment before they realized that it wasn't real. One of the perpetrators had taken the time to rip the play money into little pieces and scatter it all across the room.

Mark remembered how violated he felt when he saw the mess that they had left. He had also felt embarrassed when he discovered they had also stolen some pornographic pictures he had stashed with the money. His perverted cousin gave one of the pictures to him; it was a photograph of a woman having sex with a donkey. For some reason Mark was concerned that the thieves might think that he was the pervert, but on second thought they had taken the picture, so they must have been perverts too.

Mark, even though he still felt guilty, made the decision to look through the rest of Zella's purse while he was waiting. It felt almost like he was a kid again when he would search through his parent's dresser drawers to see what kind of hidden treasures were stashed there. Given her age and the underlying medical problems she had, Mark had a premonition that nothing good would come out of this. Looking down at the old, battered purse brought a tear to his eye. There was a bit of leather string holding her house keys attached to the outside of the purse. There were a couple of other keys there also and each one of them was color coded with little strips of tape. His mother was nothing if not organized. Inside the purse were a couple of tissues, some hard candy and breath mints. There was a small address book and a handicapped sticker that she used when her friend Delores and she used to go on the riverboat to gamble with what little she had left over from her pension and social security. Up until recently she had always been able to make the several block long walk from the parking lot into the main part of the casino. There depending on her finances she would either play the nickel or the penny slots, sometimes walking away with a few extra bucks but more often than not she would feed all of her winnings back into the kitty. The last few times she was unable to make the walk. Delores had to commission one of the wheelchairs and push Zella into the casino. This caused her much consternation. It was a point of pride that she was able to take care of herself and do things like she had always done, and when she had to ride in the wheelchair, she always bowed her head so she didn't have to look at people's faces.

When Mark went back into the emergency room he was told that his mother had been moved up to a room on the second floor. It was a private room. The hospital had once catered to the wealthy who could afford the private rooms. There was even a gourmet menu at one time for those patients not on a restricted diet. The menu came with a wine list. But with the state of health care in the country and the overabundance of hospital beds, even those who like Zella were on Medicare got the deluxe suits. When Mark walked into the room, the lights were out and the curtain had been drawn around his mom's bed. He pulled back the curtain to discover that she was sleeping. The drugs that they had given her for the pain had finally taken affect. She was laying on her side, her jaw slack and her mouth open. It seemed like every breath that she took was carefully counted and measured, like the supply could run out at any time. She had steadily lost weight over the past few years and now her body was a ghostly outline in the sea of white sheets that seemed to lap around her edges and swallow her up. Mark looked at her for a few more minutes, drew the curtains back and went home.

The next day Mark called the hospital and asked how his mother was doing. The nurse who answered the phone told him that other than being a little groggy from the medication, she was doing fine. He was told that she was no longer in pain from the arthritis in her spine. She told him that Zella would probably be discharged in a couple of days after some rehab she would be able to return to her apartment as long as there was someone in the building to check up on her from time to time.

Mark expected to see his Mom in better spirits on the third day when he returned to the hospital. He had brought her some flowers and a get-well card. As he cautiously approached the bed and gazed down at her, it looked like she was still sleeping. Her short red hair was matted to the pillow in the back and she looked almost like a baby worth a hair bonnet on. He walked over to the other side of the room and placed the flowers on the chair that sat in the corner. He took the card out of its envelope and stood it upright on the bed stand. For some reason he slid the top-drawer open, expecting to see a Bible. He was correct: standard Gideon issue. Zella was still sleeping. Mark got tired of standing after a few more minutes and pulled the chair up beside the bed. He figured that he might have a long wait before Zella woke up. A few minutes later he watched as his Mother opened her eyes. There was a wild, almost animal expression in them. Her mouth opened into what looked like a terrible scream and her eyes darted back and forth, like the rapid eye movements of a dream. She turned her head slightly and looked at him with a look of more abject horror than he had ever witnessed. It was if the very devil himself was chasing her and she couldn't get away. Mark stared back at her for a moment and then grabbed her by the shoulders and spoke her name as loud as he could. Nothing. Suddenly, out of nowhere, she grabbed his sweater with more strength than he could imagine. She sat up slightly in the bed holding on to him for dear life. There was spittle running out of the corners of her mouth. Her lips were moving like she was trying to form words that refused to come out. Finally an animal sound came out, deep and guttural. "Help Me!!" It said.

His Mother's grip relaxed a little and she closed her eyes and fell back into the bed, asleep or unconscious, Mark couldn't figure out which. He shot out of the room and ran down the hospital hall to the nurse's station. A heavyset black woman sat behind the counter, working on a crossword puzzle. She looked up from the puzzle with a look of annoyance on her face and asked mark if she could help him. He told her what had just happened. She replied that she would tell the nurse the next time that she came back from her rounds. Mark turned away and walked hurriedly down the hall, looking for the nurse. He finally caught up with her as she was coming out of the women's restroom. The nurse was sturdy looking, maybe in her mid thirties, more muscular than heavy. She looked tired like she had been lifting patients all day. Crow's feet lines were etched deeply into her face. Mark told her what had just happened and she promised him that she would be right down to take a look. Mark walked back to the room to wait for the nurse.

The nurse arrived about ten minutes later. Ten anxious minutes of Mark watching his mom not moving at all, still as death. He held her hand, and then felt for a pulse. He couldn't really feel anything. He stared at her chest and noticed the faint movement of her breathing. The hospital gown barely covered her long forgotten breasts. She had steadily lost weight over the past few years as she approached her eighties, the powerhouse in the body's cells slowly shutting down the furnace in preparation for the final winter. Mark sat and looked at how thin she had become, barely a hundred pounds. But she still had the grip; the grip that she had developed with almost fifty years of using that hand, working in the factory. Though the rest of her body had been racked and crippled with the arthritis, that hand and that arm, the right one, had remained strong. It was her secret signal to Mark, her signal that she was ok. She could still crack bones with that hand. The nurse was busy taking Zella's vitals. "Her blood pressure is a little low and her heartbeat slightly erratic, but that's not unusual for someone her age in her condition. She's fine." The nurse said. Mark asked her about his mom's inability to talk and the seeming seizure that he had just witnessed. She replied that he could show up in the morning and ask the doctor when he made his rounds, but she thought that it was just a reaction to the heavy pain medication that she was getting. "She'll probably be alright in a few days." The nurse said as she left the room in a flurry of white. "At least they no longer wear those stupid hats." Mark thought.

Weeks went by, but Zella's condition didn't improve very much. Eventually a cat scan was taken and it was determined that she had a stroke.

The stroke affected the part of her brain that controlled speech and some of her short-term memory. The decision was made to move her to a nursing home.

Brookdale Manor was a large, squat buff brick building that looked sort of like a ranch home from the fifties on steroids. There was a narrow expanse of grass on both sides and white columns in the front that resembled white washed two by fours. Parking spaces were cut at odd angles and wrapped around the place. As you entered the one-way driveway there was a sign that read "Caution There May Be Residents Walking." This was kind of unusual because none of the residents were ever observed walking once you got inside the place. There was a small sunroom at the front of the building that no one seemed to use. As you went through the second set of doors, painted white with freshly polished brass handles, you arrived at the center of activity: the "great room," as it was called. To the right was the activity center, a scattering of chairs and a solitary sofa that sat in front of a giant screen TV that was tuned into the afternoon soaps and volume amplified for the residents who were hard of hearing. Behind that was a long conference table that was usually littered with scraps of colored construction paper and dried bits of glue. In the corner was a large cage that held a variety of parakeets and tweety birds. To the right of the great room was the dining hall. This was populated with about twenty café-style tables containing only two chairs each. The reasons for this was that most of the residents ate their food out of their wheelchairs or, if they were bed ridden, back in the rooms. Usually the day's highlights were breakfast, crafts, lunch, physical therapy, and dinner. Then there was the ample time to "rest." They didn't call it a rest home for nothing. The residents used all the time they were allowed to rest.

They rested in the hallways, in the shower and in the bathroom. Sometimes it was difficult to tell whether any one particular resident was resting, or simply dead. Death was a frequent visitor to the nursing home and at least He usually brought flowers. Sometimes He would get the names confused and a resident would wake up in the middle of the night screaming: "Not Me! Not Me!" Most of the time however it was a short if not sweet visit and Death would leave quietly, past the sleeping nurse, throwing the flowers in the trash can on the way out. Sometimes He would wave the flowers around the bed for a few minutes, for He couldn't stand the smell. It seemed that the discovery was always made in the clarity of the harsh daylight. The body was wheeled out quietly and loaded into an ambulance and then it was off to the morgue. You couldn't do this at night because the morgue was closed anyway and you didn't want to get the doctor out of bed to sign the death certificate. The percentage of dead in their beds varied considerably from one day to the next.

One odd thing that Mark noticed as he traversed the hallways down to his mother's room, the room was all the way to the back of the place in the semi-private area that they reserved for the Medicaid patients who couldn't afford the one hundred and fifty dollar a day price tag. There was always a smattering of residents scattered about in the hallway. They all sat in wheelchairs and looked like a handful of bony pick up sticks randomly tossed at odd angles throughout the hall. Most of them were asleep, slumped forward in their chairs. The few that were awake sometimes called out for Mark to help them or get them a glass of water or a pill. Some didn't know where they were or what was happening to them. Mark noticed a large sign on the wall that read: "It is winter." "It is cold outside." "Today is Thursday,

23rd of February." Mark had a weird thought of some old guy wheeling himself out from his room after a long bout of dementia, reading the sign and exclaiming, "Damn! I missed an entire season!"

Mark had been spending his fair share of time in hospitals and nursing homes since Zella had taken ill. Like trying to find a good used car he had shopped around four or five different homes and "retirement" centers before settling on this one. Not that he liked the one that she was in. It was all a matter of price, location and a big factor was whether or not they took the particular type of Medicaid and private insurance that she was on.

The other thing that you noticed immediately when you entered these places besides the sadness on the resident's faces, was the odor. No matter how clean the place looked, and some of them looked a lot cleaner than the others, there was an overbearing smell of old flesh and fresh shit. It permeated the halls, the cafeteria and the recreation areas. The only safe haven from the smell seemed to be the social worker's office. He noticed that she kept the door closed and there was always a fresh stream of conditioned air flowing from the vents in the office. Sometimes as you walked down the long hallways you caught a nice whiff of a moaning senior who had just crapped his pants. The place cried out for a shot of his mother's Pine Sol. Most people remember the smell of crayons when they are growing up, but for Mark it was the fresh scent of Pine Sol every Saturday morning. Zella liked to say that her floors were clean enough to eat off of, and though the theory was never tested, there wasn't a whole lot of worry about the five-second rule when a food item hit the floor. Mark felt sorry for his mother having to stay in a place that reeked like this without the benefits of her beloved Pine Sol. All the cleaning products in the house seemed to have a Sol on the end of their names. Lysol went into the toilet bowls in the dark smelly liquid form while it's spray version went on everything else including the kitchen cabinets. She even used a little known cleanser called Barisol. Where she found that one he had no idea, but he thought that it was requisitioned from the factory where she worked. Maybe they used it to clean the grease off of the gears. His mom was never fanatical about keeping the house clean during the week. Boys will be boys and she had three of them, so some mess was to be expected. But Saturday was cleaning day just like Monday was wash day, and these two things had become sacred institutions not to be messed with. It was ok to be messy during the week, but once a week, no matter what the place received a through deep cleaning no matter what.

Mark finally navigated around all the stalled seniors in their wheelchairs and made it to his mother's room. She lie there sound asleep, her head to one side, jaw slack, mouth open. Mark pulled up a chair to the side of the bed and just watched her sleep. He knew that the old mom wouldn't like him doing this, but there were certain aspects of her personality that had changed since the stroke. Before she had been part kindly old lady that everyone in her apartment building was fond of and came to for advice and part inner city factory worker who had fought all of her life and would split your head in a New York minute. Or in her case a St. Louis minute.

As Mark sat there in the bedside chair, the strangest things would sometimes come to mind. Bits of old memories that he hadn't thought about in years. It was almost like he was recalling those memories for her and then trying to project them into her mind. He thought about the not too distant time when a man dressed only in his underwear had tried to break into her apartment.

There were many times in the past when Zella had to fend for herself in neighborhoods and situations that weren't the most pleasant. Her father had taught her three important things: one was how to drink whiskey like a man, never fall down, never get sick and throw up. Two was how to throw a short-sided straight right hand with all of your weight behind it and lastly, how to shoot a gun straight and never pull the trigger unless you really mean it. Zella never really worried about herself, but her children were a totally different story all together. Once in the old neighborhood, she put a bullet through the heel of a man she had seen peeking in her kitchen window. He claimed that he was lost and just ducked into the gangway next to her house to relieve himself. On another occasion she kept a loaded shotgun propped up right next to the front door because of the drug dealing and prostituting neighbors who lived right above her. They partied right through the night, ten sometimes twenty guys competing for the sexual favors of a middle aged woman and her two teenage daughters. *"There ensued a fearful fight, screams rang out in the night..."* One night for some unknown reason one of the revelers was thrown head first out of the second story window and Zella decided that enough was enough. She called up a few friends from the old neighborhood and after a heavily armed confrontation that only lasted a few minutes, the ladies in the attic decided that it would be in their best interests to vacate the premises. Otherwise they would have to deal with the police and if that didn't work, they would have to put up with a crazy lady firing shots at random right up through the ceiling into their apartment.

So Zella was no stranger to armed conflict. She had gotten rid of the guns as she moved into her seventies, but she still was a force to be reckoned with when it came to using a knife. And she kept a special one just for that purpose stashed in a kitchen drawer. It was a massive, heavy knife. One of those thick wide chef type maulers that came with her Ginsu set. She never used it for anything else so that it would stay sharp enough to cut a can through in just a few seconds.

On the night in question the man clad only in his underwear was dazed and confused. Thinking that he had arrived at his girlfriend's apartment, which was a few doors down from Zella's, he began banging on the sliding glass door that separated her living room from the patio. Zella was quick to react, hiding behind the curtains with the butcher knife and waiting for the guy to make it in. Luckily one of the neighbors called the police and they arrived and took the man into custody. They took him away, but not before Zella was able to get in the man's face and say a few choice words. She told him in no uncertain terms just how much flesh that she was planning to cut off of his stinking body. The Merchant of Venice would have been proud, as it was certain to come out to be more than a pound for services rendered. One of the young policemen who responded to the call told Zella to drop the butcher knife that she was still holding. She refused saying that she wouldn't put it down until the man was well out of her sight. The policeman, getting a little bit riled that a seventy something year old woman with a butcher knife was telling him what to do. Ordered her to release the weapon. Zella started saying that she would use it on him if he didn't shut up and leave her alone. Luckily the cop's partner was able to sneak up behind her and grab the weapon, but he was unable to get away before Zella was able to catch him across the side of his face with a right hook. The other cop started to laugh at his partner's misfortune, and they decided to do what the old lady wanted, not arrest her and "get the hell out of there." They told her in passing to call them if she needed anything else and Zella told them: "Yeah right, you've been enough help already."

The other seniors in the apartment gathered around for weeks to hear Zella tell the story of how she fended off the crazy burglar and the police all in one fell swoop. In their eyes she had become a hero, doing what they all had only dreamed of doing. Each time they were alone late at night in their apartment and they heard a strange noise they would think of what Zella had done and knowing that she was just down the hall, rest a little easier.

There was only one thing in the entire world that would reduce Zella to a quivering jelly, shaking mass of fear and that was Canis Lupis or in other words, the common variety dog. It wasn't really known when Zella developed her unreasonable fear of this common household pet, but it must have been very early on in her childhood. She really didn't like to talk about it very much other than tell you that when she used to live in the old neighborhood, there was a boxer mongrel who used to lie in wait for her every morning. He would then literally chase her down to the bus stop where she waited to get the 7:45 into work at the factory every morning. The dog belonged to the Syrian mob that lived next door and he was raised to be mean and nasty. He had a secret place, a tear in the fabric of the fenced in yard where he would escape to chase Zella and then quietly return home. It might as well have been a rip in the very fabric of time as far as Zella was concerned. She complained to the neighbors, but seeing the dog sitting out in the back yard they refused to believe her, telling her with a smile on their faces that maybe she should cut down a little on the bourbon that she drank each night after work.

The daily ritual went on for months. Zella would open her front door and peer cautiously outside, looking for the beast. When she was certain that he was not around she gently closed the door so as not to wake him and crept slowly down the stairs. She usually would get about a block down the street before she turned around and saw him in hot pursuit. At least he was sporting enough to give her a head start. Zella would then run like her life depended on it with the boxer in hot pursuit. There was a little shop that stood on the corner right by the bus stop that was fenced in and Zella would crouch behind the fence while the dog stood outside growling and sometimes trying to bite through the fence to get at her. Sometimes he would make halfhearted attempts to jump over the fence, scaring Zella half to death when she thought that he might make it. When the bus finally arrived, it usually distracted the dog long enough for Zella to make her move. She would usually hit the dog with whatever she could get her hands on whether it be a stick or a brick and then make it onto the bus. The dog never tried to follow her onto the bus. He knew when the game was over and he would then meander the couple of blocks home before his masters woke up, scrounging the trashcans or a little piece of dog ass along the way.

Zella really didn't want to piss off the next-door Syrians with what they considered her fantasy complaints about their junkyard dog. They were the mob that pretty much controlled the city at the time, and being friends with them did carry certain advantages. A payoff here and a handout there and you could go about your business without the annoying intervention of the police department or the local government. She would have to take matters into her own hands, even if it was a little risky. She was desperately afraid of the animal and she was also hell bent on revenge. She didn't like the way that the dog looked at her with the "is that all you got?" look on his face when she hit him with the stick. And the incident that happened last week was the final straw as far as she was concerned. Her son Mark was playing out in the back yard when the boxer snuck through the fence and decided to try and have the boy for lunch. The red pepper that the Syrians had been feeding him to make his belly hurt and keep him mean was getting to be a bit to much and he needed a bland diet of boy flesh to sustain him for awhile. He waylaid the boy from behind and was just about to take a bite out of the tender flesh when Zella heard all of the commotion and Mark's screams. She had a pot of boiling potatoes simmering on the stove and threw the potatoes on the dog, scalding his back. The dog, who was almost as immune to pain as a Pit bull, stood up and took notice. He stared Zella right in the face and growled his revenge. He would extract that revenge come Monday at the bus stop. Zella knew that action had to be taken before then.

The neighborhood that Zella and Mark lived in was bounded by the Barst-Tebbie housing projects; nasty broken high rises that harbored every manner of petty criminals. They pretty much stayed out of the two-block area that was literally owned by the Syrians, but it was an uneasy truce. The hoodlums still had kids and the kids were hungry a lot. Even though this was the sixties and Zella talked a lot about what those damned "niggers" were up to on the television, marching on Washington and the lot, she always seemed to have Black friends from work hanging around the house. Her door was also always open to any of the kids that happened to pass by and notice the smells of home cooking wafting through the door, no matter what their race or color. All of this was a little confusing to Mark, who would hear his mom talking all of the racist shit and then come home from school and find the house full of people of "color." Zella's explanation was that there was a difference, these people happened to be friends of hers. After feeding the kids sometimes Zella would give them some spare change to run down to the corner store, or sweep out the yard. Sometimes the duty was to keep an eye on Mark so he wouldn't get into any trouble on the street. Mark wasn't told about this of course, and sometimes it would surprise him when he was about to get into a fight and a bunch of strange kids came out of nowhere and kicked his opponent's ass and then disappeared into the alleys.

Zella called an emergency meeting of her "posse" that afternoon and emptied the cookie jar of all of the money that she had saved up. She put a contract out on the dog, half of the money now and half when the damned beast was dead. Early the next morning the kids showed up at Zella's door while she was waiting to run down to the bus stop. They took her across the street and then into the alley that ran behind the Syrian's house. The boxer lay dead in the alley, covered with bricks. He had a surprised and painful look on his face, Zella looked down at him and smiled. She dug down into her purse, beneath the Wrigley's Spearmint gum and retrieved the roll of money that she had stashed there and paid off the gang. Two of the boys picked up the rotting carcass and threw it into the trash can. The next time the Syrians saw Zella they looked at her kind of funny, but nothing was ever said. Although they probably suspected that she was behind the death of the dog, they had to admire the way that she had it done. She was a woman after their own heart and they would allow her this transgression. After the dog wasn't a pet, he was a bodyguard, an enforcer, and he was expected to die a violent death. There was also a stash of puppies under the back porch that included the boxer's sons and daughters, growing fast and ready to take over in just a few weeks.

Mark was just about nodding off sitting in the chair in his mother's room. The only sounds he heard was the occasional clang of a bed pan and the whir of the oxygen machine sucking oxygen right out of the air that sat next to the bed. The nurse who had been by earlier had told Mark that this was a new generation of machine that replaced the old iron bottles that they had used before. This thing actually was able to directly take the critical component right out of the room air. No more need to buy the stuff under pressure, even though the machine was big and bulky and cost a pretty penny right off of the bat. Mark opened his eyes fully and was startled by the bright fluorescent light that ran across the wall atop of the bed. For a moment he had forgotten where he was and felt a small connection with what his mother was going through, not knowing where she was most of the time, or even which day of the week it was. He walked over to the bed and smoothed oiut the sheets that swaddled around the frail woman in the bed. He thought that he would try to wake her up in a few minutes nad try to get her to eat something. The home had suggested that he allow them to insert a feeding tube, because she would eat very little. Mark had decided early on that he wouldn't allow it. During a brief period of lucidity Zella had remarked how nasty the food was here and had forced Mark to taste a bit of it. She was right. He understood why she didn't want to eat it. Why anyone would was a puzzle to him. He gently shook his mother's shoulder, but she refused to wake up. She mumbled something that Mark couldn't understand. At times she would lift her arm and groan and Mark would hold her hand. Sometimes she would come around for a few minutes and other times she would be out of it all day.

Just then Mark heard some commotion in the hall along with a few of the seniors saying something like "nice boy." Mark wondered what the hell was going on. Just as he was about to leave the room to find out, a middle aged butch looking lady came marching into the room with a German Shepherd dog that was the size of Stockholm. The dog put his paws up on the bed just as Zella was waking up. She was staring at the animal, her eyes open so wide that Mark though for a moment that they would bleed or pop out of her head. Her mouth was frozen into an O shape, like a scream was trying to come out but got frozen in her throat. The butch-looking lady was trying to explain that she was from an organization who brought pets around to the nursing homes and hospitals to visit with the elderly. It helped reduce stress and lower their blood pressures. Mark tried to explain that with Zella's morbid fear of dogs, this wasn't going to help her blood pressure very much. Zella had her right arm lifted up and outward over the bed railing and she was moving it towards the dog like she was trying to pet it. Her hand moved along the top of the dog's head and down across his right ear. But when she got her hand just below the dog's muzzle, the hand looked like it had taken on a life of its own. It clamped down on the dog's windpipe with a grip that made the huge animal whimper. Zella had what amounted to a death grip on the animal's throat. It took a few minutes for Mark and the dog lady to realize what was going on and help get the animal out of Zella's grip. Mark told the woman that his mother doesn't like dogs and was, as a matter of fact deathly afraid of them. The woman gave the standard reply that this was a specially trained animal that would harm a flea, but Mark told her that it was his mother and not the dog that was the problem here. The woman sniffed a little of the room's recycled air up her nose and walked out of the room to "visit" with the next room. When Mark went back over to his mother's bed, it looked like she was having a seizure: her eyes were still wide open and she was convulsing. Mark just watched, knowing that there was nothing that he could do. After a few moments, Zella stopped moving and Mark went over to the bed. He noticed that her chest was moving up and down. At least she was still alive. Her right arm, the strong one that had very nearly choked the dog, came up and she gripped Mark's hand, her signal to him that she was all right. He gently put her hand back down to her side, turned out the bright light over the bed and went down the hall to the vending machine to get a cup of coffee.

The coffee vending machine was in the employee's lounge. When Mark entered the small cluttered room it was empty except for two overweight women, one Hispanic, the other African American. One was chewing on what appeared to be a stale sandwich while the other one had her head down on the table, apparently taking a nap. She raised her head when Mark entered the room and they both looked at him as if he didn't belong there. There was an air conditioner in the window, angled so it looked like any water from it might leak back into the room. The air in the room was a mixture of food smells from the microwave, stale coffee and dried disinfectant. Mark fumbled with the change and finally got it into the machine. He pressed the button that had the picture of the coffee with cream on it but instead he got black. Oh well. The two employees got up and left, so Mark decided to sit down for a minute and finish the coffee before he went back into his mother's room. The cup only held about a thimble full and the paper cup was so hot that it burned his fingers. He noticed that there was music playing over the tin speaker that was mounted Muzak-like in the dirty tile ceiling. It was playing an old Rod Stewart song, Maggie May. Mark listened to the mandolin riff about halfway through the song and remembered the night that he and his girlfriend at the time, Kay had taken Zella to see her first rock concert.

The United Universal Amphitheater was a medium to large sized venue that sat in an open area near a major river and a gambling casino. It held about twenty thousand people and had a large area that was grass seating where people could sit on their blankets and scratch mosquito bites or even bring along a folding lawn chair as long as they promised not to throw them at the stage. Mark had been a Rod Stewart fan since the early seventies when he heard his brother singing "Tonight's the Night" at the corner bar during sing along night. He had just gotten his first apartment and his first real stereo that was capable of shaking the walls late at night. He was in the midst of buying every album that he could find and putting them on his first credit card. He bought all of the other Rod Stewart albums that were out at the time, despite the admonishments from his friends that the singer's voice sounded the way that it did because...well you know the story. After that he moved on and bought up all the Who and the Rolling Stones work that he could find, softened a little by various collections of Van Morrison and Jimmy Buffet. Zella lived downstairs at the time, moving in with a lady named "Big Barb" and talking Mark into taking their old apartment so she could keep an eye on him. Mark took the first Rod album that he had bought downstairs to let his mom listen to it. She played the thing on an old record player with two tiny speakers that she had gotten as a gift for agreeing to purchase just twelve more records the upcoming year from the club that she was joining. The first words out of Zella's mouth when she heard the raspy-throated singer was "quick, somebody get that guy a cough drop." But over the next few years she caught a glimpse of the rock star on one of the talk shows and kind of fell in love with him, saying that he was the most "good looking ugly guy" that she had seen. Zella was now in her early seventies and had just finished getting both of her knees replaced because of arthritis. It was announced that Rod was coming to town and Mark asked her if she wanted to go. She told him that she had never been to a concert before, especially one of this magnitude, but she was willing to go if he was. Mark went down and stood in line several hours the next Saturday to get the tickets. He scored some pretty good ones, center stage in the seated area about sixteen rows back from the stage.

The night of the big concert slid in well oiled. There were stars in the sky and a gentle breeze blew over Fifth Avenue. Mark sat in the car with his Mom and the girlfriend that he had at the time, Zinnia. He stared at the long line of cars that were ahead of them and watched the taillights blink on and off. The prisms in the plastic reminded him of bee's eyes. Compounded and glazed, as were his own. Mark was a nervous wreck. He had visions of his mother keeling over onto her artificial knees about halfway on the long journey that they would have to make from the crowded parking lot of the ampitheatre to their seats. If she made it that far, her fragile heart would probably give out when Rod was about halfway through Maggie May. He had smoked a little, a couple of hits, before they set out for the concert and now he wished that he hadn't. The stuff was just making matters worse, making him more paranoid than he already was, and that was a lot. They had allowed plenty of time to get the ageing Zella to the concert, since she still had problems with climbing stairs and he had no idea how many they would have to transverse when they finally made it there. After what seemed like an eternity, they finally found a place to park, pretty close up actually, in the handicapped area. It was a good thing that, even though she didn't drive, Zella had went to the driver's license bureau and had procured one of those blue handicapped parking signs that you hung from the rear view mirror. It was hard for the old gal to walk on the gravel that made up part of the parking lot, but she seemed to be on better footing when they got out of the solid asphalt. At the outer gate one of the attendants told them that the concert was wheelchair accessible and even offered to try to find one for them. Zella then became very adamant that, "Damn it, he had walked this far and had every intention to make it the rest of the way." They stopped to rest and bought beer at the concession stand about halfway to the seats. Zella was animated and talking to a lot of the people that were strolling about, getting high and ready for the concert. Mark nervously chugged his beer and then went back and waited in line for another one. They were six bucks apiece and when Zella found that out, she refused a second one. There was a time when she could have out drank almost anybody there, but in that area she was well past her prime. This was really the first drink that she had taken in many years, citing the reason that it gave her such a pain in the side that it was no longer worth it.

Most of the people that had come to see the concert were couples in their thirties to early forties. Most of the men didn't like Rod, but went at the urging of wives and girlfriends who thought that the aging rock star was still pretty hot. And the guys didn't mind that the women would sometimes get so turned on that they would jump their bones practically before they got off of the parking lot.

Zella was busy saying hello to everyone and telling them that this was the first rock concert that she had ever been to. No Mark was feeling a little self-conscious that he had brought his mother to a rock concert and was worried what the other people there might think. The support however for his mom's first time experience seemed overwhelming, everyone there congratulating her and telling her that they hoped she enjoyed the show. They finally made it to the area where their assigned seats were and one of the ushers helped Zella into her seat. She propped her three-legged metal cane on the seat next to her, but moved it onto the floor when a couple sat down there. The show started about forty-five minutes late and this gave Zella plenty of time to get aquatinted with the people next to her. Mark had never seen her so outgoing and talkative, and merely nodded his head when she introduced their neighbors to him.

The show started with a bang and Rod launched right into "Maggie May" and most of the twenty thousand people were up on their feet in no time. Mark halfway expected to look over to see his mother passed out from the loudness of the sound or at least have her ears covered with her hands. Instead he saw that she was up and dancing in the aisle wit the next seat couple, seemingly having the time of her life. Mark's girlfriend was dancing on the right side of him, so he decided "what the hell" and he nudged his mom and started dancing too. This type of behavior lasted pretty much the rest of the concert and Mark was a lot more tired than Zella was by the time they had made it back to the handicapped parking area. After they got back to Zella's apartment and Mark had walked her to her door, she threw her arms around him and tanked him for letting her have one of the greatest times of her life. As Mark walked back to the car, he was fighting back the tears. His girlfriend asked him if his Mom had enjoyed the concert. "Yes." He replied. "And she certainly deserved it. "

Chapter 15

Mark looked down at his Mom. Her right arm was twisted at an unnatural angle underneath her body. The oxygen machine whirred and whined, still sucking the air out of the room, leaving an acrid and sour smell. He looked down at the urine bag that was fixed to the bottom of the bed's guardrail. It was filled with blood that had an orange tinge to it. His Mom's eyes were closed but tight and tense. She was wrapped in a drug-induced sleep and from the grimace on her face he could tell that she was not having pleasant dreams. She stirred a little and then opened her eyes and stared at him like he was a tall cool glass of water and she was dying of thirst. A tiny spark of recognition flashed across her face. She managed to moisten her lips enough to form the word hello, but it took awhile to come out. Mark got the small plastic cup with the straw and the thickened water and held it in front of her. She took a small sip and twisted her face into a frown, the one side that was paralyzed refusing to go along with the other side. "Would you rather have a Pepsi?" Mark asked. He knew what her response would be. It was one of the few small pleasures that she was able to still enjoy. For years while she had been working in the factory her breakfast had consisted of a cold Pepsi, an aspirin and a cigarette. She had never drunk coffee, saying that she loved the smell of it but couldn't stand the taste. She shook her head yes and managed half of a smile. Mark went down the hall, past the nurses station and put a crumpled dollar that he had stashed in his pocket into the machine. He had to re-insert the thing several times before the machine finally gave up its prize. As he walked back to her room with the can of soda, once again he had to dodge the residents that were strewn about in the hallway, some ignoring him and others reaching out to try to touch something that was alive.

Back in the room his Mother had fallen asleep again and he felt sorry that he had to wake her. He cracked open the drink and poured a little into the plastic cup that had held the water. Then he mixed in some of the gooey powder, the cornstarch that would make it the consistency of thick nectar. That way the stuff would slide down her throat more easily and not choke her. He went over and rubbed her right arm briskly, right above the elbow. This seemed to wake her up. He positioned the straw in front of her mouth and she sucked at it greedily. Several times he had to withdraw the straw and tell her to slow down a little. He imagined that years ago she had to do the same thing for him when he was a baby, and now the situation was reversed. She was able to finish most of the liquid, but then put her hand on her stomach to indicate that she was full. Mark asked her if she wanted a little of the soup broth and Jello that he had brought in for her. She waved her hand in the air: no. Just then the nurse came into the room and told Mark that the director of nursing at the home wanted to speak to him about his Mother. He walked out of the room and followed her down the hall to a brightly lit office that sat in the corner. Inside was an older lady wearing too much lipstick. It seemed to be smeared upwards toward her nose, possibly to cover the wrinkles there or maybe she had just received a sloppy kiss from one of the orderlies. She motioned him to sit down on one of the swivel chairs that were lined up against the wall. She told him that his Mother was still not eating enough, only taking a few bites and then spitting out the rest, telling them in her limited way that the food sucked. "She is still losing weight, as I understand that she has been doing for some time." She said. "If we don't insert a feeding tube now…within the next couple of days, then she will surely starve to death." Her face was solemn as she put the emphasis on "starve" and "death." Mark looked at her and blinked his eyes. He told her that he would have to think about it for a couple of days and then give her his decision. She told him that was Ok but time was a critical factor in his decision and he should let her know as soon as possible.

Mark went home that night and got on the computer. He looked up everything that he could find on "intubation" as they called it. There were two options: one was to cut a hole in his Mother's stomach and put the plastic tube in through which they would pour the gruel that would feed her and keep her from starving. The other option was to stick the plastic tube down her throat and directly into her stomach, neither one of them seemed very pleasant. Although most of the medical community and the nursing homes were for the intubations, there were a couple of interesting web sites that argued against it. It was an "end of life decision" they argued and it carried with it a large risk of complications and a lot of restricted mobility, as most of the patients would try to pull the damn tube out of either their stomachs or their noses. It was better to let them starve to death, which might sound cruel, but it really was a natural way for the body to shut down when it got old. a sort of weaning off of life process so to speak.

Mark returned to the nursing home the next day and told them that he would not allow them to put in a feeding tube. They seemed to be a little upset, the nurse at the floor station more so than the director, because she would be the one that would have to try to shove food down Zella's mouth. Mark offered a different solution. He was a pretty good cook and knew what his Mom liked to eat, so he would fix the meals at home, with lots of seasoning and bring them in to her, every day if need be.

Over the next couple of weeks, Mark was a fixture at the nursing home. He bought an ice cream maker and made fresh ice cream for Zella. He cooked pasta and loaded it up with lots of garlic and fried chicken. He went out and bought White Castle hamburgers; anything at all to get his Mother to eat. And eat she did. Not very much, most of the time it was just a few spoonfuls of each of the items that he brought, but at least she was packing in three meals a day even if they weren't square. Mark liked the time that he spent feeding and interacting with his Mom even though at first, he thought that he would dread it.

On a number of occasions Zella had a deep, dark and mysterious visitor that came to visit her in the middle of the night. He entered the room like a suffocating cloud, a dark mist that would leave her gasping for air. Each time she looked into his cold and bitter face, up came the strong arm and she pushed him away. She had become familiar with him and at times even called him by name. He wouldn't let her up out of bed, but that was ok, she took her small pleasures anyway that she could get them. The smile on her son's face, a breath of fresh air coming through the window, a ray of sun swirling up dust bunnies on the furniture, and her wishing that she could get out the rag and dust it. She knew how to pull up the inner strength that she still had, even after the stroke and survive. Survive like she had always done for her almost eighty years on the planet.

It was a Saturday that Mark last came to see her. After a slow start, he thought that she was remarkably alert. She had even begun to talk a little where you could understand her with the help of the speech therapist. Mark fed her the favorite lunch of pasta followed by vanilla ice cream. She had become an ice cream hound, eating up the main course almost too fast to get to the desert. She asked Mark if he was doing all right and if he needed anything. Even in the state that she was in she was always worried about her son. Mark told her that everything was fine and left early to enjoy the rest of the day.

About ten the nest morning Mark got a call from the hospital. He had better get out there to see his mother because she was fading fast. Mark was a little annoyed; he had received this kind of phone call before. A number of times the hospital and the nursing home had called saying that Zella's blood pressure and oxygen rate was dangerously low. But then by the time he got to the emergency room they always had her stable and she was usually awake and talking. Sometimes Mark thought that she pulled that sort of thing just so she could have visitors. Mark asked the nurse on the other end of the line what the problem was this time. After all he had just spoken to the doctor about his Mom a couple of days ago and all things considered, everything seemed to be going fine. The nurse replied that Zella's white blood cell count had suddenly shot way up and that she was going into septic shock. Mark knew that she had a urinary tract infection and the blood in her urine, but he had no idea that it was so serious. Infections like that were routine nowadays and could be easily taken care of with antibiotics. There was so many other things that could have done her in. The words "septic shock" however made Mark's heart leap up into his throat and then fall down into the pit of his stomach. He knew that not many people, even healthy ones survived that condition. He jumped into his car and drove the fifteen minutes to the hospital.

When he got there he noticed that the door to his mother's room was closed. Not a good sign. A nurse motioned him to go into the room, a stern, sad look on her face. A priest stood by the side of the bed, reading the Lord's Prayer. It was too late. Zella lay there twisted in the bed, her neck arched to one side, trying to take one last desperate breath that never made it to her lungs. Mark noticed that her right hand, the one that had possessed so much strength in her life, was frozen it what appeared to be one last attempt to grip something; one last attempt to tell Mark that she was ok. Mark remembers looking down at her body. There was nothing left there but a dried husk. She looked like a rat caught in a trap. Mark felt guilty for feeling such a thing. The priest reached out his hand and put his arm around Mark. Mark bowed his head for a moment and then left the room. When he got into his car and turned on the engine, the words came from him out of the radio....*"her face at first was ghostly, turned a whiter shade of pale."*

Part 111

The Final Destiny

Chapter 16

Cloud no longer had any idea of where he was or who he was. He could see, if that is what you want to call it, only light and dark. He felt scattered, broken up into the million bits and pieces that he once was. The light of the human spirit was just a tiny point that was soon extinguished. The only true thing that existed was the Void. The Universe that he had called his home and all the other countless Universes didn't fare much better. They were just larger flashes in the pan. To try to explain anything in human terms was to alter and ultimately lose its meaning. The Universe was just a bitch and a whore, constantly in labor, giving birth, and God was the impregnator. Then there is the universe that we create in our minds, the egocentric one that thinks that the tiny little microvolts coursing through the soon to be rotting flesh that is our brains amounts to anything. Things started going to hell when Adam bit into the apple and Eve did the dirty with the snake. The ancient knowledge was packed away in a suitcase and shipped off to Detroit, first class UPS. Then Darwin came along and even though it wasn't his idea, showed that it wasn't from dust to dust, but rather from slime to slime. The second law of thermodynamics slammed the last nail into the coffin. (Nail it tight to keep the motherfucker from getting out.) The whole universe has an addictive tendency towards chaos. Black holes sprout like cancer throughout eternity and kill the stars. Even eternity it turns out doesn't last forever. Humpty Dumpty sat on the wall, was shot with the destructor beam and disintegrated into a trillion electron particles, what a shame. Heaven and Hell are simply states of mind, but the mind is without boundaries. The point is that there is no point, don't try to make one out of nothing, just go with the flow.

What comes around goes around and we are no different from the countless numbers of universes that have been here before. Don't think that we are anything special. Cloud is back lying on his cardboard bed in the cold abandoned warehouse. It is like he never left. How many lives lived and lessons learned to come back to this? How many more to go before you're back in the Void?

Down the street from the warehouse sits another warehouse of sorts. A large gray building that used to stock hats and gloves, but now serves as a warehouse for the homeless. The Right Reverend Harold Cake and a small beady-eyed man with a pencil moustache named Brice run the place. The two started out nearly thirty years ago with a tiny little soup kitchen on the other, but equally bad side of town. It was called the Rottwell Evangelistic Center. The Rev. Harold was somewhat of a radical back in those days, telling his small flock of followers to get up off of their couches and do something to help the poor and the homeless while they worshipped Jesus.

Reverend Cake is known about town for being able to stretch a buck. This not only applies to his quest for feeding the homeless but in his personal life as well. He was always proud of telling everyone that his bank account only held about thirty dollars at any given time and that he had worn the same threadbare blue suit for about the sum of twenty years. Even that he got at Goodwill for the grand sum of about fifteen dollars. All this at the time when a lot of the other television evangelical types were living in Mansions in Bel Air and driving around in fancy cars: Cadillac's and Mercedes Benz. Reverend Cake ran a small broadcast station out of the front room of his house. This was to save up room at the homeless shelter. He was very particular about what other uses the shelter was put to other than to house and feed the homeless people that wandered in off of the streets. After all he was on a mission; a mission from God himself. And he was sure that he had heard Him correctly. It wasn't like go ahead and get yourself rich and live the life, but rather like Jesus said and the quote that the Reverend was most fond of: "What you do to the least of you, you do to me."

Early in the morning Reverend Cake would show up to greet the trucks that delivered the coffee and day old donuts to the shelter. There would be several tables that held the aluminum foil lined cardboard boxes. The Reverend would then walk along beside the donuts, blessing and counting every one. Then he would pry the lids off of the coffee pots and peer inside. God help you if you were a volunteer and he caught you pilfering one of the donuts or a stray cup of coffee. He told all of the volunteers that there was a Seven Eleven right down the street and you were welcome to take a break and go down there and get you some refreshment. The stuff that he was able to beg from the locals was for the homeless and just for the homeless.

Over the years the Reverend was involved in his share of controversy. As a matter of fact a lot of the folks in this rather large midwestern town considered him a Liberal. There was one point that he even started talking about things like waste disposal and saving the environment in addition to people's souls and the unborn babies. This caused a little bit of a gasp in his constituency who could rightly well tolerate him cooking up rabbits at Easter to feed the homeless and burning effigies of Santa Claus at Christmas time. After all, Jesus was the reason for the season; it wasn't about Jolly old fat guys and small furry creatures that bred like crazy. But this little bend to the left was viewed as maybe the Reverend was losing it, but most of the flock didn't seem to stray.

On Sunday mornings the Reverend left the preaching at the church to his partner, Brice. Brice sort of looked like the Vietnam veteran who spoke through the voice box on the television series South Park. At times he sounded a little like him also. He was a former homeless person whom the Reverend had rescued from the brink of despair. Turned around from the evils of drugs and alcoholism for the very noble purpose of showing others the way to the light. When the Reverend wasn't around, Brice liked to show that he was in charge and some of the volunteers thought that he was sort of an overbearing henchman. The Reverend, on the other hand, was tall and outgoing, friendly and pervasive in a country sort of way, a purveyor of the Word in a thin blue suit that seemed to getting thinner as the years passed away.

The Reverend was giving his Sunday sermon in his television "studio." The studio was located in the back of a warehouse. There was a makeshift stage made of unfinished plywood with some plastic flowers scattered behind it. The pulpit was starting to peel away some of its laminate in the more well worn places and the solitary microphone was getting a few bare wires here and there. The station was run by a 50,000-watt faulty tower that would give up the ghost and rise to heaven at the slightest suggestion of a thunderstorm. On many occasions the Reverend prayed off the storm clouds, asking the Lord to just hold them back long enough to get the broadcast in. On this Sunday the Reverend had some special musical guests, a country gospel team of Slim and Zella Mae Fox. Well they weren't really anything special as they appeared on the program most every Sunday that they could pump enough oil into the 1972 cargo van they owned and make the trip from the town of Mondosi that was about 150 miles one way from the city. Slim was of course big and fat and he combed his oily, thinning white hair straight back over his forehead. Zella Mae on the other hand was the opposite to his Jack Sprat and was thin as a wire with a beehive hairdo that at times was known to go from dripping honey to squirting out vinegar. The Reverend had an old upright piano that Slim would bang out the tunes on even though there were a couple of keys that weren't working. He played the thing so loud and so fast that no one noticed anyway. Most of the audience was either drunk or stoned from being on the streets that night before so it really was like preaching to the choir. Zella Mae really sang just about as well as Slim pounded on the piano, loud and off key, but at the end of every performance, the audience stood up and clapped and cheered anyway. In the summertime a lot of them did that to get a little of the air circulating because the studio wasn't air-conditioned and in the winter it was to generate some body heat. Slim had a small forehead and wore a pair of thick glasses that sometimes slid down his nose when the sweat started flying and the room started spinning around.

After the concert was over the two stood outside the building and handed out cards that gave directions to their used furniture store where the homeless could get some inexpensive furniture if they ever got beyond the point of being homeless.

The Reverend was getting more and more Righteous the longer he got in the tooth. For the past couple of years he had been busy fighting city hall trying to get an empty federal building that was right up the street from his warehouse. The founding fathers of the city, however, were dead set against it. They wanted to tear down the building and replace it with a parking garage. They had intentions, along with a local developer, to refurbish and old movie theatre that was within walking distance of the federal building. They would then run second run art movies there and concerts from washed up rock acts that couldn't fill the larger venues. The Reverend wanted to expand his homeless shelter into the building. By law he had every right to purchase the building, but he was eventually denied because the city sent building inspectors to the warehouse and pointed out numerous building and fire code violations nad gave the Reverend a limited amount of time to repair them. Alas all of the money that he had set aside to purchase the building had to go to repair the old one. About all he could do about the situation was to get on the television and rant into the faulty microphone.

The other pet peeve that was making the back of the Reverend's neck get all sweaty and gritty was Nora Robinson. Nora was the small town pastor of a church located just a stone's throw from the little town where the Reverend spent his childhood. She was now the small town preacher who had made it big. While the Reverend pumped away at his tiny 50,000 watt station, Nora had made it national by focusing on the business side of Christianity. And it was a huge billion-dollar business to supply all the music, churches, T-shirts, books and all the other stuff that was needed to quench the thirst that people had for Jesus. There was even a debate at one point on which international preacher He would choose to air his return to Earth. The smart money was on Billy, after all he was the preacher to the presidents, but he was getting kind of old and frail and might see Jesus before He came to see him. Nora however was in the prime fit of her health and only 45 years old, Her kingdom here on Earth might just last for a considerable amount of time.

There was a shiny new black Mercedes sitting in the driveway of her 1.2 million dollar home in the rich old part of the suburbs inhabited by dysfunctional beer barons and novo rich stockbrokers who had made it rich during the internet boom. She didn't have her own TV station yet but that would change soon. In the meantime she paid the Reverend about $100,000 a year to carry her program. In a couple of months she would drop the sleazy little worm and reach millions of fans who were willing to send her twenty bucks for her "get rich" prayer.

The Reverend on the other hand happened to watch one of her broadcasts and took offense to her mention that the truly poor and homeless got that way because it was their own fault. God's monetary blessing were out there and rather than spending the money for material things like food, etc. they should send a little bit of it to her to get truly blessed. After all most of them were on welfare anyway and used all the surplus cash to buy liquor and drugs and engage in elicit sex. Nora was a little kinky on that end too, she enjoyed putting leather on her husband Pete and strafing his back with a cat o' nine tails until just the slightest trickle of blood came to the surface. She also liked to watch videos of the extreme Christians down in South America who crucify themselves ever year around Easter to atone for their sins. Some of them walk for miles on their knees until they are scraped into a bloody pulp and then use their own cat o' nine tails to whip their backs. The only difference is they embellish the whips with small pieces of broken glass to really get the religious juices flowing. People watching along the way hope to catch a few drops of this blood that is shed for Christ and wash their faces in it; a kind of reversal of roles so to speak.

After the Reverend found out about Nora's tirade against the homeless, people who were the least and therefore elevated to the most, he was summarily outraged. He called the office of Nora's ministry and told them that she was kicked off of the air. Then he went on his television station and told everybody the truth. He was certain that the loss of revenue and the loss of some members of her viewing audience would probably take a bite out of him financially, but he didn't care. He was steadfast in his beliefs and he was also on a mission from God. God told him in a dream to be as much like Jesus as he humanly could. There were no promises as to what would happen if he obeyed God's word, but he was certain that it was the right thing to do.

Nora on the other hand was outraged to hear that the Reverend has dropped her like the hot Christ potato that she was. That night she strapped the leather onto her husband twice as tight and whipped him twice as hard.

The old hand painted bus that the Reverend used to scour the streets and underpasses for the homeless was about on its last cylinder. It was a resurrected school bus that was painted about as many colors as Joseph's coat in the Bible. As a matter of fact that was what the members of the congregation affectionately referred it to. "Bus of Many Colors" was even hand painted on the side of the bus. It burned oil like crazy and the only thing that was keeping it from automotive heaven was numerous cans of STP Oil Treatment. As a matter of fact that was about the only thing that was left in the crankcase. The thing also had worn out front end joints and the steering was so loose that the driver had to keep moving the steering wheel from side to side just to keep it from running off of the road. The brakes weren't so hot either, as the engine was in the back of the bus and even the slightest amount of pressure on the brake pedal would cause it to lock up and go into a spin. But even without hazard pay and a few precarious near misses, there was never a shortage of volunteers to drive the thing, including sometimes the Reverend himself.

On this particular April night the weather was unseasonably cold. There was a slight mist in the air that would make the bus even harder to navigate. Roy Smithers, the volunteer and long time member of the Reverend's "Homeless Posse" was down with the flu and called in sick. Several frantic phone calls failed to produce any more volunteers on such short notice, though the Reverend was able to get two of the homeless residents to join him. Both of the men had been staying at the shelter for several months and helping out wherever needed, mostly preparing food in the kitchen.

One of the two men was named Matt and was the younger of the two. Just talking to him you could tell that he "wasn't quite right in the head." Anyway that seemed to be the way that most people referred to him. Nobody went as far as to say that he was retarded or mentally challenged, there was just something that wasn't quite right about him. If pressed, nobody could quite come up with what that "something" was, it just wasn't right, or maybe it just wasn't there. Matt was short and a little stocky and he speech was ok, but really slow, not slow in the sense that he spoke slowly, just slow in the sense that he had to think about what he was about to say for a really long time before he said it. He was also bald in spots and this caused him to shave his head to the extent that a lot of people thought that he was a Buddhist, that was until he started talking. He had small facial features and a turned up nose that made him look like a bald dog. It really wasn't surprising that Matt had turned out the way he did, his parents were children of the sixties who never grew up and had used a lot of drugs on the night that he was conceived. The sperm that his father released that night were really stoned and a lot of them had just swam in a circle, really not in the mood to fertilize an egg at that particular time. One of them however had ingested too much speed and broke free from the rest of the herd and went for it. He enjoyed a brief moment of rest and repose with the egg right before he died. But the DNA diamond ring that he gave her was flawed and the result was Matt.

The other of the two volunteers that night was a lot older and had a lot more bones to pick clean with society. His name was Bill and he was really a three-time loser, only you had to multiply that by three to get to the correct number. Tall and lanky with along beard adorning his face that he refused to shave off, not for the prison guards and not for Jesus. The Reverend had suggested that he tidy himself up a little so as not to offend the homeless that they were going in search for and Bill just looked at him and laughed in his face. He told the Reverend that he was a homeless person too, and that was how most of them looked. The Reverend, who had seen his share, agreed and then confessed that it wasn't the homeless that he was worried about, it was more like the news media who sometimes followed them around looking for a laugh when there weren't more important news stories to cover. Bill told the Reverend that he, of all people shouldn't be worried about who he was hanging around with and the Reverend also agreed with that. Bill was dirty and smelly and still used alcohol and crank when he could get it. The combination of the two made him even more mean and nasty than he usually was. He didn't care for his partner Matt but was able to easily manipulate the younger man into doing what he wanted him to do.

Bill was a pretty good mechanic when he was sober and was able to get the old bus rolling with a couple of toothpicks, a rubber band and a string. On the night in question, Bill had a bottle of rock gut whiskey hidden on the bus and a pocket full of speed lining his greasy overalls.

The two men helped the Reverend load a couple of boxes of the care kits onto the bus that he gave out to the homeless that he passed on the street. The care packages held a toothbrush, some toothpaste, a comb, some shampoo and a miniature version of the Bible.

The left wheel of the shopping cart had become loose over the years. It was getting harder and harder for Myrtle to push the damn thing around. It was probably time for her to steal a new one, an updated version with all of the modern advantages. Plastic. The newer ones were made of plastic. red and gray plastic. They were a lot lighter and easier to push than the old metal ones, the one like the one that she pushed around every day. The one that held all that was important and precious to her. Myrtle was forty-five years old and getting a little wrinkly and heavy. She had been living on the street for a long time. She used to sell what was between her legs and push a needle filled with everything from heroin to Drano into the veins in her arm, but that was a long time ago. Nowadays she had regressed back to a hunter and gatherer. Mostly gatherer. She was a collector of things. Things that she put in her cart and prized as her precious. Food was on that list and it was pretty far up, but it had declined somewhat in the last few years in importance. She had gotten a little heavy from a society-imposed diet of left over pizza scraps and fast food. It was amazing what variety you could get living out of a dumpster. She did that most days for all of her meals. Except for the holidays. They were the special times when she got depressed and remembered the family that she once had. On those occasions she went to the inner city mission and listened to the sermon by the Reverend so she could get a hot meal of turkey with all of the fixings. The rest of the time though, she shunned the speeches, they made her feel uncomfortable. She liked to think of her self as the las6t of the independents, not having to rely on anybody to survive in the cruel world. It was getting harder and harder though for two reasons: one was that the code of the street was breaking down. There was a time when the gentlemen of the street deferred to the ladies, offering up some of the food and cheap wine to them when the times got tough. Now it was different, it was literally dog-eat-dog, and sometimes if you found one that had died and was fresh enough, that was what you had to do. The other thing that was getting worse in Myrtle's life was the way that she viewed reality. Of course reality was an illusion anyway, but there were outside influences that were slowly creeping into even her jaded view. It was starting to interfere with the way that she conducted her day to day, the way that she didn't brush her teeth and comb her hair. In a word she was starting to see things that some people would say weren't there. At first they were just little annoyances, little specks in the corner of her eye. But then they started hogging more and more of her field of vision and the worst part was when they started talking to her and telling her what she should do. They hadn't become demanding enough yet to influence her decisions, but she was afraid that they might in the near future.

Myrtle had the rusty old shopping cart with the broken wheel filled with everything that she held near and dear to her. A lot of the space was filled with old newspapers. She picked them up from park benches and soaked with soda sitting in waste cans. She hardly ever read them anymore because they were filled with conspiracies and plots against her. It was all THEIR doing, but if you pressed her about it, she could never really say who THEY were, but she did have her theories. Newspapers came in handy though; they were excellent sources of insulation, working just as well as blankets in the wintertime and fans in the summer. She would sleep in the park in the summer, with the birds chirping in the trees and the muggers just a shout away. Most of the time they left her alone unless she bothered talking to them, as they knew she didn't have anything and what she did have, stank. In the winter she would usually tough it out in an abandoned building or roll some drunk off of his steam grate. When it got really bad and really cold, she would swallow the word of the Lord and sleep at one of the shelters. She often wished that the government would acknowledge the presence of the homeless and take the whole issue out of the hands of the Church. She considered them the worst, more evil than Satan himself. They held things like food and warm blankets out in front of their noses like carrots. They were free money wise, but they came at a much greater cost: you had to promise them your soul. They wanted to "save" it, package it up in a Sunday suit and ship it off to the Promised Land of the Third Baptist Tabernacle.

Fate has an ugly head; there is no doubt about it. Sometimes it wears makeup: eyes heavy with greasy liner and bright red lips dripping with blood. But make no mistake about it, it has snakes for hair and a pustule in place of a nose. Myrtle was making her way down Tenth Street, pushing her wobbly cart in front of her. She had earlier misplaced her trousers and had wrapped the all-important newspaper around her lower torso to avoid the draft. If you looked real close you could see that she had a mostly used roll of toilet paper wedged tightly between her butt cheeks. It served a dual purpose: she never wiped and it slowly absorbed the brown liquid that came out and it also prevented anything from going in. It seemed that someone was always trying to put something in the openings in her body that were designed to let things that were nasty go out, but that was another story altogether.

On the particular night in question, things were happening pretty fast and Fate was laughing with delight, but Satan had nothing to do with it, as his lawyers would later attest to at the hearing, where He was found to be innocent.

Myrtle looked up to see the old church bus screeching down the street like an airplane headed for an important government building, the Reverend fighting the two men at the wheel for control. The brakes were locked and there were sparks coming from the front wheels. The van tipped from side to side before crashing into the Mercedes that was coming from the other direction. Nora was driving the Mercedes and had a momentary lapse of awareness as she was trying to talk on the cell phone and check the satellite navigation system at the same time. It seems that she had made a wrong turn off of the highway on her way to an important business meeting and had ended up in a very unsavory part of town.

The Mercedes exploded on impact, frying Nora in the process. The two men who were fighting the Reverend aboard the bus were thrown clear of the bus, both of them landing in the grass and getting up and staggering off into the night. The Reverend however, was not quite so fortunate. He was trapped in the bus, both of his legs shattered into little pieces, and bled to death before the ambulance could arrive. The flaming carnage ended up just a few feet from Myrtle and her shopping cart. She held a piece of newspaper up in front of her face to protect her from the heat, but it burst into flames. She made her way to the emergency door at the rear of the bus and took the bags of toothbrushes and the Bibles and loaded them up into her cart. There were also several grocery bags of ham sandwiches that she was able to gather up before the bus started burning. They were nice and toasty. All in all it had been a pretty productive night for Myrtle, she had enough food to last for about a week and she didn't have to listen to the Reverend go on and on about hellfire and salvation to get it. She adjusted her toilet paper roll and moved slowly down the street. Things were a little bit different for the Reverend and Nora. They both ended up frozen in time, both experiencing the burning hell that they both had preached about for so long. Nora's last thoughts about the money that she would never be able to spend and the new house that she would never see built, and the Reverend about all the poor people that wouldn't be fed. Not by him at least. So it looks like that in the end, good intentions don't really matter after all. Just being in the right or wrong place at the right or wrong time…and survival, but nobody does that for very long.

Chapter 17

Cloud woke up from a sound sleep feeling lightheaded and physically lighter. He rolled over in the bed and tasted hair, long black hair. He reached up and pushed the hair back out of his face and noticed that it came almost down to his shoulders. It felt thick, clumped together and scraggly. Like it hadn't been washed in about a week. He looked at his hand as he pulled it away from his face. It was small and brown with flecks of purple fingernail polish on the nails. It was a woman's hand. He looked around the room. It was a small dimly lit place surrounded by wood paneling. He could almost stretch out and touch both opposing walls with his arms. There was a small aluminum window on the other side of the room that was levered shut, but it still let a crack of sunshine to filter in. Cloud got up out of bed and opened the flimsy paneled door that led into the other room. It was a small kitchen with an even smaller living area beyond it. On the table sat a grungy plastic bong, the bowl filled with a tarry residue. Dirty bong water had spilled out of it onto the square kitchen table. The sink was filled with dirty dishes. He realized that he was in some kind of a trailer. One of those old silver rounded Air Stream numbers with an ancient Chevy truck parked out in front of it. He would scope out more of his surroundings later, but right now he had to piss in the worst way. He felt his way through the dark trailer, not bothering to take the time to find the light switch, and found the bathroom. He unzipped his pants and reached in to find his penis. There was nothing there! He felt around a little more, felt hair and pubic bone and a moist area but nothing more. Fuck it. He was about to burst. He relaxed his bladder and felt the warm liquid gush out all over the front of his pants. Shit. He realized that for the time being, until he found out what had happened to him, he would have to sit down to pee. He finished urinating all over himself as he was too far along to stop in midstream. Peeling off the sodden, tight fitting jeans and throwing them on the floor, he dried himself off with a dirty towel that he saw hanging over the bathtub.

He stood there in front of the mirror looking at his new body. He was definitely female, that was for sure. Dark skinned, Hispanic looking, maybe early twenties. His breasts were small but firm. He ran his fingertips over them, squeezing the nipples and felt a little shiver in his spine as they erected. He looked down between his legs seeing the dark patch of coarse and curly hair there. He slid his fingers down across his clit and put his middle finger into the soft folds below it. He felt a little bit ashamed, like he was violating the previous owner of the body. He brought the finger up to his nose and sniffed; pretty powerful. He lifted up his right arm and sniffed again; pretty rancid smelling. He realized that he/she probably hadn't taken a shower for quite a few days. He slid the soap scum encrusted shower door open and saw several roaches gathered around the drain, drinking from the water hole created by a leaky faucet. He reached over next to the toilet and discovered that the roll was out of toilet paper. There was a small cabinet over the toilet and he opened it to find several partial rolls of paper. Not bothering to put one back on the dispenser he tore off a few sheets and captured the roaches. One of them was able to escape his grasp and hurriedly crawled over his thumb. He quickly shook the thing off into the commode followed by the soggy crap paper and flushed. The toilet made a bubbling sound and then a sound that was something akin to an eighty year old man hacking up phlegm early in the morning. For a moment he thought that the thing was going to overflow, but then the shitty-looking brown water finally went down. Cloud then looked around the bathroom for some cleanser or even some of that scrubbing bubble stuff to clean the shower stall before he got in it, but found nothing. "Oh well." He thought to himself. "I'm probably dirtier than the damn shower, so what the hell." He turned on the water and the pipes finally released their treasure after a few moments of moaning and groaning. The only problem was that the water was ice cold and made Cloud jump back with a shriek. He was surprised to hear his voice. It was higher than his usual voice, but low for a woman. He grabbed the tiny sliver of soap that was in the dirty dish and quickly scrubbed himself down, concentrating more on the smelly parts underneath his arms and between his legs.

Cloud dried himself off with another dirty towel, avoiding the one that had the urine all over it. He walked back into the bedroom and looked into the clothes closet. The pickings were pretty scarce, another pair of jeans with holes all through them and a couple of black T-shirts and a black dress that was made of denim and came all the way down to his ankles. As he was looking into the bedroom mirror he noticed something that he hadn't noticed before. One of his legs from the knee all the way down to the ankle and most of his right shoulder were covered with tattoos. On his shoulder was a peacock with the head of a vulture and there was another skull on his leg with flowers growing out of the eye sockets. One of the eye sockets anyway, there were worms crawling out of the other one. It made Cloud feel a little creepy just looking at them. He wondered just what this girl was into anyway. Then he realized that this wasn't some other body that he had possessed, but rather this was he, either in another life or on a different plane of existence. He had been thinking about this lately. Sometimes when he left his body it was like he was revisiting a past life, he wondered if there was such a thing as visiting a future existence. If there was he hadn't been there yet. Other times though, the surrounding definitely seemed contemporary, which led him to believe he was being thrust into some kind of parallel universe. He could understand paying off bad karma by reliving part of his past lives, but what was to be gained for his soul if he had one, by being thrown into an alternate reality? He was starting to think that there was no order of intelligence to the universe. Maybe it was all just chaos, and he was trapped in some kind of unthinkable cosmic sinkhole.

Cloud pried himself from looking at his new body in the mirror and went back to the closet. He chose a pair of raggedy black jeans that were way to long for his legs and one of the black T-shirts. After dressing he went back to the mirror and looked at himself one more time. It was as if he was some kind of voyeur adjusting his binoculars as he was gawking at the young girl who lived next door. He noticed that the shirt he was wearing also had several holes cut into it, as did the jeans. Looking closer, he saw that the holes were there for a purpose. They had been cut to correspond to the places on his body that had tattoos on them. Pretty clever, he thought to himself. She was able to show off the ink without removing her clothes. He guessed that it was some kind of preview. He noticed that he had a rancid, bitter taste in his mouth and went back into the bathroom to brush his teeth. He found a frayed toothbrush and a tube of paste that was very nearly empty. As he started brushing he felt that there was something odd about the way his mouth felt. He rinsed his mouth and stuck out his tongue. There was a large metal stud right in the middle of it. It felt as if he was constantly rolling around a marble in his mouth. He didn't care for the sensation, but he had no idea on how to get the damn thing out of his mouth. He noticed a couple of other things as he was staring at his new face. His top lip had part of it missing. It didn't come all the way down to meet the bottom one. He believed that he had the makings of a cleft lip. He guessed that the girl either didn't care about it or never had the money to get the surgery to have it fixed. The other thing that he noticed was that his face was full of holes. There were several over both of his eyebrows, one over his bottom lip and one in each of his cheeks. So this was the piercing thing that seemed to be all the rage with some of the children nowadays. At first the whole concept didn't make any sense to him. Then he remembered the strange markings and scars that he had seen on some of the older members of his tribe, and he could see how such things might attract the young, even if they had no idea what the purpose was for.

His revelry was interrupted by a tinkling sound. At first he thought that it was water leaking in the bathroom, but then he realized that it was coming from the bedroom. He entered the bedroom and traced the sound to the bed. It was coming from underneath one of the pillows. He lifted up one of the pillows to find a small cell phone vibrating under it. After a few seconds of trying to figure out how to answer it, he finally found the right button. He tentatively said hello into the thing, wondering how anyone could possibly hear him. The young female voice on the other end asked: "Ang, is that you?" Cloud replied. "Yes." "I was worried about you." The voice on the other end of the phone replied. "I haven't been able to get a hold of you for the past couple of days…what's happening?" Cloud replied that he had just been very busy. "Well, I'll be over there in a couple of minutes." The voice said back.

It was actually about twenty minutes before Cloud heard the knock on the flimsy trailer door. Cloud peered out of the diamond shaped window with the crack in it that graced the middle of the door. He cracked the door open about an inch and the girl on the other side pushed her way in. "Boy, you been acting strange lately, even for you." She said. Cloud just turned and walked the two feet across the room to the couch without saying anything. The girl, whose name happened to be Susie, looked like a carbon copy of Cloud except that she was a lot lighter. Her face was filled with piercings, she even had some in her nose and a bone looking thing shoved between her nostrils. Her head was shaved down to the bare scalp on one side and on the other sat some very closely cropped bleached blonde hair that looked like it was changing color from the sunlight. Both of her arms were covered with tattoos of some kind of cross between a winged bird and a dragon and all of the metal in her mouth made her speech slurred and spitty. Her bottom lip hung down a little bit from the weight of the silver ball and this made her look petulant. Her jeans were even more hole-ridden and ragged than Cloud's.

The two looked at each other for a couple of minutes before either one of them spoke. Finally Susie opened up her arms and grabbed Cloud around the waist and kissed him fully on the lips. There was a clash of metal that caused Cloud to step back a little. "Hey best friend." Susie said. "You look like shit!" "Thank you." Cloud replied and sat down on the couch. It smelled of spilled beer mixed with semen and vaginal juice. "Looks like you been hitting the crank pretty hard lately, or are you just depressed?" Susie asked. Cloud told her that he had been just feeling a little down the last few days, that's why he hadn't called her. "A few days?" Susie replied. "It's been more like a fucking week." "I was beginning to think that it was because of what happened last week." Susie said. "Refresh me." Cloud replied. "Don't you remember?" Susie said, her lower lip dropping even more into a frown. Cloud shook his head. "You know." Susie spit out, a drop of it landing on Cloud's forehead. "When we were both drunk and lying on your bed…the thing that happened between the two of us. Must have been pretty bad if you don't remember." "Oh no, it was great." Cloud replied. The thought of them having sex gave him pause for thought. Susie went on to describe what had happened that night, how after the sex, Cloud started talking some really strange shit. About how he wished he could just hurry up and go to prison because he was tired of making all of his decisions by himself and he really wanted someone else to run his life. Then he started talking about how he wished he had been born back in the sixties so he could have been a follower of Charles Manson. Susie asked him if he really would have carved a baby out of a living pregnant woman like one of his followers had done and he replied yes. He had told her that he thought it was a cool thing to do. Then Cloud had went on talking about he wished he had a boyfriend that was hooked on Heroin so that way if he couldn't get him off sexually, then he could at least watch him shoot up and get off that way. "You were really talking some weird shit sister." Susie said. "What in the hell were you taking anyway?" Cloud made up a story about going down to the clinic and getting some antidepressants that had an unexpected effect on him. He told Susie that he was feeling much better now. She told him that he needed to stay off of that bad shit and just stick with the recreational drugs. "Just do what I do." She told him. "Every couple of months or so I take a little break, stay at home cocoon-like and just meditate. Get in touch with my spiritual side." Cloud told her that he didn't know if he had that much will and determination.

Susie asked Cloud what he wanted to do. "I dunno." he replied. "Just hang out I guess." Susie edged a little closer to him and put her arm around him.

He could feel her hot cigarette breath on his face. "You want to go into the bedroom and fool around like we did before?" She asked. Cloud replied no. He told her that all he really wanted to do was get a little fresh air and maybe get high. He was thinking to himself that what he really needed was a stiff shot of whiskey, maybe scotch or Jack Daniel's. He thought it was strange how addictions and desires translated even over several lifetimes. No matter which body he was in, he still felt the craving for booze. He had never been all that hot on other drugs; they always strung him out too much, complicating his daily hangover. But he felt that he could blow a little weed just to calm his nerves. He hoped that Susie had some; he was up for going out and getting a drink.

Instead she suggested that they go over to some guy named Joseph's house. The only problem was that he lived way out in the boonies in a place called Grubville. Cloud wasn't sure whether the place was named because they had a lot of worms, or because somebody found some food there. Anyway he thought that it was a stupid name and didn't feel like making the hour and a half drive to get there, but Susie seemed to insist and Cloud didn't want to piss off his new best friend right off of the bat.

The ride to Grubville was long, hot and torturous. Cloud resisted all attempts by Susie to start up a conversation. A dark cloud had settled over him. He was depressed. Hell he had been depressed through most of his former lives, but he was too busy coping to notice. A few facts about his life had trickled out during the ride. He had just turned twenty-one years old and the birthday party given to him by the few friends that he had left was quite a blast. At the end of it was when he and Susie had "gotten it on" so to speak. He/she lived in the trailer with her mother, though mom wasn't there too awful much of the time. Instead she chose to stay with her alcoholic boyfriend. She was an alcoholic also, so it was the best of both worlds. They enabled each other to get up out of bed and get to the wine. About once a month though, Gus would sober up enough to realize what he was laying next to and beat the hell out of her for the realization. She would then drag herself over to the trailer and spend a few glorious days with her daughter. The days were filled with laughter and sunshine. Mom got all weepy and poured her guts out and Ang was obliged to get out the paper towels and clean it up.

They finally arrived at Grubville and it seemed like friend Joseph lived in well, another trailer. A thought ran through Cloud's mind as he looked up at the rusty painted white collection of metal with the flat tires underneath and the broken screen door. The trailers were like the broken down old car that sat out on concrete blocks in front of so many of them. They represented dreams of the future when there weren't any. The cars would someday be totally restored. "All she needs is a new tranny!" They would say. "And maybe a couple of coats of paint." In reality the car, like the trailer, would sit there for the next twenty years until they were towed away for non-payment of rent, or the owner went to jail or his liver exploded. His swollen corpse would be removed, the place fumigated and made ready for the next occupant who would brag to everybody what a great deal he had gotten. Both the car and the trailer had the potential to move, to run away from all of the mess, but neither one would. One of the saddest days in any trailer trash history is to have to sell the wheels and the undercarriage out from underneath the trailer. To hock one's means to escape so to speak. It was different in the city. The people there were just as much trapped by the harshness and poverty, but at least they realized it from the start. The 150 plus year old rat infested buildings were not going to move until the wrecking ball came along, and then they at least had company as the whole block was demolished. Literally, there goes the neighborhood. In ancient Ireland there was the cult of the head. Bury a horse's head in the wall and the new foal will be born alive and healthy, the old horse's spirit rejoicing in its new body. In the city it was the rats that were interred. Sometimes more than one bloated corpse underneath the floorboards that was stinking up the place. The other thing that Cloud noticed in the brief time that he had spent in trailer country was the sound of sawing and hammering early in the morning, especially on Saturdays. It was like the people who had some kind of subsistence jobs wanted to take one last small jab at the dream by building something before they went out and raised hell on Saturday night. After all they may not survive. If they did, they spent Sunday recuperating and then next Saturday tearing down what they had built the weekend before. After all they needed the lumber.

Clod thought that Joseph could use a little of that spare lumber as he and Susie stood outside of the trailer on the rickety, portable steps waiting for Joseph to come to the door. Susie acted like they were the stairways to heaven, the way she fidgeted and jumped up and down on one foot.

Finally Joseph arrived, first looking out of a peephole carved in the door so he could see who was there. He was a sight to see. Tall and lanky he looked like a country cross between Chong and Jerry Garcia of the Grateful Dead. His forehead was pockmarked and he was sporting a burn on the end of his nose. The rest of his body was hairy as well and on top of his scarred nose sat a pair of wraparound sunglasses, the kind that the bikers wear.

"Well yee 'fuckin haw!" He announced. "I ain't seen you two bitches since the flap door on the moon sailed over the horse ranch!" Cloud had no idea what he was talking about. "Come on in and stick your jams into the marshmallow." He said. As he turned around to lead them into the living room, Cloud noticed that Joseph was wearing a pair of black leather pants. They definitely defined the roundness of his somewhat flat butt, offsetting the overhang that was at the front of his belly pretty well. He motioned them to have a seat and started saying something about how some people preferred the taste of cucumbers to that of pickles. He then motioned to the bong that was sitting on the coffee table and offered the two ladies a smoke. He filled the still smoking bowl with a small pinch of weed, reached inside the pocket of his leather overalls and took out a small amount of white powder which he delicately added to the mixture. Taking a silver Zippo out of his other pocket and striking at the lighter for what seemed like forever, he finally got the kerosene soaked thing to ignite. Sticking his face into the bong hole he applied the flame to the drugs and inhaled more deeply than Cloud thought was humanly possible. He held his breath like a buried Guru and then finally exhaled a cloud of smoke that practically filled the room of the small trailer. He then passed the thing to Susie who took a hit almost of the same magnitude and passed it over to Cloud. "Football!" Joseph exclaimed. The two girls stared back at him, Susie choking a little. "Football!" Joseph said again. "Pass it!" He made a gesture like a quarterback, his arm finishing the throw by falling limply into his lap. "Oh I get it." Susie said, laughing as she turned and looked at Cloud, who was still holding the bong. Both of them just stared at Cloud, who reluctantly picked up the lighter and applied the flame, almost burning her finger in the process.

The hit was powerful, acrid, and not at all pleasant despite all of the ice chips that were in the bong water. Cloud felt like someone had punched her in the throat and her head was spinning. "What did this loser cut his choker weed with anyway, Clorex bleach?" Cloud thought. She couldn't help but cough. The harsh smoke had stirred up a bit of debris that must have been hiding in her throat since she was a baby. Her dark skin turned even darker as she struggled desperately to cough up the Lugie. She noticed that both Susie and Joseph were staring at him laughing. She got up, excused herself and struggled to reach the bathroom. The violent spasms in her stomach forced the vomit into a projectile that cleared her throat on the way out. She couldn't find the bathroom light switch and ended up puking in Joseph's bathtub. "Served the fucker right!" She thought as she wiped her face on what she thought was a towel. Turned out the "towel" was a crusty pair of Joseph's underwear. Silk boxer shorts with pictures of Teddy bears on them. The one bulb in the bathroom light shorted out just as Cloud was looking at the redness that covered her eyes like a dark cloud. She stumbled back out into the long dark hall of the trailer and towards the light in the living room. As she passed through the kitchen she noticed that both Susie and Joseph had taken off their clothes and were going at it on the couch. 'Jesus!" Cloud thought. "Doesn't this bitch have any class at all?" Joseph was sitting on the couch with Susie on top of him, his big hairy belly almost touching her tits as she moved up and down on his cock. Cloud stood in the doorway for a few seconds before the pair noticed her. "Come on, join us!" Susie hollered, a little out of breath. "The water's fine!" Cloud was about to excuse herself and apologize for interrupting the two when Susie jumped up off of Joseph and ran across the room, grabbing Cloud. Joseph followed, his ample sausage swinging in the wind. "Do we have to do everything for you!" Susie exclaimed. With that they pushed Cloud over onto the couch and fell on top of her. Cloud was screaming and calling the two everything in the book. "I love it when you talk like that!" Susie yelled out. In a matter of seconds Cloud's clothes were removed against his will. Joseph once again assumed the position that he had been in before on the couch, sitting upright and stroking himself. Susie forced Cloud's mouth down on Joseph's cock. "Suck it bitch!" She whispered into Cloud's ear. Joseph put both of his large hairy hands on the top of Cloud's head and held it in place. He then thrust himself vigorously into Cloud's mouth. His pubic bone crashed against Cloud's face, causing her lip to bleed. She had to keep her neck arched back as far as she could just to get air into her nostrils. Susie was busy playing with herself and stroking Joseph's balls. Joseph moaned and Susie whispered into Cloud's ear: "Honey, his balls are getting tighter!" "Get ready for it!" With that Joseph exploded into Cloud's mouth. She felt the hot liquid at the back of her throat. She thought that there was no end to it. Finally he pulled out of Cloud's bloody mouth. Susie put one of her hands over Cloud's mouth and used the other to massage her throat like someone trying to get a dog to swallow a pill. She had no choice but to gag or swallow. After swallowing several times she finally got the stuff to slide down her throat. "Now don't get pregnant." Susie told her. Joseph was sitting in a chair across the room, firing up the bong again. Cloud felt degraded, betrayed and humiliated. If this was what it felt like to be a woman, then he hoped that he would hurry up and die and come back as something else, an ant or a dog perhaps. She curled herself up on the corner of the couch and refused to talk to the other two as they went about the business of getting totally stoned, not to mention shit faced. Finally Susie decided to say goodbye to Joseph and motioned for Cloud to get ready to leave. As they were exiting out of the rickety trailer's front door, Joseph grabbed her and mashed his smelly face onto hers. Holding her by the ears, he first stuck his sordid tongue down her throat and then sucked her lower lip in between his front teeth. Biting down hard enough to draw blood, he sucked the liquid into his mouth. Her lip stung and she tasted her own blood mixed with his smelly spit. She spat the mixture back into his face and slapped him before she joined Susie in the car.

Cloud remained silent while Susie talked and talked about how great Joseph was and how great was the drugs that he supplied them. Cloud thought that it was probably crank that got mixed in with the weed. The stuff certainly didn't make her talkative. All she felt was overwhelming anger, shame and a nervous feeling in the pit of her stomach as she fidgeted in the seat like she had to go to the bathroom.

About half a mile up the dirt road that led to Joseph's trailer, the car started acting up. Something must have been wrong with the alternator because the headlights got dimmer and dimmer and finally went out. The engine was still running as they pulled over to the side of the road. Susie got out and looked in the trunk. She pulled an old greasy flashlight from the toolbox. Amazingly it still worked and was pretty bright. She instructed Cloud to shine the thing out of the window onto the road in front of them. "All we need to do is make it a couple of miles up this road to the filling station that we passed on the way in." Susie reassured her. Cloud said nothing in return. She thought that it was a stupid idea, but couldn't think of any alternatives. She sure as hell didn't 'ant to try to go back to the trailer. If she never saw that place for the rest of eternity it would be too soon. The flashlight trick seemed to work pretty well as long as the road was straight. Whenever there was a turn though, they would run off of the road. Cloud thought that Susie was driving too fast and told her several times to slow down. Finally the tires skidded in the gravel and they ran into a fence. The right rear tire was stuck in the mud. Suddenly two headlights appeared in the distance. The light got brighter and brighter until the pickup truck carrying the two men stopped in front of the car. The two men were wearing cowboy hats, jeans and boots and were obviously drunk. They stayed in the truck for a few minutes surveying the situation and talking among themselves. The one on the driver's side finally crushed the empty beer can that he had been holding and threw it out of the window. Both of them then got out of the truck. Cloud noticed that one of them wore a beard and the other one had no front teeth. "We almost didn't see you two ladies." The one with the beard said. "What's the matter, you stuck?" Susie explained what had happened with the lights on the car and her idea about the flashlight. As she was explaining she got closer to the bearded man and unbuttoned the top of her blouse. Cloud noticed that both of the men had fixed their gaze onto that area. One of the men told Susie to open the hood of the car and told the other man to get the tools out of the back of the truck. "It's probably just a loose belt." The man said, slurring his speech. Susie opened the hood and the man told her where to look for the alternator. As she was bent over the front of the car, the man popped open another beer and pressed himself up against her. Susie didn't seem to mind. Cloud was starting to panic; she couldn't stand the thought of another man forcing himself on her in the same night as Joseph. The dude with no teeth was walking towards her saying something. She reached down into the toolbox and grabbed an adjustable wrench. When the man was in striking distance, she swung with all of her might. If he would have had any teeth the force of the blow would have probably knocked most of them out, instead it just fractured his jaw and sent him flying to the ground.

The last thing that Cloud remembered was the sound of a big bass drum as the heavy tool came crashing down on her skull. She felt a soft and tender kiss on the lips. "Oh no!"

"Not again!" She thought.

Chapter 18

Cloud opened his eyes to a blinding yellow light. He soon realized that it was the sun shining into his face through an open window next to the bed. He felt warm and fuzzy, actually a little bit hot, but there was a warm breeze carrying the melodies of songbirds through the opening. As he sat up he noticed that there was no bounce of innersprings on the bed. It was more like a big pile of covers, one piled on top of the other. The room he was in was bright where the sun came through the window, but there were areas that were dark. The room had a musty odor that seemed to be mixed with just a hint of spoiled food or dead animal despite the breeze. Or maybe it was the breeze that was bringing the smell in from the window. Cloud looked down to see that he was dressed in some sort of white gown. There was a sleeping cap perched askew on top of his head, a sleeping cap? He wondered if maybe he had been a character out of some kind of fairy tale in one of his previous lives. He had to keep things in focus. Here he was again, either dead or having one hell of a dream, and thrust into someone else's existence. No it wasn't someone else. It was he revisiting in a reality that was slightly askew from well, reality.

Cloud noticed that there was a closet on the other side of the room, a closet that had no doors. In the closet were a couple of plain men's suits, some ruffled shirts and a four-cornered hat. If he had to guess what time period that he was in, he'd have to guess that it was somewhere late Middle Ages. Of course he could easily be off several hundred years as he certainly was no historian. Cloud put on the jacket and trousers, though it seemed a little warm for the jacket. The jacket appeared to be hand sewn. It was sturdy and durable but roughly made. Cloud walked through the house but didn't have far to go. There was a small kitchen with no lighting fixtures, not even gas. Just candles and a sort of hearth with a big black rusty pot hanging over it. Again there were no doors in the place and no locks. It must have been a time or an area where everybody trusted each other. He could find no bathroom and no running water. There was however, one more room that was filled to the brim with papers and books and what appeared to be plant samples. Cloud walked through the open door to the outside. It was a warm and pleasant day. A small path on the right led off into a fenced in garden. The garden had a few rose bushes, but mostly seemed to contain herbs. He noticed right away that it certainly smelled better than the rest of the outside. That was probably the reason that it was situated on the bedroom side of the house with the breeze coming from the East blowing the fragrance right over the sleeping occupant.

It was jut then that Cloud noticed the little man staring through the open window at him. "Doctor?" The man inquired. "I see that you are awake sir!" "When will you be leaving?" "Leaving?" Cloud responded. The man looked at him quizzically. "The trip." The man replied. Cloud told the man that he had fallen that very morning and his head was a little foggy. "You really must have taken a good blow to the noggin to forget about the trip!" The man said. "Such an important trip and a life saving one at that!" Cloud asked the man to refresh him about the trip he was taking because it seemed that he knew so much about it. "Ah, up to your old ways again I see." The man said. "Quizzing me on what you have told me, that's it!" "Well I'll do the very best that I can to relate it back to you sir."

The man told Cloud that he, the good doctor had been working on a treatment for the plague, the Black Death, for some time now. He was on his way to a few of the neighboring towns to try to stop the horrible disease before it made its way to the town that he lived in. He told Cloud how the village was almost deserted most of the time know and how they had sealed off the wall around the town and barricaded themselves in their houses. The one stranger who had sneaked past the barricade and gotten into the town was promptly hung in the public square without the benefit of a trial. The good doctor was an Alchemist and a herbalist as well as being a physician and had been working diligently in his alchemist's garden to develop a concoction that would if not cure, at least slow down the spread of the disease. He had come up with a mixture of rose hips, cloves. Aloeswood, mercury and a few other secret ingredients that he was sure to do the trick, but he needed to test the concoction on a few of the real plague victims before he was certain that it would work. He would try to treat the disease in three different ways. First he would brew a tea out of his ingredients, second he would pack the curative herbs and the heavy metals into a "bird's beak." A bird's beak was a long conical object that was filled with the herbs and then tied around the person's face, just in case there were any "bad vapors" in the air. The good doctor Cloud still practiced most of the remedies that were in vogue at the time like blood letting and testing the body's four humors, but he liked to be innovative and used a lot of his own remedies as well. The four humors were black, red, yellow and white bile. It wasn't allowed at that time by the church for human bodies to be dissected. When a person's skull was split open either by an accidental injury or during a battle, it was thought that the big mushy white and gray stuff that was contained in the skull was a mucus-producing organ. This thing supplied all of the different types of mucus that the body needed. The red mucus was of course, blood. The white was that which held the bones and ligaments together, the black was fecal matter and the yellow, of course, was the urine. In the medical view of the Middle Ages we were all a pretty squishy mess. Disease causing organisms, bugs like bacteria and viruses were completely unknown. It was believed that most disease was caused by an imbalance in one or more of the body's humors. Things to increase or cut down on the production of these types of mucus were all the rage. If it was believed that you had too much blood then a gash was made in one of your arteries or a big fat slimy blood-sucking leech was applied to your arm. There were plants and extracts to purge you of yellow and black mucus by either stimulating your kidneys or your bowels. Pus was considered one of the white humors and the treatment was the same as for an overabundance of the red: stick a leech on it. Trepanning was also in favor. This was to cut a small hole in your head and let some of the evil vapors out of your skull. The urine of a small boy was said to be important in the alchemist's quest not only to cure disease but also to be spiritually pure and turn base metals like lead into gold.

Some of the medical knowledge of the times that Cloud had amassed was slowly coming back to him. But in reality he knew that the Black Death was caused by some kind of bug. He was trying to remember what he had read so many years ago in one of his more modern textbooks. Rats. What was the cause? He dismissed the neighbor, telling him that he had some important work to attend to before he left town. As he was cleaning out one of the dusty cupboards, moving around one of the dusty bottles he was startled by a huge rat. He smashed the thing repeatedly with the bottle that he was holding in his hand, but the damned thing just started back at him with bloody eyes and then took off. "That was it!" He thought to himself Rodents! The plague was caused by rodents! Not just the infestation of the dirty pests but carried and transmitted to humans by the fleas that fed on the rats. He was racking his brain to think of how Europe finally rid itself of the disease. The best that he could remember was that they didn't. It had wiped out over half of the population before it went south. He couldn't single handedly get rid of the disease himself and change history, he was certain that would screw up everything else, the drop of water in the rainforest thing. He tried to think of the children's story about the pied piper. Didn't he create some kind of song that mesmerized the rats and then he would just walk them out of the village? Or was that some other kind of animal? He couldn't think. Well at least he knew that he might be able to help the neighboring town and save his own by eliminating the rat problem. If only he had some D-Con.

He wasn't getting rid of the medicines that he had prepared though. Being somewhat of a Shaman himself in his previous life, he valued a lot of the folk remedies because he knew that some of them, like aspirin for example, had roots in scientific fact. He grabbed a few of the bottles of rose hips and a few of the masks. Hell those things might not have any effect on the plague, but they might work well against the flu. On second thought, he wondered if there was some way to make a lotion that could be rubbed on the body that would kill fleas? Hmmm. He would have to look into that. After packing he sat down and wiped his forehead. With all of these heavy clothes these people wore it was a wonder that the fleas could even get through to bite them. He noticed that there wasn't very much light left in the day and wasn't about to try to travel to the next town by night. There was no telling how many desperate people were on the road and what they might do. Better to wait until the morning. That way it would give him a little time to check out the town and see what kind of people he was fighting for to try to save their lives. He put on his square shaped hat and walked outside.

Though it seemed that his house was out in the country, it really wasn't that far away from town.

As Cloud walked through the streets of the small village, he noticed that there weren't many people out and about. Advance word about the spread of the plague must have already reached the town. Way off in the distance at the end of Main Street he could see the big house on the hill. Not quite a castle, it still was about as close as one could get for the times. He wondered how the Lords and Ladies were addressing the disease problem. Were they taking any precautions at all or did they just barricade themselves in the walled house, stock up on supplies and let the townspeople fend for themselves. He smirked knowing that the rats that carried the fleas that carried the disease would eventually find their way to the castle, even if they hadn't already. He then realized where all of the smell was coming from. There was a gutter that ran squarely down the center of the narrow street. It was filled with rotting garbage. The town must have relied on the occasional heavy rain to wash the putrid stuff to wherever it was washed to, and obviously it hadn't rained in awhile. It was filled with rotting food debris and human waste. They must just carry their shit out in buckets and dump it in the middle of the street. Cloud noticed that there was a tavern on the corner of the street called the Iron Helmet Inn. Above the front door of the place was the namesake; a rusty old gray helmet perched on a wrought iron hanger. He decided to go inside. The place seemed to be filled with a fair amount of people. Seems that even the threat of the plague couldn't keep the locals from enjoying their drink and merriment. Inside the place smelled of sweat and stale beer. Several of the patrons acknowledged Cloud as he pulled up a chair at one of the empty tables. They seemed to address him with a certain amount of respect. He wasn't sure if that was because they owed him money or because he was the only doctor in town and they might have to rely on him to care for them if they got sick. A girl who looked like she was right off of the bottle of a St. Pauli Girl approached Cloud; the only difference was that she had dirty gray hair instead of the blonde that was on the label. She perched the wooden tray up under her arm and thrust out her hip. She was maybe in her late twenties but living the life in the Middle Ages made her look like she was forty going on sixty. Dental hygiene must have not been at a premium in the town because it seemed that everyone he saw had a mouth full of rotten teeth. The serving girl was no exception. Cloud ordered up a beer and a plate of food. He hadn't realized just how hungry he had become. He had no idea how long it had been since his last meal. The girl brought out a wood cup full of cloudy beer and a plate of some kind of meat and some moldy looking bread. When Cloud complained she told him that supplies in town were getting pretty scarce and he was lucky to be getting anything at all. She then told him that what was on his plate was actually not too much worse than what they were used to eating. Cloud then remembered that this was the Middle Ages and not the Waldorf Astoria and his stomach told him that he had better take a chance. He took a sip of the beer, which tasted like warm piss. It had a foul order about it like something had fallen in the vat, a rat or two possibly. Cloud tried not to think about it and concentrated on the food. The meat was dried, tough and chewy, but it had a smoky flavor that was ok. The bread on the other hand, tasted like the bitter mold that covered it. He was able to get the food down with the aid of another beer. At least the stuff tasted like it had quite a bit of alcohol in it. Cloud sat at the table drinking for the next couple of hours.

The other people in the bar were pretty quiet, a few of them walking up to
his table and inquiring how things were going and whether or not he had
heard any more news about the plague. He told them that he didn't know,
but he was getting ready to travel to the neighboring town and find out, see
if he can help. He told them about the possible treatment he had developed.
A couple of them replied that if he left the town, he probably wouldn't be
allowed to return because of fears that he might be infected. He tried to
explain to them how the disease was spread, but they kept telling him that it
was reparations from God for some unthinkable sin that they had
committed, but didn't know what it was. Finally Cloud just shook his head
at their ignorance and tried to get up to leave. He suddenly felt violently
sick to his stomach and the room was spinning. He was able to stagger out
of the tavern and into the street. The cobblestones had taken on a bright hue
and were literally jumping up at him like piano keys. The windowsills were
lips that shouted out his name as he went past them. The last rays of the sun
came down in waves just like rain. He stopped, staggered out into the
middle of the street and vomited. The stuff looked like fluorescent green pea
soup. The acrid beer stung his nostrils. The nausea was like an ocean wave
that started in the pit of his stomach and ended with his chest taking the full
brunt of the hurricane's high tide. It finally ended when he passed out in the
gutter of the street, the last few dry heaves being solely the result of his
reflexes. It was still dark when he came to and he noticed that his face was
sore and his wallet was missing. He guessed that some drunken passerby
had seen the state of his misery and the fact that he was wearing fancy
clothes and decided to take advantage of the situation. He felt a little better
having purged himself of the rancid food and beer, but he was still shaky

and disoriented. The streets were dark, not even having the advantage of being lighted by candle let alone the benefits of the electric streetlights that he was accustomed to. The southerly breeze was now gone, being replaced by the stagnant mugginess of the summer night. The resulting stench from the open sewer in the street didn't help his queasy stomach all that much, but he struggled to his feet and walked down the dark street in the direction that he thought was home. The narrow street soon opened into what looked like some sort of Town Square. He noticed that there was a different stench here than what lingered back in the street. The smell of the rotting garbage was replaced by the smell of rotting flesh. There was a large ornate building right ahead of him that was accented by a large tower in the center. In front of the tower was a wooden platform that held the hanging rope of a gallows. There was a small lantern on a pole next to it that lit the scene. There was a corpse hanging from the rope and from the look of his body, he had been there in the summer heat for quite a few days. His body and face were grossly swollen and badly decomposed. Large areas of the flesh had rotted away and the rope had cut all of the way through the man's neck, which was held at an impossible angle only by what was left of his backbone. The eyes were missing, looking like birds had picked them out. Cloud pulled up the sleeve of his jacket over his nose to keep himself from retching again. He wondered if the eyes had been picked out while the man was still alive, or if his neck had been mercifully broken when the hangman pulled the rope, sparing him the agony. Around the man's neck there was a piece of parchment paper stating the crime for which he had been hanged. It was something quoting an obscure law against bringing the plague into town. So this was the way that they treated the victims of the disease, hanging them by the neck and letting them rot away to a skeleton.

Cloud noticed something very unusual at the man's feet. Someone had placed a small wooden box there that was full of soil and had a few tiny green leaves sticking out of it. On the front of the box was carved the word: "Mandragora." The Mandrake root. Cloud remembered from his training that the root was used prominently in Witchcraft. The poisonous plant with the root that took on the shape of a human being was believed to have very strong magical powers. It was thought that on the rare occasion it was found growing underneath a hanging tree and fertilized by the dead man's blood and semen that invariably dripped out of the body, had especially deadly powers. The problem was when you harvested it if proper procedures weren't followed, you could be killed doing it. The little root that looked like a man would scream so loud when he was pulled out of the ground, it would kill you. Special dogs were trained to take care of that problem. They would pull out the plant and be killed while you waited a safe distance away. Cloud guessed that the person who placed the box at the hanged man's feet wanted to bypass that problem. He must have thought that he could just carry the box back home and gently extract the root. Cloud wondered if he had any of the roots growing in his Alchemist's garden.

The night air was getting a little cooler and that helped cut down on the stench a little. It also cleared his head and made his stomach feel a little more like it should. He realized that he was heading in the wrong direction and started walking in the other direction, leaving the hanged man to sway gently in the breeze; strange fruit hanging from the tree. Eventually he found his way back to his house just as the morning sun was beginning to peek across the horizon. He fell into his bed exhausted, with just enough energy to pull off his puke stained shirt and trousers. His last thought was that he would have to delay his life saving trip to the next town until he was feeling better. Later that day, a little after noon, Cloud awoke and realized that he was starving. He remembered reading somewhere that a lot of the peasants in the Middle Ages suffered from Ergot poisoning. It came from eating the cheap rye bread that had been stored in the cellars that allowed the hallucinogenic mold to grow. Someone had surmised that was the reason for all the witchcraft hysteria and the burnings. It was easy to imagine your neighbor flying around on a broom after ingesting enough of that stuff. You might even conjure up the devil or at least a couple of minor demons. The rich folk up in the castle could afford the more refined white bread that was made of wheat instead of rye, so they escaped much of the poisoning, but the mercury they used to tan the leather slowly seeped into their brains and got them anyway. Cloud was in the kitchen of the house looking at some dried meat and vegetables that were in the cupboard when he heard music outside of his window. He tossed the ingredients into the big metal kettle and added some water. There was still a little bit of fire in the hearth. He added a couple of pieces of wood and stirred up the embers before going over to the window to see what was causing all of the racket outside. It was a parade! The people of the village had assembled all of the children, dressed them in costumes that were right out of the Brothers Grimm and had them march down the cobblestones. Several men and women with instruments followed closely behind. The children marched in unison and waved colorful handkerchiefs over their heads. Cloud walked outside to watch and in a few moments the parade was gone. Marching around the corner onto the next street. An old man with a wizened cane strolled slowly past. Cloud stopped him and asked him what the parade was for. The old man looked surprised and told Cloud that he had participated in the parade just last year, last year in happier times. Cloud told the man that he had fallen down and was suffering from a little bit of memory loss, but was taking a tonic that he had prepared himself and he was sure that he would be fine in a couple of days. The old man told him about the parade. How it had started a hundred years ago to commemorate the anniversary of the children saving the town from the Russian invaders. The walls to the town had been breached and the residents were outnumbered and outgunned. The commander of the Russian army was very fond of children and had several of his own. In a last ditch desperate attempt to save the town just as the soldiers were marching in, the local school teacher assembled all of the town's children and had them march down the center of the street right in front of the Russian army. They pleaded with the general and waved flags in the air. The general was so touched by this movement that he spared the town. The old man told Cloud that he wasn't quite sure if the story had any truth to it, or if it had been modified over the years, but the village still celebrated the date that it was supposed to have happened every year without fail. It was the town holiday and everyone was required to participate. It was also a day off of work with pay for everybody. This year however, with the plague looming over the town, the turnout was low and the mayor had waved the fine for not participating because of the special circumstances. The ones that did show up did so because they feared that there wouldn't be any town or children left the next year to celebrate.

Cloud walked back to his house and sat at the kitchen table, finishing his stew. The meat and vegetables were dried, so hopefully he wouldn't get sick. The thought of the children marching made him even more determined to fight off the plague before it wiped out the town. He would prepare for the fight today and leave for the neighboring village the next morning.

The next morning broke hot and humid. Cloud was up early, before the sunrise, assembling all of the tools of his trade. He worked steadily and focused by candlelight, fill up two large leather bags. One contained the medicine that he hoped would help cure the disease, the other some food and water, enough to last for a few days. He was afraid to consume the food in the next village, not only because of the sanitation, but also because of the unpleasant experience that he had a few days before with the moldy bread. He carried his supplies out to the carriage house just as the sun was peeking through the morning clouds. He tossed the saddlebags over the back of the dark horse just as he looked up and saw a huge rat staring down at him, perched on one of the rafters. He made a mental note to deal with the hideous creature when he returned. That was IF he returned. He had no idea of what awaited him when he arrived at the plague infested neighboring town. The village wasn't very far away in modern travel terms, but it took him almost a full day to get there. He stopped a couple times in the woods, once to water the horse and the other time to pluck some fresh fruit from an apple tree and enjoy a few minutes of peace underneath. He finished the apple and then took some dried rose hips out of his pouch and sprinkled them with some powdered cloves. He knew that the vitamin C in the rose hips and the oxyalic acid in the cloves was almost like an antibiotic. Maybe if he dosed himself enough it might help keep him from getting sick. He wasn't quite so sure if the stuff would have any affect on someone who was in the advanced stages of the disease. He would soon find out. He got back on his horse and hurried towards the town, he really wanted to get there while he still had a few hours of daylight left. As he approached the village he realized that it was worse than he had thought. He encountered two bloated and decaying bodies along the way. Their bodies were covered with the boils and carbuncles that had festered and turned black, thus giving the plague its name. Another fellow staggered past him, holding a bloody cloth to his face. Cloud did not stop him, figuring that he was in the advanced stages and beyond his help. The town was in a shambles. Bodies littered the street and the decomposing flesh made Cloud take one of the bird's beaks that was filled with aromatic herbs and incense out of his pouch and cover his face with it. He looked a strange figure in his long black coat, four-square hat and bird's beak tied to his face as he rode through the town.

Cloud walked up and down the streets of the desolate town looking for signs of life. Even the tavern was empty, half glasses of beer sitting stagnant on the tables. As he approached the church he thought that he saw a flickering of light from within. As he approached the huge red doors of the gothic cathedral he noticed that someone had painted a large black slash across one of the doors, signifying that the plague had gotten inside. As he opened the door the rusty hinges made a sound like a thousand rats being burned alive. Inside he could see several people slumped over in the pews, hands clenched together in prayer, in a last ditch effort to appeal to a God long dead to save them. In the middle of the aisle was the lifeless body of a woman who had partially sewn herself into her own shroud. Just then he looked up to see a tiny face peering at him through the door to the rectory.

The face disappeared, closing the door behind it. Cloud hurried down the aisle to find that the door was still open. As he peered inside a knurled hand reached out and grabbed his cloak. He saw that the man was wearing a black shirt and a frock. There was a large boil on his forehead and a beard on his chin. "Your appearance frightened the child." The man whispered, pointing to the bird's beak hanging off of Cloud's face. The man noticed the leather bag that Cloud was carrying. "Are you a doctor?" The man asked. Cloud replied that yes he was, here to try to help with the plague. He explained that he had some ideas and medicine that might help if he wasn't too late. The priest told him that the disease had already wiped out more than half of the town's population and that the rest of the residents had either fled the town or barricaded themselves in their homes. Cloud asked the man if there were any men in the town that were able to work. "Maybe a handful." The priest replied. "Why?" He asked. Cloud told him that the first thing that they had to do if the town was to be saved was to clear the streets and houses of all the dead bodies, get rid of the rotting garbage and then try to get rid of the rats. He had a special powder that would drive the creatures out into the open where they could be caught and disposed of. "It's a fine time to be worrying about cleaning up the town." The priest told him. "This is a time when the people need to be turning to God and asking for forgiveness that he should visit such a horrible circumstance upon them." Cloud tried to explain to him that it was the rats and not God that was killing them; more specifically the fleas that the rats harbored. The priest looked at him strangely. "Even if you are correct." He said. "Most of the men are afraid to get anywhere near the bodies, fearing that they will catch the disease. But if you wish, I will ring the church bell to call a meeting. Most of them should still come, wanting to find out if I have heard any news."

Cloud followed the priest up the stairs to the church's tower. The priest grabbed the rope that was attached to the huge iron bell and tugged at it three times. The sound reverberated throughout the tower, spilling out into the streets. "It might take a few minutes for them to gather." The priest said as he tied off the rope and descended the stairs. "Let's have something to drink."

The priest led Cloud down into the basement of the church and lit a candle. The tiny light barely illuminated the musty room, but it was enough to see the large brown rats scurry for cover. The priest moved aside a few empty bottles that looked like they had at one time held wine for the sacraments. There was an earthen wear ceramic jug covered with dust and cobwebs sitting behind them. It was unmarked except for a couple of pictures of herbs scratched into the side. The priest found a couple of dirty wine glasses and poured some of the contents of the jug into each one. He raised his glass. "Here's to your success and god's mercy." He said solemnly. The liquor was dark amber in color, was strong and sweet and tasted thick on the tongue. Smooth at first, some of the honey laced mead cloyed at the back of the throat, sticking there and burning the tonsils. Cloud didn't care, even though at this point he wondered how much lead had leaked out of the painted jar, but oh well. The priest poured another drink. This time it tasted like almonds and hazel nuts with maybe a little wintergreen thrown in for good measure. Cloud noticed what looked like an old alter sitting in one corner of the room. There was what looked like an ancient illuminated manuscript sitting on top of it. He walked over to the book and asked the priest what it was. The book was from the bible, made before the invention of the printing press. It had been illustrated and hand copied with meticulous care by the monks that once occupied the monastery where the church now sat. The father told the story of how the monks had sequestered themselves here, on a very ancient pagan site before the town even existed to protect themselves from the heathen invaders that were invading the countryside. To wile away the long hours the monks prayed and copied the bible, adding beautiful pictures of the characters and fancy intricate designs to the work. Since paper and supplies were extremely scarce, they milled their own paper from the surrounding forest and made the brightly colored ink from the bodies of ground up insects. The manuscript that Cloud was looking at and two others that were inside the altar were the only ones that were left. The others had disappeared when the old monastery had been torn down and replaced with the church. Rumors had circulated that the church itself was behind the disappearance, taking the beautiful artwork and destroying it because it had contained "elements" of the old pagan stories that the monks had Christianized.

Suddenly there was a knock at the church door and the priest looked up from his drink, telling Cloud that it must be the men assembling for the town meeting. The two men walked outside to greet them. They were a ragged bunch, most of them wide eyed and staring, the rest staggering around like they were drunk. A couple of them dressed in robes, stood silently with their hands clasped together, praying.

The men were talking excitedly amongst themselves so much that Cloud had to strain his voice, which was already somewhat foggy from the liquor, to get their attention. It looked like a couple of the men were carrying weapons. One of them struggled to conceal a rusty broadsword underneath his cloak, while a few of them stood there, looking numb, holding on to their clubs. What they planned on doing with the weapons or why they needed them against the priest, was hard for Cloud to figure out. Maybe they had come to the church for the answer to the plague and as their children and families slowly perished, that answer became more and more elusive. As Cloud looked over at the haggard man of the cloth standing next to him, he felt sorry for the man. That was as a man and a fellow suffering human being, but he did not feel sorry for what he had represented. Through all of Cloud's extraordinary experiences since he had "died" or whatever had happened to him, one thing was sorely for certain: his faith in religion certainly hadn't increased. As a matter of fact, it had seriously dwindled. His spirituality had increased however, or maybe it was a kind of faith in the universe. A sense of steadiness, no matter what the constant of change turned out to be.

The last thing that Cloud remembered about the Middle Ages and the plague was the sensation of his body slowly being torn to pieces by the rats. Unlike the other incarnations, he wasn't really sure how he had died. The thing that he was aware of was that this time his spirit or whatever you called it, had lingered around longer than the other times. Maybe it was the energy of the mass deaths, or the fact that he and the priest had died at exactly the same time, or maybe even that there was a certain amount of processing that had to be done and the highways to hell were paved with good intentions. Anyway, the agony of this passing certainly seemed to take longer. He looked down at his decaying and bloated body and watched it dissolve. At first it was picked to pieces by the rats and a gaggle of birds. They were black greasy creatures that seemed to carry evil intent in their eyes. Then when there wasn't much left of him except the bones, the insects came and finished him off. The rats made one last futile attempt to knar at his bones which were now bleaching in the mid day sun. Then finally his concept of time began to speed up and he actually watched his remains turn to dust and the street change beneath them. He looked down at his tanned arm, rippling with muscle to see that he was holding a machete. It was slippery in the intense jungle heat.

Chapter 18

Cloud heard his breath come out in ragged heaps as he struggled to make his way through the thick jungle floor. He heard shouts and screams and the clashing of more machetes in the growth up ahead. He looked down and noticed that he was wearing combat fatigues. They we made out of thick, heavy material and stuck to him like leather against sweaty skin. It was hot, but at the same time clammy. His feet hurt from the heavy outdated boots that he was wearing. Then, the struggling sound that was coming from up ahead quieted down a bit and all he heard was the heavy grunts of the other men and a sort of muted sobbing sound. He followed the impromptu trail that the soldiers had made and came to an opening in the jungle. There were six other men gathered around in a circle. There was another man, dressed in more traditional clothes, in the middle of the circle. He was on his knees with his hands over his face. One of the men, heavyset with the beginnings of a potbelly, spoke something in Spanish. Cloud knew that he had never learned the language, but he could understand what the man was saying. It was something about "the revolution, in this case, would be televised." Cloud thought that it was odd that the man would quote something from the American sixties over a man who was obviously a prisoner.

Suddenly, the kneeling man tried to make a run for it. One of the soldiers quelled his effort with a quick thrust of his rifle to the man's face. This seemed like a signal for the rest of the group to join in. Cloud watched in horror as they beat the man and then held him down. The heavyset man stood over the squirming body and lit up a cigar. He then pulled a large hunting knife out of a holster attached to his belt. Holding the cigar clenched between his teeth, he grabbed a hold of the man's dark hair and pulled up on it violently. The man, who must have been in his late twenties, suddenly looked like someone out of a Chinese wood carving. Slowly the commander began pulling the sharp knife across the man's head, cutting off his scalp. Soon the knife was covered with blood and you could see specks of the man's skull showing through the red liquid. The prisoner was still trying to move, but his movements were more like convulsions now, no longer deliberate. You could tell that he was going into shock. The scalp came off easily and now the commander held it up like a trophy. His eyes appeared a little glazed, but there was no show of emotion on his face. Then a different vision flashed across Cloud's perception. He was no longer in the jungle anymore, but rather in the middle of a large group of people on a flat level ground that could have been somewhere in the American Southwest.

He found himself looking down at the wounded man lying beneath him. Cloud's painted face was swollen with rage and he felt an intense hatred towards the white man struggling at his feet. Cloud let out a yell that he really didn't know he had in him and his movements were almost trance-like as he cut off the man's scalp, and held the blood drenched hair and skin up for all to see. Then he felt a sharp burning pain in his lower chest as the bullet tore through him.

"Get the camera out, you idiot!" One of the men in the jungle was shouting at him. "We have to get the film footage!" Cloud fumbled around in his backpack and produced a small video camera. "Is the film rolling?" The commander asked. Cloud nodded. With that the commander pulled the prisoner's pants down around his ankles. He grabbed the man's genitals and began to cut them with the knife. The man's eyes opened and he began to move again, only this time a hideous scream escaped from his throat. Then he was still but still breathing, his breath coming out in short, gasping spurts. There was very little blood, just a red splotch right below his abdomen. The arteries that once supplied his private parts with blood were now in spasm, clenching tightly to prevent further loss of blood. The commander held the withered genitals up to the camera and screamed: "This is what happens to those who support the old regime!" He then threw the handful of meat into the dying man's face and instructed Cloud to turn off the camera.

The men spent the rest of the day making their way through the thick overgrowth of the South American jungle. Finally, as the sun was setting, they started to make their way home. There was an occasional grunt of exertion, but other than that the men rarely spoke. Except for the commander, who grunted out orders between puffs of cigar smoke.

It was dark before they arrived at a makeshift village. The village consisted of a few huts made out of mud and straw and a spare piece of tin. Most of the huts had fire pits in front of them. Cloud seemed attracted to one of the huts that was on the perimeter of the village. As he approached, a woman came out to greet him. She was about middle-aged, with dark brown skin and high cheekbones framed by a stern lower jaw and sloping forehead. Her hands were dirty and there was what appeared to be a splotch of soot smeared across her face. She didn't speak, but instead handed Cloud a bowl of some kind of gruel. He realized that he hadn't eaten all day and he was hungry. The gruel/soup tasted gamy with a little hint of fish, or maybe it was some kind of lizard meat, or that of a turtle. It tasted thick and greasy with a bitter aftertaste. Cloud swallowed it quickly. He wanted it in his belly as fast as possible without having to linger on the taste. There was a small wooded bucket of water in the corner of the hut and he reached his hand into it, taking a small sip and spitting the rest of it out onto the dirt floor. The woman remarked that water was still in short supply, most of it being gathered from condensation off of the leaves.

After he finished eating, Cloud took off the outer layers of his sweat-soaked uniform and placed them in a pile. He looked at the woman, who averted her eyes from him and then picked up a small bundle of clothes and moved away from him. Cloud recognized the bundle of cloth as being baby clothes, about the size that would fit a small infant. The woman gripped the clothes to her breast and rocked back and forth, humming softly to herself. Cloud instinctively knew that the clothes had once belonged to his son, who was now dead. The details were hazy, but they slowly drifted into his memory like water through a grease-clogged pipe. They felt thick and oily, with stringy fibers of hate flowing through them. He knew that he blamed the politicians that had come to power in his tiny country for the death of his child. He knew that he must fight and kill them, even if it meant giving up his own life. As he rolled over on the makeshift bed and fell asleep, he saw the shadow of the woman flickering in the firelight.

As Cloud slept he had a dream. He was in a beautiful garden. It was like the ones that they had in Rio. Everything felt clean and there was the small of flowers and the sound of water running. A cool breeze replaced the horrible heat of the jungle. There was a marble fountain in the middle of the garden. It was obvious that was where the sound of the running water was coming from. The water was blue in color, like that of the ocean, and the spray from it tasted salty. The water flowed over several tiers of the stone fountain to a basin filled with flowers at the bottom. As hard as Cloud looked he couldn't tell where the water went. It just seemed to be sucked up by the flowers as soon as it reached the basin. Then he noticed that there was a crack at the bottom of the fountain and there was a small trickle of water leaking out, but not nearly enough to account for all of it. The trickle of water seemed to follow a regular path down the hill that the fountain was resting on to a gravel path that led into some trees. Cloud decided to follow the path of water to the edge of the trees. As he approached the forest, it seemed that the water was changing color. It was no longer a clear blue, but was taking on a reddish tint. He couldn't see very far into the forest, as it was pretty dark under the canopy of trees. As he stood at the entrance he reached down and touched the water with his finger. He put his finger up to his mouth and licked it. The water tasted like blood.

He wiped his finger on his shirt and spat out onto the ground. He noticed that there was a soft, murmuring sound coming from inside the woods, sort of like a breeze ruffling the leaves, but not quite. There was a part of him that wanted to go back and just sit in the peaceful garden, but there was also a desire to see what lay ahead on the path. He ventured on into the woods and the light at the end of the trail behind him grew dimmer and dimmer the further he walked. The forest seemed to be aglow under a purple midnight sky. There was a sliver of a crescent moon overhead. A luminescent butterfly floated past him and landed on a plant that he had never seen before. Suddenly he the sound of flowing water, and as he looked down, he realized that he was standing in the middle of some kind of a stream. The water wasn't very deep, maybe only a couple of inches, and he watched as it swirled against his shoes, but not over them. The he heard a child's voice. It came from right beside him. "Let's go down the stream daddy." The voice said. Cloud looked to see a small boy, maybe five or six years old, standing next to him. The boy was small with dark hair and big almond eyes that glittered in the moonlight. He was wearing a pair of raggedy pants that seemed to be cut off right below the knee. The boy tugged on Cloud's hand and the force of the pull was enough to tip him over and make him fall into the shallow water. Then it seemed that he and the boy were on some kind of water slide. The ground was level but it seemed that with just a thought, they shot forward at a really fast pace. The boy was laughing gleefully and holding on tight. Cloud felt giddiness in his stomach and a profound sense of joy that he had never felt before. It felt almost like he was that young boy with all of his sorrows and inhibitions stripped away and he was enjoying all of the sensations and movements of life.

The boy and the man came to the end of their joyous water ride through the forest. They had slid for what seemed like miles, but neither one of them was wet or muddy. Cloud looked up and saw that they were sitting under what seemed to be a tree bearing strange fruit. The fruit looked like some weird combination of an apple and a peach. Cloud reached up and pulled down a couple of pieces and handed one of them to the boy. The first bite was incredibly sweet and juicy, but Cloud noticed that the more he ate of it, there was a strange bitter taste that lingered long after he swallowed. He wondered if the boy tasted it too, but if he did, he showed no signs of it. Cloud noticed that the colors at the edge of the forest seemed to be changing, getting lighter. There was a separation, a line of white, just above the horizon. He knew that soon it would be time for him to leave.

When he awoke from his dream he was no longer in the hut next to the woman. He seemed to be in the embrace of some kind of giant mechanical arm that spidered out across the ceiling above him. There was a dim light off to the side in his field of vision. Things melded together and began to come into focus. He realized that he was once again in the warehouse in Chicago.

Chapter 19

The stabbing pain in Cloud's stomach brought him a brief moment of lucidity. He tried to breathe, but the air around him felt like it had turned into molasses and what little air that he could drag into his lungs must have been laced with battery acid, it burned so intensely. The cardboard box that he was lying on was soaked with the blood that had leaked out of his mouth and his nose. The congealed blood had formed into a plug in his nose and had encrusted his lips. The empty whiskey bottle was lying on its side like a pointy-headed fallen soldier. Cloud tried to move, but he couldn't lift his legs, move his arms, or even roll over. The weird thing was that he didn't feel weak, just the opposite, but his body felt too heavy to move, even with the illusion of added strength. He thought of the boy and a woman walking together hand-in-hand through a filed of tall grass. He was behind them, struggling to keep up. Their movements seemed fluid and graceful, while his were heavy and slow.. They were all moving towards a figure that was in the distance, sitting under a tree. The man was dressed in ceremonial Indian gear in front of a small fire. The flames were green in color and the smoke that curled up from it seemed to have all of the colors of a rainbow mixed in. As Cloud moved closer, it looked like half of the tree's leaves were also on fire. There was no smoke rising from the burning leaves. The woman and child arrived where the man was sitting before Cloud. Without saying anything, they sat down across from the man. It took some time for Cloud to reach them because it seemed like every time he got closer, the three of them got a little farther away. At first Cloud felt an intense desire to reach them without really knowing why? Then the desire turned into need as he felt himself growing weaker. At one point he thought that he would never get there, but just as he was about to stop trying and give up, he realized that he was there, standing over them.

The man looked very old and was wearing a complete headdress of feathers. There was a pipe lying on the ground beside him. On the other side was what Cloud recognized as talking stick. The stick that was passed around the circle and whomever held it had the right to speak to the group. The old man motioned for Cloud to sit down. As he sat there a small white feather drifted down from the sky and landed in the center of the circle, right next to the fire. There was a small glazed pot on the ground in front of the old man. He picked it up and offered it to Cloud. It contained what appeared to be a murky green tea. Cloud took a sip. It tasted incredibly bitter, but it made him feel better. Then the man picked up the talking stick and offered it to Cloud. As soon as the stick touched his hand he began to speak. He couldn't control himself, the words came fast and furious, a mile a minute. It was like Cloud was relating a condensed version of all of his life's stories to the group. When he finally finished he handed the stick back to the elder. The woman and the child stood up and each embraced Cloud, first the woman, then the child. Cloud looked into the elder's face. He smiled at Cloud. It was the last thing that he saw.

www.ingramcontent.com/pod-product-compliance
Lightning Source LLC
Chambersburg PA
CBHW031200020726
47499CB00002B/428